MADE IN YUGOSLAVIA

Vladimir Jokanović was born in Osijek in 1971. He started his medical studies in 1990 but as the clashes began he moved first to Zagreb and then to Belgrade. His family scattered across the world except for his mother, who stayed in Osijek under solid bombardment from federal forces. Jokanović finally moved to Novi Sad, Serbia, and completed his novel there in 1994. He still lives in Novi Sad. *Made in Yugoslavia* is his first novel.

Cathy Porter is a writer and translator. Her most recent translations include four plays of Karal Čapek and Ludmilla Ulitskaya's *Funeral Party*. She lives in London.

Zeljana Zovko was born in Mostar in Bosnia and Herzegovina and lived in London from 1992 to 1999. She now works as a public relations assistant at the Presidency of Bosnia and Herzegovina for the Croat Member of the Presidency. She lives in Sarajevo.

Vladimir Jokanović

MADE IN YUGOSLAVIA

translated by

Zeljana Zovko & Cathy Porter

PICADOR

First published 1995 by Matica Srpska originally entitled *Esmarch*

First published in English 2000 by Picador
an imprint of Macmillan Publishers Ltd
25 Eccleston Place, London SW1W 9NF
Basingstoke and Oxford
Associated companies throughout the world
www.macmillan.co.uk

ISBN 0 330 48059 6

1 3 5 7 9 8 6 4 2

A CIP catalogue record for this book is available from
the British Library.

Typeset by SetSystems Ltd, Saffron Walden, Essex
Printed and bound in Great Britain by
Mackays of Chatham plc, Chatham, Kent

I would like to thank the following people who supported me and helped me get this book published: Elemer Botos, Milica Bujas, the late Judita Šalgo, Zoran Mirković, Svetozar Koljević, Jadranka Milanović, Chris Hedges and Andrew Nurnberg.

MADE IN YUGOSLAVIA 1991

PART ONE

OSIJEK 1991
The Anarchitects Together Again

1

BILI COMES HOME

It was time for Bili to come home from the army. It was the last Tuesday in June, and he was returning from Ljubljana via Zagreb on a cheap cattle-truck stinking to the roof of onions, piss and spirits. The train was always at least half an hour late, so his brother Greg and friend Luka took cover from the heat in the empty station restaurant.

Greg's Dalmatian tram-driver friends were in there, grumbling about the Serb outlaws from Knin who had ruined the tourist season, and eyeing up two hungry-looking Romanian showgirls or hustlers who looked bored to death at the next table.

'Jesus, Stipe, they're not that bad,' Jure, the younger of the tram-drivers, was urging his friend. 'We could shag them as sort of first aid.'

'Knock it off, Jure, I have to drive that clunker in a minute.' Stipe jerked his shoulder at the empty red tram parked outside the station.

'I could take it once round the town for you, lover-boy,' offered Greg, finishing his second beer.

'C'mon, join in!' Jure said.

But Greg bashfully refused. 'Thank you, boys, I'm faithful to my Katarina, anyway they're not my type.'

'Don't warp the boy's mind,' said Stipe. He turned to

Greg. 'That girlfriend of yours is very nice, but why did you let her go to university? Like I'm better off with my law degree? As if there's any law round here anyway.'

Stipe wanted to discuss law, justice and women's rights, but Jure was in a hurry to annex a piece of Romania, and the conversation ended.

They ordered two beers for the girls, who appeared to be more in need of food, but despite their generosity Ferenc the waiter told them they had no hope of getting the back room for another half an hour. Trilateral negotiations followed between the drivers, the waiter and the ladies. Leaving their empty bottles, Greg and Luka went outside.

They were crossing the yellow paved square with 30 degrees under their armpits when they heard the hoot of the train, and hurried to the platform.

The train had stopped about a hundred yards from the platform, and thick yellow smoke was belching from the windows of the carriages. Crowds of madmen were stumbling out, falling down, swearing and weeping, then picking themselves up again. When Luka and Greg approached, they smelt the familiar fragrance of tear gas.

The last passenger to appear was a young man in combat fatigues, with a gas mask on his head and a large army kitbag slung over his shoulder. He glanced right and left, then kicked two smoking canisters across the platform. Bili was back.

Lifting the mask off his shaved head, he greeted Greg and Luka with a big smile, and there followed much thumping of backs and shoulders, pinching of cheeks and slapping of Bili's shaved head, until their noses started running and their eyes filled with tears – more from the tear gas than emotion.

The tram was filling up with people now. Greg went to the restaurant to take a piss, and Bili and Luka climbed aboard. Most of the cattle from the train were in there, identifiable by their streaming eyes. The rest of the passengers looked at them suspiciously and somebody asked them what had happened on the train, but most were more interested in where the effing driver had disappeared to. Two old women recognized Bili, and stumbled off with tear-filled eyes to the back of the tram. The boys took their seats, and Bili put his bag in front of him.

A moment later, Greg climbed in through the back door. 'What's the problem, no driver? Don't cry, folks, I'll drive you!' he said, moving down the aisle to the front.

Some of the passengers tried to talk him out of it, but he would not reconsider. 'Hell, I won't let honest people wait while those animals drink themselves legless in there! No way! Let's go!' So saying he eased himself into the driver's seat and pinged the bell.

When they saw he was serious, people started jumping out but few made it. Greg was in his best beery mood, happily whistling an old hit from a popular children's film as the tram ploughed through the streets and over the empty crossroads, pinging all the way.

'How are your studies going?' Bili asked Luka as they passed the Faculty of Law (he didn't know that Luka had dropped out).

The tram finally came to a halt. Greg opened the door and the passengers tumbled out as fast as they could. Then he dropped Luka and Bili near the old Papuk cinema, and tore off again down Kapucinska Street.

Bili and Luka sat on a bench by a pillar covered with

posters from the previous year's elections, Croatian independence referendums and other rubbish. Concerts used to be advertised here, but times had changed. The town was quiet, not a dog on the street.

Stripping off his unpopular YPA shirt, Bili sat in his vest and produced from his bag a number of hand grenades, an assault rifle, a spare-parts bag, more tear-gas canisters and various other bits and pieces.

'This stuff is cool now,' he said.

Nodding, Luka stretched out on the grass by the bench and stared up at the sky. Bili leaned his big shaven head on the bench, and gazed into the middle distance.

Crowds used to hang out here at this time of day for no other reason than to chat. 'Vapping', it was called. Vapping here would be the town's best-looking girls and all its best-known faces. The 'vap' was like a midday roll-call, where your best friends would collide with your worst enemies. You only began to worry if any *didn't* turn up. Since most of them practically lived to be seen here every afternoon, their absence could only mean one thing: they were dead.

'So where are all the cruisers?' Bili asked in a loud voice.

'Gone,' Luka replied.

'About fucking time. I was waiting for someone to chase that scum off the streets,' Bili said, and they were quiet for a while until the tram drew up again. This time it was driven by Stipe. Greg got off carrying a wooden box used for packing fruit, smiling seductively.

'I bumped into a fruit stall on Cesarčeva Street, and this sort of stuck to the tram,' he explained, laying the box on the bench and kissing his brother on his shiny head.

'Shit, I missed you, brother!' Bili hugged him.

Greg looked embarrassed. 'Wow, the kid's gone soft from the gas. What's in the bag?'

'More gas.'

'Man, this town will be a valley of tears.' Greg suddenly became serious as he looked at the tell-tale bulges in the bag.

They infiltrated the downtown tram. Greg started up a conversation with his old friend the driver, while Bili and Luka guzzled peaches from the box. On all of the seats someone had written with a firm hand: 'USTASHE ONLY!' The guys kept standing.

Bili's account of the tear-gas incident was as follows:

'It's a no-smoking carriage and everyone's puffing away. Fog, smoke and pollution, worse than London. The minute I try to open the window all the old women jump on me. What am I thinking of, exposing them to draughts, there are small children in the carriage, blah, blah. I don't argue, I just find myself another seat. So then what do I find? A teenage slut in the club, her belly would be up to her teeth if she had a tooth in her head, smoking like a chimney! On your way to Osijek for an abortion? I ask her. A quick blow job in the first place would have saved you the bother. I change seats three times and finally end up in the corridor, where they're eating smelly sausages and onions and God knows what. That does it. I chuck out two canisters of tear gas. Some wanker opens the windows, and the draught carries the smoke through the carriage. The driver flips, the train stops. End of story.'

They had finished all the peaches and were starting on the apples.

'How about we go to Kopika this afternoon for a swim?'
Luka suggested. The day was terribly hot.

'This evening we could get a gig together. Is Koki in town?'
Bili asked.

Koki, the fourth member of their band, had returned from
Zagreb and was hiding out from the rest of them revising for
his medical exams.

At that moment they saw Maria and Bea heading towards
them from the bridge. Just the stuff to give the troops. Bea
was Bili's ex, Maria was Luka's who knows what. Since the
massacre in the village of Borovo they weren't really on
speaking terms.

The two women had noticed them and stopped to change
their route, but Bili stood up to meet them.

'Try not to make a complete fool of yourself,' Greg advised,
but Bili was making of himself what he wanted.

It was all very awkward. Bili had split up with Bea in March
during one of his weekend leaves, but even before that she
had been going with Koki. Actually it was hard to know
which of the two she was with, since they were forever
handing her back and forth between them.

Greg munched an apple and watched the three of them
with philosophical detachment. It was impossible to hear
what they were saying, but their energetic gesticulation
defied the heat. Bili and Maria were doing most of the talking and waving, with Bea clearly wanting to be somewhere
else.

The conversation ended and Bili returned, patting his head
to check if his hair had grown at all. The women passed,
giving Greg, Bili and Luka a wide berth, and disappeared off

to their homes; from their clogs and rucksacks it was clear they had been swimming.

'What are you sulking for, we were talking about you. You should thank me for getting you back with your girlfriend!' Bili said.

'It won't be that easy.' Luka frowned.

'I said we'd do a gig tonight at ten. Make sure Koki's there.'

'So we're together again,' sighed Greg. 'I was hoping the Anarchitects would never play another note.'

They were generally regarded as a truly awful band, but no worse than any other in town. The peak of their fame came when graffiti saying 'ANARCHITECTS' started appearing on buildings all over town. This won them a certain reputation with the young people, and an even bigger one with the police, who hauled them into the police station to check their handwriting and box their ears. They were promised a sound beating if the graffiti didn't stop and were faced with the dilemma of whether to continue their happy career or go straight like good boys for the rest of their lives. Eventually their love of life prevailed, particularly with the more weak-minded members of the band.

Luka was mulling over all this as the Bilek brothers stood up to leave, clearing the last of the apples from the box.

'Listen, in half an hour we'll be back to pick you up and take you swimming, you'd better be ready!' Bili shouted as he disappeared with his brother.

2

SWIMMING
Dirtier than the Political Scene

When he was seventeen Luka's parents had divorced. Since then he had been living with his father in one of the blocks of flats on the Sjenak estate. His old man was a builder who worked at the Institute for the Protection of Cultural Monuments, specializing in the restoration of old family houses; there were plenty of these in town, and while he was working on his fancy façades his own was falling apart. Luka's mother was a nurse. In the summer of 1968 when she had Luka she had been a beauty, and even in 1991 she was still a good-looking woman. She had bequeathed none of this to Luka. From her he had inherited his short temper; from his old man he got his mean looks. His sister Mirjana had got the combination right. She was three years older than Luka and had already been in full-time employment for almost four years. Just as he was scraping his way out of his gymnasium she arrived there to teach literature. Then she had got tired of living with her mother and had married a socialist fairy-tale prince, after which Luka heard nothing but good about her.

He was in his third year at university, still resitting some of his exams from the first year and studying, like most of his pals, in the Economics Faculty canteen. His skinhead mate

Bogdan, known as Bižo, introduced him to some lucrative retail arrangements and during the golden days of Ante Marković they really had some big money coming in. Sometimes they even made managing directors' monthly salaries on a single move, and Luka was the deputy director. But the magic didn't last. In January the state showed the first signs of fatigue, everything started slipping, and the masses in town fell into a Croatian trance. At Luka's faculty, students from Herzegovina founded countless patriotic societies, and the Croatian Democratic Union advised a few liberal professors to fuck off. Some Dalmatian lads held debates in highfalutin political rhetoric in Luka's beloved Economics Faculty canteen, and he and Bižo, half-Serb unionist mutants, set up mainly as a joke, their Association for Peaceful Cohabitation, of which they remained to the end the sole members.

In May, when Luka was retaking his exams in Roman law for the last time, he watched a crowd in the assembly hall celebrate the replacement of Tito's portrait with the popular Croatian chessboard emblem. Before hanging it up, the students came one by one to kiss the new icon, then a bigoted hulk from Imotski named Anto Krolo stretched his arms to the ceiling and hung it on the wall, and Tito found his place in the toilet.

'What do you say to this, Mijatović?' one of the Imotski clan asked Luka.

In an outburst of resigned inspiration Luka lived out his last academic dream by throwing his student ID card into the toilet along with Tito.

Soon after this he met Bižo in the canteen, where they blew the last of their food tokens on beer, aborted the Association for Peaceful Cohabitation, and henceforth devoted themselves to more serious business.

Bižo's export–import corporation had already hit the rocks; the Croats had discreetly stopped buying from him, and the Serbs in Osijek were wisely closing their shops, which left Bižo up to his neck in shit with two tons of imported chocolate long past its sell-by date that he couldn't get anyone to buy. His father got the sack and his mother was made redundant, and the former up-and-coming businessman and president of the Association for Peaceful Cohabitation was reduced to selling ice creams on the street.

Luka got a job as one of the new census takers. He witnessed some scenes that would make a pig puke, but he was paid good money. He had stopped seeing Maria because of her Aryan crap; he considered Bili's Good Samaritan intervention that afternoon pointless, but the kid was fresh from the army and didn't need a crash landing into reality.

Things with Koki weren't good either. Frankly Luka couldn't stand him. Tall, skinny, hunched as a camel, Koki was always on the edge of things. At school the other kids had bullied him, kicking his arse, spitting at him, punching him in the face and leaving him alone only when they didn't know what else to do to him. He was all fingers and thumbs – every bone in his body had been broken, every tendon distended. He had spent half his dreary life in hospitals and rehabilitation centres, and the only attention he ever received from anyone was from the doctors who changed his bandages and stitched him up. Inevitably he fell in love with white coats. It was only at university that he began to achieve something. For the first time he could hold his head up. After just two more years in Zagreb he would realize his dream of being a doctor, and screw everyone who had pushed him around.

Luka dialled Koki's number and waited a good fifteen minutes before he finally got through. When he did, there was no way he could persuade him to come until he mentioned that Bili was back. Shitting himself at the idea that at Luka's garage Bili might reclaim his Bea in his absence, he nobly agreed to be there at nine. Luka hung up with a mixture of pity and disgust for him, and a good feeling about tonight's gig; it would be just like old times.

Just then the first two bars of 'Lili Marlene' blasted out below the window, and Greg's VW swooped up. Luka rushed round the flat grabbing his swimming things, and by the time he came down from the sixth floor the brothers were raving in the heat. The VW was black, and an excellent heat conductor. Once, during the summer holidays, Luka had fried an egg on it for a bet, like they used to on tanks in the army.

Greg drove his car more ferociously than the tram, he knew he could fool around, he had a top-cop uncle. But even he had to slow down on the bridge. An unusually large number of cops and members of the Special Police Force dressed in US combat fatigues were milling about, and it looked as though something serious was about to happen.

'Look at the way that idiot's holding his rifle.' Bili pointed to a policeman carelessly balancing the tip of his gun on one foot as he talked to a Special Police Force guy resembling a lizard in his green uniform. These games with weapons were becoming dangerous; two days before, a cop had shot himself in the hand while playing with his rifle in Ante Starčević Square, and Luka's neighbour, Dr Mitrović, spent four hours in the operating theatre stitching him up.

They passed the police without being stopped, and soon they were walking across the hot asphalt to the legendary Copacabana beach, dirty and neglected as ever.

Trying to play smart and not burn his feet, Greg trod on a bit of broken glass left in the grass after some high-school booze-up. The blood gushed from his foot. He gasped and hopped around, and a group of boys and girls sitting on the grass nearby started laughing. Although normally a calm person, Greg was sensitive to girls' smiles and he overreacted, kicking one of the boys in the head – not too hard, since he did it with his wounded foot, but hard enough for the boy to fall back on the grass. He sat up with blood on his lip looking worried, and the laughter stopped.

'The blood's mine, it's on the the house!' Greg showed him his foot.

Luka and Bili stood tall. 'It's okay, the kid seems to have had enough for the moment,' said Bili, waving his hand to the flustered girls. Then the three friends went off down to the river, marching like heroes of the beach and trying to avoid the litter of broken glass that flashed at them from the grass.

On all sides loudspeakers were blaring out speeches from parliament. It was a historic moment: for the first time since 10 April 1941 the country was preparing to become a sovereign state and declare its total independence. This had little effect on the beach, where beautiful girls with big breasts and tiny swimsuits ran about playing volleyball. It was a feast for tired eyes; Bili's pride awoke from its long army sleep, and his swimming trunks were unable to hide the fact.

'What's happening, kid? Your lift working again?' Greg asked.

'It's all right, I'll get it wet in a minute.' Bili smirked.

Men played cards in the grass. Some guys kicked a football in the sand. Others played frantic ball games in the shallow water. At least no one had broken their back this year.

'Nothing's changed, everything's exactly the same,' Bili said, disappointed.

'What did you think, we'd fall apart without you?' said his brother, looking over at the other side of the river where some boys were slipping their boats in the water.

'Look at those gorgeous women, brother. It's good to be back!' said Bili suddenly, ogling two girls as they passed by with provocative smiles. 'So let's swim!'

He dipped his toe in the water and threw in first his brother, then Luka. The Drava was cold, with a yellow scum of soapy effluent on top, as well as numerous branches and other bits of rubbish, so nobody really enjoyed swimming in it very much. Greg's cut foot was still hurting and he was floating on his back with his mouth closed, trying not to let any of the crap in. The water bore the two of them along. A couple of powerful strokes brought Bili level with them, and in another minute the current had swept them all to the other side. Climbing to the showers, they were dirtier than the political scene. Greg was limping and in a bad mood. 'Let this be your last idiotic idea today,' he said to his brother sullenly.

Bili was too busy chasing little boys out of the showers to reply. Luka turned the water full on. There was a ton of trash in his hair.

'Why did you grow it so long?' Bili asked disapprovingly.

Luka pretended not to hear. He wouldn't even consider cutting it. Maybe he would grow a beard too, Chetnik-style.

They walked to the children's swimming pool and found Bižo selling his ice creams. It was obviously the worst place on the beach, since only small children swam here without their parents. Bižo was wearing sunglasses and a baseball cap with a cloth at the back to protect his neck, and listening to his Walkman. The loudspeakers droned on. He looked miserable.

'I'm going crazy here,' he informed the others. 'This is a fucking sweatshop – just me and the loudspeakers.'

A deafening medley of patriotic Croatian songs rang on and on, and the conversation was run at the tops of their voices.

Bižo took a beer from his cooler and opened it. 'I've sold six ice creams and drunk three beers. Profit – nil!' he shouted, the veins on his neck bulging from the effort of making himself heard over the music.

'Where's the rest of your gang?' Bili shouted back.

'Drinking at Njaka's most likely. I might go there at six when I finish.'

'Come to our gig tonight,' Luka said as they were leaving.

Bižo waved his hand and propped his feet on the cooler. Fuck the gig, it didn't interest him. 'Take care if you go to Njaka's. Lager's gone nuts. The others are okay, just him.'

'What happened to Krišna?' Luka asked. Krišna was a

friend, the most normal one of Bižo's crowd. Her father was an officer. Luka hadn't seen her for over two months.

'Don't ask me, she's not been around for weeks,' said Bižo in a quieter voice, noticeably wearying of the conversation.

Greg and Bili had already moved off, and Luka had to hurry to catch them up. 'What's the rush? Do you need a shit?'

'We didn't want to disturb your private conversation,' Bili said peaceably; Bili didn't want to talk about Krišna and Lager, and whatever Bili didn't want to talk about didn't exist for him.

They went back down to the beach, rolling around in the sand and pelting each other with mud, and everything was as it used to be. Then they lay in the sand, muddy as pigs, and whistled at the girls.

Burying himself in sand, Greg outlined his plans for his forthcoming wedding. He had left his job in Germany to get married, but things kept being held up. First Katarina had met a mechanical engineer in Zagreb, and this had taken a while to sort out, with Bili requesting endless compassionate leave to clear things up and Luka making several trips to Zagreb. After this Katarina said she didn't want to get married until she graduated, which was hard for all the parties concerned. Now she had just one more exam to take.

'See, Luka, we're going to hire a tram, clean it up, put a trailer on the back for the band, and eat and drink till dawn!'

The idea wasn't in itself that original, since trams were used every year for May Day, Workers' Day and the opening of the Youth Summer Festival. But they weren't normally used for weddings.

'What do her parents think?' Luka asked.

'It's no skin off their nose, it'll hardly cost them anything. All they care about is that we have it in church. You know what, I had to get christened and confirmed and take First Communion all in one go. I never knew it was so hard to become a Catholic. But I'm not complaining, people will talk about this wedding for years to come.'

'Knowing you, smartarse, you'll spend your wedding night in the tram,' Bili said, standing up in the sand and going back to the showers.

They drove back in the stiflingly hot VW, and ran into a long tailback at the bridge. The police were searching someone. Actually they were searching everyone; they didn't want unauthorized fireworks on the day independence was declared.

'No one fucks with me, we could be held up here for hours,' Greg said, driving to the head of the queue and stopping before the police.

'Hey, guys, I'm clean as a white swan! Let me through or I'll lay an egg before my turn comes!'

He then dropped the name of his illustrious uncle, and they let him through with a salute.

'That's democracy for you,' he observed wisely.

Luka pointed to Bili's bag of weapons on the back seat. Shaking his head, Greg clenched his teeth and his hands on the wheel, and turned the car towards Njaka's place.

Njaka's club for alcoholics met in the basement of his grandmother's house. A happy brewery employee, Njaka was able to get beer at bargain prices, and they mostly drank that. His girlfriend, Biserka, toiled away in the biscuit factory opposite the brewery, so they had plenty of biscuits to eat. In every other respect too they complemented each other perfectly, and you couldn't have found a better-matched couple.

The decor of the basement was more than a little kitsch, with its scorched flags, its car number plates stolen from every country in Europe, its abnormally enlarged photographs on the walls and its collection of mismatched seats: there were seats from various cars, a whole row from the old Zvečevo cinema, a bench from the park, another from the Health Centre waiting room, a bus seat and an old toilet off the train.

In the middle of all this, Njaka sat on one of the cinema seats like a king on his throne, deep in thought, drinking beer and incessantly filling up the bottle with vodka. He was in one of his basement depressions.

'This place could do with a clean-up,' Greg said, looking around.

'Shut up, Greg, you're as sober as a traffic warden, I can smell the fruit juice on your breath. Just as well your brother here is in a decent state. Hi there, Luka!'

This remark about looking decent referred to Bili's shaved head. Njaka threw each of them a bottle of beer. The beer crates were laid out to form the pattern of the Croatian chessboard symbol, thirteen white and twelve red squares, the latest thing in bar decor.

The only other person there apart from Njaka was Biserka, whom they called either Bisa or Serka (Shithead), depending on their mood. She was at present too busy shaving her head to greet them. Greg sat down on the toilet seat, holding his beer. Bili and Luka stood observing Biserka's ritual. She nicked her scalp, and a little blood fell on her shoes.

'Put a jug down, we'll make black pudding,' said Bili, but she didn't jump at his suggestion.

'All for beauty,' she said, inspecting the damage in the mirror.

'Why don't you get yourself done too, Luka? An ugly head like yours doesn't need hair.'

'Right,' mumbled Luka, sitting down beside her and looking at the picture of Krišna on the wall. 'Say, d'you know what's happened to Krišna?'

Bisa was about to say something when somebody crashed headlong down the stairs into the basement in a failed attempt to enter quietly. It was Lager, already very drunk, shouting at the top of his voice.

'Fuck it, we've guests! Bili's back! Greg's here! Luka! Sorry, I've had a few!'

Greg and Bili bent over the beer crates playing chess, trying to ignore Lager as he stepped out of the shadows.

'What the fuck is that outfit?' Njaka balanced his beer bottle on two fingers.

Lager was dressed in paramilitary camouflage uniform with a red beret at his waist. He was bursting with confidence. 'They accepted me in the Croatian Defence Force! My training starts tomorrow!'

'You'll make bacon for the Chetniks, fat boy!' teased Biserka, looking at him in the mirror.

Ignoring her, Lager pulled a bundle of notes from his pocket and waved them over his head. 'I got paid too — thirteen thousand!'

Njaka solemnly poured half the beer from his bottle on to

20

the floor. 'A libation for your sinful soul, charming young boy in the corner!'

Without replying, Lager strode to the wall, tore down the photograph of Krišna and threw it on the floor. Then he pissed on it. He pissed and pissed; he must have had at least five beers before he arrived. Luka disliked this carry-on. Krišna was the only woman who had overlooked Lager's nocturnal bed-wetting and snoring and slept with him; he should have carried her photo in his wallet, instead of treating it this way.

He leaned over to Bisa again. 'What happened to her, no kidding?'

Bisa didn't say a word, just concentrated on her shoelaces.

'You talking about Krišna?' Lager turned to Luka, zipping up his flies.

'Yeah,' said Luka. He couldn't get out of it now.

'She had the sense to get out, as if you didn't know.'

'Where to?'

'Over there, where all you lot are going.' He jerked his shoulder east.

Nobody said a word. Luka knew he was talking about Serbia. Bižo had warned him. For a moment he considered breaking a bottle over Lager's head. But this was bigger than Lager, this was a reservoir of fucking political shit waiting for the dam to burst. Luka knew – just another word and he'd get a tanker of it. Greg and Bili were still playing chess. He felt very lonely. Greg hardly managed to make it a draw. They both stood up.

'We're off, we were going to invite you to our gig but we see you're fully booked up,' Bili said to the others, and they left.

Njaka caught up with them by the door at the top of the stairs.

'Don't let Lager wind you up, Luka. You know what he's like when he's had too many.'

'I don't know anything any more,' Luka said, more to himself than to Njaka, and climbed into the car.

Greg started the engine, driving less recklessly now that it wasn't so hot and the streets were filling with people. On Ante Starčević Square a Very Important Meeting was taking place, one more meeting that would go down in history and had become a normal part of everyday life during the past months. With so much history around, you started feeling like a tourist in your own town.

They turned into Šamačka Street so the cops wouldn't stop them with a bag full of firearms. They had had enough excitement for one day.

3

THE MIDNIGHT PICNIC

At nine o'clock sharp Luka was at the garage. The sun was down, the massacre of the mosquitoes had begun. He opened the door and looked at his old man's wrecked Renault 4; he had crashed into it with Bižo's van while his Fiat was being serviced, and had had to sell the Fiat to pay Bižo and his father for the damage.

He pushed the car out of the garage and inspected Bili's drums, covered in a protective film of dust. On the wall behind them was a big photograph of the Anarchitects, taken when they were about to hit the big time. It felt like a million years ago. Where had he been all those years? It seemed wrong to be playing tonight.

Just then he heard footsteps approaching the garage, and Koki appeared carrying a synthesizer under one arm and an accordion on his shoulder; he had obviously taken seriously their invitation to play. 'How are you doing?' he asked Luka.

'Don't ask.'

'Who could be well today?'

Koki went to the corner where the instruments stood draped in plastic sheets. He pulled the covers off, raising clouds of dust that made him cough like a mule. Koki was allergic to dust. Sand, water, wind, draughts, food, cigarettes, alcohol – you name it, Koki was allergic to it; his life hung by a thread. He started fiddling around with the speakers and the amplifier while Luka dusted the drums and tapped the cymbals.

'I can't believe we'll be able to play on this stuff,' Koki said. 'The band broke up, the gear's broken up.'

Luka didn't like that. 'So why the hell did you come? You don't care about the band, you've better things to do.'

His voice echoed through the empty garage. It was no good, Koki would never be like them. Bili had picked him up like a stray dog off the street. He did his best to be one of them, but he would never make it.

Luka sat on an empty beer crate and watched him.

'It could be worse.' Koki leaned over a speaker. 'I know guys who'd give us a thousand Deutschmarks for this.'

'Are you serious?' Luka asked him.

'You think we could get more?'

Luka looked at him; he was deadly serious. He really hadn't a clue.

Koki finally plugged in his synthesizer and started running through his favourite songs. Luka loathed all of them. Picking up his guitar he bashed it until his anger passed. They had just started jamming when Bea and Maria descended on them, pretending to applaud. 'You deserve a kiss for that,' Maria declared generously, throwing her arms around Koki.

'Save it for someone else,' Luka snapped. She was giving them away as if she wanted to give everyone herpes.

'I didn't mean you, anyway. I just wanted to welcome our man back from the capital!' she told him.

The capital! She was getting on his nerves with her political swipes; with her, everything was the fault of the one-party system. She was being incredibly irritating, and she looked incredibly good.

Koki was kissing Bea now. Luka greeted her coolly, then turned to Maria. 'Take it easy, I don't want geography lessons in my garage, okay?' He eyed her the way he might eye a nice-looking girl.

Her gaze softened. She smiled. 'Hello there,' she said.

At that moment the Bilek brothers turned up. Greg carried his bass-guitar. Bili was wearing a terrible orange wig and carrying two bottles of vodka, one of them half empty. Koki went up to embrace him, and he threw off the wig to get a kiss on his shaved head. They both laughed, ordinary guys.

'Boy, your head's like a light bulb, we could connect you to the mains and switch you on!' Koki said.

'Koki, my son, I could die of happiness that we're all together again,' Bili said, passing him the vodka.

Koki drank heroically, put the bottle down and exhaled like a dragon. 'Let's play for the girls!' he said, his eyes shining like in the good old days of the Anarchitects.

Luka grabbed the bottle and finished it off; the vodka burned his throat as it always did – some things never changed – then he switched on the light and jumped on the rickety stage, raising a cloud of dust. Bili sat down at the drums, Koki took his accordion. Greg and Luka picked up their guitars. While they were tuning them, Maria opened the other bottle and swigged it like a man. Bea was more ladylike and sipped hers. The mood was good. Good music hung in the air.

'Ladies and gentlemen!' Luka's voice shook with excitement.

'Bili's home, let's welcome him back! The Anarchitects and – "Dirty Old Town"!'

Koki had just struck up the opening bars on his accordion when one of the cables overheated and caught fire. In two seconds the garage was filled with smoke and the smell of melting rubber. Everyone jumped up, and Luka emptied an entire fire extinguisher on the amp. That was the end of it, as well as their carefully planned gig. Giving it up as a bad job they finished the rest of the vodka.

There was nothing else for it but to go fishing. The moon was full – of what, no one knew for sure – and Greg maintained that the fish bit like crazy in the moonlight. None of the others knew anything about fish, but they didn't mind eating them once in a while. Armed with fly rods belonging to Luka's old man they piled into Greg's VW and set off for a spot that Greg recommended as the best place for catching them.

They stopped at the nearby corner shop for bread and bottles of wine, then they drove down the straight road to the village of Bilje. By the Csingi Lingi Csarda restaurant Greg turned off the main road on to the dirt track leading to the Old Drava Lake. Luka and Maria were squashed together on the back seat, and in all the jolting he managed to put his arm around her. She didn't resist, and he kept his arm there until the car came to a stop by the lake.

While Greg sat down by the bank sorting out the rods, the other five lit a fire and sat around it happily with the guitar and the accordion, waiting for him to make his big catch. He fished for nearly two hours, and with every minute that passed, his hopes of catching anything dwindled.

'Oy, quit shouting, I'll never catch anything at this rate!' he burst out at last.

This was the moment Bili had been waiting for. Going to the VW, he came back with a green hand grenade.

'Okay, brother, stop fucking about, the army's taking over,' he said, hurling it into the calm water. Greg barely managed to jump back from the deluge that rose in the wake of the muffled explosion. An offensive grenade is only slightly stronger than a simple firecracker, but a mass of fish and baby frogs rose instantly to the water's surface, their stomachs glowing pitifully in the moonlight.

Everyone crowded around to look. Taking off his trousers, Bili waded into the water to remove the catch. Luka joined him, and they chucked the dead and maimed fish on to the grass, where they thrashed about helplessly until Greg and Koki finished them off in an ethical and humanitarian way with a hammer. Bili came out of the water and he and Luka threw frogs at each other, while Greg cleaned the fish to make the famous Baranian carp-on-a-spit to serve to the drunken company. The fire was down and the embers were just right for the fish. Maria and Luka sat back to back on the grass while Bili and Koki boozed and broke the idyllic silence of the place arguing about the meaning of life. Koki had drunk himself into a semi-stupor when he finally stood up and made a public announcement:

'THE PURPOSE OF LIFE IS NOT TO SHOUT DRUNKENLY IN THE MOONLIGHT! NO! THE PURPOSE OF LIFE IS TO SURVIVE IN AN ALIEN ENVIRONMENT! THAT IS LIFE, MY FRIENDS!'

His words had quite an effect on Bili, who stood up,

grabbed the speaker by the collar of his jacket, and roared in his face, 'Sit down, you wanker, you haven't a clue what life's about!'

Koki managed to pull himself away.

'LIFE IS A CONTINUOUS STRUGGLE AGAINST THE ENTROPY IN AN IRREVERSIBLE PROCESS!' he persisted, yelling so loudly that even the distant stars trembled in horror.

After he had announced this important scientific truth he was overcome by fatigue and hit the grass. Seeing him in this sad condition, Bea put aside her half-eaten carp and wept quietly. Bili was instantly at her side offering support, whispering in her ear and drying her tears, and five minutes later he was leading her off to Greg's VW.

Greg thought sadly of the suspension and shrugged. Then he turned to Luka and Maria with more helpings of carp.

'You two want fish?' he shouted to his brother in the darkness.

'No thanks, we've got some!' Bili shouted back, and Bea laughed happily.

Koki lay on the grass like a dead man, while the others sat around the fire with their fish and wine. Maria and Luka faced each other. The sparks cast a yellow glow on their faces. Maria's was partly covered by her long hair, and as he looked at the spark in her eyes he knew they had almost made it up. They finished eating. She sat with her back against a tree, and he lay down with his head in her lap.

'You remember 15 September 1988?'

'Of course I do,' she said, stroking his hair.

That was the day he had finished his army service; for both of them, a passionate sexual memory.

When Luka opened his eyes next morning the first thing he saw was Maria, stunning in sleep, and Koki pacing round the dying embers like a sick dog. Bili and Bea were returning from an early morning walk in the wood, exhausted but happy, and Greg was gutting the rest of the fish. What a beautiful, promising start to the day, Luka thought. Maria yawned and stretched next to him. It didn't look very ladylike, but it was sexy enough for him to get an erection. She noticed, and smiled at his swelling crotch without saying a word. To solve the problem, he rolled over on his stomach and watched Koki throwing up in the beautiful still waters of the lake. They were all watching Koki in fact. Greg wished he had his camera, and thought what an excellent picture it would make for his archives.

'Hey, shall we take photos this afternoon?' he said as Bili and Bea swallowed their fish and bread. 'It's going to be a great day for it.'

Koki crawled over to them, clutching his stomach with one hand and wiping his mouth with the other; in one night he had travelled back down the road it had taken evolution millions of years to cover.

'Wow, you two look hot and hungry!' Greg teased Bea and Bili, but they didn't notice. 'So are we taking pictures or what?'

Koki grumbled his discontent, but the others were all more or less in favour.

Greg dropped them home, and Maria stayed with Luka to tidy up the garage. Or rather he tidied it up while she ate one of the apples from Greg's box. She helped him push back his dad's car, then jumped on the bonnet with her mouth full of apple.

'Hey, give me a bite of that,' he said.

She bit off a piece and held it between her teeth, teasing him with it. He leaned over, put his hands on her hips, took the apple from her mouth with his and kissed her lips. She kissed him back lazily, absorbed in her thoughts, looking over his head to the ceiling of the garage.

He moved back. 'What's the matter, Maria? What is it now?'

Her eyes were trying to avoid his. She turned her head and said something he couldn't hear. Then she said again, 'We haven't been getting on lately, Luka.'

'What's that got to do with it?' he said.

'Just yesterday we were fighting like dogs. How can I be sure that afterwards . . .' She took his hands from her hips and jumped off the bonnet. 'I have to go. See you this afternoon.'

'Yeah,' he replied.

Maria left, and he was alone in the garage. He kicked one of Bili's drums, and that calmed him down a bit.

4

THE ZOO: INSIDE AND OUTSIDE

That afternoon at around two o'clock Luka met Bili at the footbridge over the river. They waited for Greg, who had gone to see the priest about the wedding; it was now just a matter of setting the day. They sat down in the shade of the dense poplars and Luka took off his trainers and pulled up tufts of grass with his toes, while Bili reported all the details of the previous night's encounter with Bea. His feelings were warmer for her again.

'I can't handle her thing with Koki. I ask her what she sees in the fool, but she can't answer. God, man, she's like a child!'

'Yeah, right,' Luka said, thinking that what Bili knew about children could probably fit in an ant's arse.

He wasn't keen to pursue the subject, and was almost glad when Koki turned up and started whingeing about his stomach. His arrival cooled them both down wonderfully. His eyes, framed in green circles, darted about like a lunatic's. 'I should never have got so drunk,' said the future doctor in a voice full of suffering.

Koki went on in this vein for a while, until they saw Bea and Maria come into view. Maria smiled at Luka. Bea didn't say anything to Koki, just clung to him like a leech as usual and threw him compassionate looks as if to say, 'Are you feeling better, darling?' The others were well aware of what was happening; Bili pretended not to notice and lay on his back with his knees up, staring at the sky.

Maria sat down next to Luka. 'Where were we?' he asked her.

High above them a plane traced a trail of chalk across the sky like a silver mosquito. Maria unlaced her trainers and kicked them aside, and he lay with his head in her lap again, holding her foot. Beside them Koki and Bea were necking like a normal couple.

Maria turned to Bili on the other side of her and pointed at his legs, poking palely out of his shorts like two cigarette papers.

'How did you get your knees so nice and white, Bili?'

'It was all the washing they made us do in the army,' Bili said.

Luka looked at Maria's legs, tanned and freshly shaved. 'Sweetheart, yours are so dark you must have the sun between them!' he said.

He looked up at her face. She was watching Koki and Bea, biting her lip. Turning to face him she laid a cool hand on his neck and bent over him, spilling her long brown hair over his face. He slowly pulled her hair back, and they looked into each other's eyes. Then she put her lips to his and moved them slowly, as if whispering something to him, and he was numb to everything but the warmth of her breath on his mouth. She drew back quietly, the kiss ended, and she let her hair fall over her face again, moving her hand and pressing her

lips together as if trying to remember something, some taste
from long ago.

Koki and Bea were virtually shagging by the time Greg
appeared with news that made everyone happy: 'The wedding's
in ten days, folks! Everyone's invited, you'll all get your
invitations when I've printed them!'

After this announcement he suggested they take off for the
zoo.

They took a few pictures of the bridge, then crossed over
to the Baranja side, spreading out in a column some hundred
metres long. Overhead the sun blazed mercilessly like a giant
H-bomb. Greg and his brother walked in front, and Bea and
Koki followed. Maria and Luka lagged behind. She was
collapsing in the heat, so he held her hips and swung her on
to his shoulders, and she sat there comfortably all the way to
the gates of the zoo, where she climbed down and they
wandered with the others to the cages.

The last time they had visited the zoo was when they were
all at primary school. Now they were the only ones there, not
even the keepers were to be seen. They stopped first at the
monkey house. The animals seemed rather depressed, maybe
because they hadn't been included in the last amnesty, Luka
thought; it would be good to see them on television, bragging
about all their years behind bars. Greg came equipped with
sweets and peanuts, which aroused some interest among the
monkeys. The rest of the company moved on to the big cats,
who were in a state of even greater distress. Panthers, lions
and tigers stared yearningly from their cages, rattling the bars
and uttering threatening noises. Then all of a sudden a

trapdoor in one of the cages flew open and chunks of meat started pelting down from the sky, hitting the concrete floor with a deafening thud. It was three o'clock, feeding time. The sight of all the bloody carcasses and powerful gleaming teeth was pretty disturbing and, since the bars offered no psychological protection, Luka and Maria went off to watch the beavers mating like maniacs in their little fur suits in 30 degrees. Maria stood gazing at them in a trance; she loved fur, and she loved watching these beautiful creatures doing their tricks. Beavers left Luka cold; it was Maria he wanted. He took a picture of her against the beavers, then she took one of him; two photos made in heaven for the family album.

The others were still by the big cats.

'Listen,' Luka said to Maria, deadly serious. 'Tonight, anything could happen!' He grabbed hold of her leg.

'Stop that, naughty!' she said, mimicking the lisping tones of Bea, who had left the tigers now and was advancing towards them. She was slightly taller than Maria, with earthquake tits, blue eyes, blonde hair up and down, and a desperate need to seem twenty years younger and always adorable.

'I'll never complain again about you belching like a pig,' she said to Luka in her little girl's voice. 'That tiger belched so loud I could have slapped him!'

'Right,' said Luka. 'Have you seen the beavers?'

'No, I haven't,' she pouted. 'What are they up to?'

'Same as you were last night, darling,' Maria said unkindly, then the three boys caught up with them and they dropped the subject.

They walked around a small artificial lake filled with ducks and other water birds. In the middle was a little island overgrown with trees, bushes and vines like a jungle, with unearthly sounds echoing from it. In the shallow water surrounding the island, flamingoes stood on one toothpick leg scratching their backs with their bills and rummaging around in the mud. Circling the middle of the lake were parties of ducks and swans. Along the edge, willows dipped their branches into the pondweed, offering an ideal breeding ground for Osijek's famous mosquitoes.

But the creepiest animals in the zoo were the birds of prey. Condors, vultures, eagles and other proud poultry sat two by two in their cages like fattened-up turkeys, sluggish from heavy food and inactivity. Only one of the eagles had any sharpness in its eyes; all the rest looked as if they were stuffed with sawdust. Even if someone had opened their cage, they would have just gone on flying around it in two-metre circles. The more you looked, the more depressed you felt.

They walked on and soon came to a pleasanter sight. Camels, antelopes and zebras, giraffes, bison and llamas all lived harmoniously together in a large sandy enclosure like happy cartoon creatures, nibbling away at the grass just as they did at home. One of the llamas spat at the less cautious visitors, but they already knew him from their school trip years before.

Luka's favourite animals were the bright tropical birds. They looked as if they were made for fun. The craziest of them, a red, blue and yellow parrot with a black beak, kept blinking and laughing at itself in a mirror, then coolly took a shit.

After this they went to the reptile house to cool down and check out the snakes and lizards. It would have been more logical to let them out in the sun, but head office obviously didn't want them too active. Reptiles, like communists, once spent time shaking the planet, then inexplicably collapsed, leaving behind the pale ghosts of past power in concrete pools and glass cages. In those terraria, real classical tragedies were taking place. The friends watched as the snakes uncoiled slowly in the corners while little white mice cowered before them, paralysed by fear.

'How come those poor mice are in there?' Bea asked, touched by the rodents' plight.

'Because snakes won't eat anything that's not alive,' explained Bili with his usual sensitivity.

'How horrible!' Bea was genuinely upset.

What a piece of work was this woman, a walking theatre of the absurd; if she had seen that mouse anywhere else, in her room, or in her bed for instance, she would have gone crazy and stayed that way for days. Some girls' emotional circuits are so weirdly programmed it's not surprising that the ones who piss standing up invariably end up paying the bill.

They passed the piranhas and other fish, and Greg took pictures of a sleeping elephant, and some kangaroos jumping over their hut. By now they had exhausted all that Osijek zoo had to offer.

The company trailed back along the riverbank, sick at the prospect of making the long return journey on foot.

'Come on, Greg, not even the Foreign Legion would march in this heat,' moaned Bili, his skull streaming with sweat. 'Pay for our ferry tickets and I'll wash your car for you.'

Greg took pity on them and paid for the ferry. The ferryman looked suspiciously at his unexpected crowd of passengers, and they moved slowly across the river. Sculls shot past with rowers sweating like drugged pigs, one could only shake one's head at the youngsters' efforts; the heat was too heavy for anything more strenuous. Maria and Luka sat embracing on the bench and watched the light break over the little waves. There was something magical about the water rippling past them that made them think of their lives, and they were quiet until the boat reached the jetty and the land adjusted itself to their feet.

Greg suggested they visit the Castle area to take more pictures, but no one else fancied the additional four-kilometre trek, so he went off with Bili, Bea and Koki to Koki's place to develop the films, and Luka and Maria found themselves alone.

She gave him her hand and they walked along the path by the river, just like they used to do in the old days. The heat slowly ebbed away, remaining only in the asphalt beneath their feet. As they cut across to the park the gravel path crunched like a column of marching soldiers, even though there were only two of them. From the tennis courts animal shrieks rang out, as if the players were in deep pain, as one can be over shallow things.

Maria wanted to sit down on a bench. She was tired and relaxed, and something in her eyes made Luka feel confident about the outcome of the evening ahead. At last a good night was coming, a darkness he wasn't afraid of, a darkness completely unlike the darkness that ruled his thoughts, about the present and the future, about people who chased yellow balls over the red sand, studied at university, hung out in bars and cafés, made speeches and listened to other people making speeches. The future made no sense, it was just a lovely, made-up fairy tale that would never happen. There was only one place he wanted to be now, and that was between Maria's legs and deep in her eyes, somewhere even deeper inside her, like a cloud in her soul, where he could float free of all thoughts and needs. Sometimes he would see a spark from that place, and her look of calm surrender, far above all the petty everyday bullshit. That was the only light he had the will to follow.

'Shall we go to my place?' she said in a subdued, almost timid voice.

Luka nearly fell of the bench. He had been to her house only once. Once in five years. Maria's parents didn't like him. If they knew him, they would dislike him even more.

'Your folks out?' he said, looking into her eyes, where the spark seemed to have become stronger.

'They're away for a few days,' she said.

'How about Marian?' Luka had no wish to bump into Maria's brother, a rabid Croatian patriot.

'He's been out for the last two days getting ready for some rally,' she said, meeting his eyes — or his eyebrows or his mouth, he wasn't sure which.

'Let's go to my place instead,' he said at last. His old man had nothing against Maria, although his ideal woman was a senior nurse or physiotherapist; the old man was hardly ever in these days, which made Luka suspect that one of them must be on the scene.

Another thing he had against Maria's room was the photo on her wall, which had given him the shits the moment he had seen it. It had been taken on some church trip to Rome, and showed her kissing the Pope's hand. He couldn't help it, the root of his aversion was clearly the usual petty pathological jealousy; but Maria saw all sorts of other things going on here, and her innocent relic had been the source of several heated arguments between them.

As they walked along Istria Street they saw a large crowd of people gathered outside the Army Club. This must be the rally Maria had been telling him about. There was a noise too, a familiar, almost intimate noise, which made Maria's flesh creep. She dropped Luka's hand, and he listened. The noise from Vukovar Street brought back an avalanche of memories from his army service days...

People ran towards the noise like brainless animals, and Maria ran with them. Luka took the short cut by the high-school playground. Later he couldn't explain to himself the force that had propelled him there. He sprinted like an Olympic medallist, and arrived at the crossroads of Klein and Vukovar Streets in time to catch a historic moment. A group of furious youngsters stood hurling stones at a couple of army vehicles while a crescendo of noise thundered from the downtown garrison. The earth shook. Luka's knees trembled from some strange emotion, and he was unable to move. People kept running up, and he stood frozen by the crossroads where for centuries people had been hanged or executed according to the fashion of the day, but this stoning was something else.

Crowds were running from the town now like mad people, picking up stones that others had thrown, and hurling them again and again, cursing all the motherfuckers; Serbian, Chetnik, communist and Bolshevik bastards. The tanks' armour-plating jingled carelessly as they roared down the street as if in someone else's dream.

Just then a little red Fiat swooped up to the crossroads and came to a dramatic halt, and a suntanned young man in trunks and flip-flops (he had evidently been swimming) climbed out and walked calmly away, as though it was someone else's car he had parked in front of an advancing tank.

It was a T-55 with a bucket for digging, making it look like an ant in desperate search of an entrance to its anthill. The tank hooked up the little Fiat and pushed it along for a few seconds before squashing it against the side of a nearby bus. There was a faint squeak of metal, like the sound of chalk being scraped across a blackboard, and the car was flattened, fit for the history books.

A shower of curses and stones poured out after the green machine as it creaked on indifferently up the street. Luka could almost hear the curses hit the ground in the dull silence that followed. People were bending down and grabbing anything that came to hand, making projectiles out of broken bottles and bits of metal from the squashed Fiat. But the column passed, and no more cars appeared after that. The whole spectacle had lasted maybe thirty seconds.

Then Luka saw Maria. She was coming towards him slowly and breathing heavily; the running had worn her out, and her face wore an expression of utter astonishment.

'Shall we go home?' he said.

Silently she gave him her hand. The crossroads were almost deserted now and the crowds were dispersing. They crossed over to a quiet side street. Maria was still breathing hard, her palm hot and sweaty in his hand. Their hands separated and she leaned against a wall, waiting for her breathing to slow down. Luka waited too.

She looked up at him, her eyelids glistening, her lips trembling. 'They're going to kill us all!' she said.

'No one's going to kill us,' he said, putting his neck against her warm wet cheek. He desperately wanted silence, and her in that silence.

'Why are they doing it?' she asked, and the way she said it made it sound as if he were the one doing it. They had been through these stories a million times before; long, ugly stories that he didn't want to hear or have anything to do with. Guys like Lager with their bullshit. Luka's father with his gun, under his arm by day, under his pillow at night. Newspaper headlines. The TV news. Election posters. Anonymous letters. Anonymous telephone calls in the night. Pre-election promises and threats. Historic emblems and history textbooks. Drunken morons shouting on the streets of their quiet town at night, and he would wake up shitting himself with fear. A bunch of dirty tricks to drag you unawares into the same kind of shit you were watching only yesterday on television, taking place in some other corner of the planet, but now hugging and dragging you in, drowning you in it.

No, he didn't know who was doing it, or why, but both of them had already been pulled into it. Somewhere at the back of his mind lay a faded black and white photograph taken before his father was born. It was of something they never talked about at home, and his old man had shown it to him only after the communists had packed their bags and gone. It was of Luka's grandparents and his aunts and uncles in their old-fashioned romper suits. All had disappeared in one of the many massacres of the last war, leaving behind no explanation, no warning, just the photograph, and now he could feel the same thing beginning to happen all over again.

Maria was still talking. She was repeating the shit from the newspapers and TV, all that stuff about the Serbs being guilty of everything: killing the cops in the village of Borovo, putting up barricades around Knin, blocking the roads to the seaside. It was the thing about the seaside that got to her most. Then she replayed the scene with the poor guy and his little Fiat. Whose side was the army on? They almost killed him. Did Luka think she was stupid and couldn't see where it was all leading?

Then he reminded her who had promised to send him floating down the river Save and the Danube, all the way to Serbia. And what about the anti-fascist traditions of the people of Borovo village, and the fact that the sea belonged to everyone, and that the army listened to their High Command not to him, and that the 'poor guy' had deliberately parked his Fiat in front of the tank? And as for the last question, yes, she *was* stupid, and no, she didn't know where it was all leading. Blinded by rage now, he told her that as far as he was concerned she had the sovereign right and freedom to fuck whom she pleased and never to call him again. Even on the phone. Not even when she was at home on her own.

He would never forget the way she looked at him. If he hadn't just had her he wouldn't have turned his back on her so calmly. He walked away as if afloat, and was dismayed to discover that the charge of his anger was diminishing. Soon it vanished altogether and he regretted his big mouth. He turned back to Maria, but she was standing in the middle of the street shouting at some shithead to drop dead. As the street was empty he realized she must mean him, so he walked home, taking a roundabout route to avoid passing her house.

The crossroads were quiet, with just a couple of cyclists returning from swimming and a few stones lying on the ground along with the front page of a three-day-old newspaper.

The walk home took for ever. In the flat he found his old man shaving in romantic mood. He saw Luka was in bad shape and suggested he could use a haircut, but Luka said he might as well cut his name too, Croatian-style, and there the conversation ended.

He dialled Bili's number, but there was no answer. Realizing they were probably at Koki's place, he called there. That stupid bitch Bea answered, and was surprised to hear he wasn't with Maria. Then Bili came on. Luka told him he felt like hell and needed to get drunk, and that at least two people would have to carry him home. Bili said he would get drunk with him, and that Greg could drive them both home.

5

THE NUN RAPIST AND THE HIP FUCKER

At Koki's place Bea had made a nice pizza, and they sat drinking Bamboos and watching the Croatian news. The main item was the incident at the crossroads; there had been a camera there, recording everything. Then Koki left to take a bath, and Luka went off with Greg and Bili. Bea saw them out, looking at Luka as though he were a hardened criminal. She was dying to find out what he had done to her best friend, and he knew she would leap to the telephone the minute they were out of the door, but he didn't think Maria would feel like telling her.

Darkness was falling as they left Koki's building, and patriotic music was starting up from the hotel terraces. One night they had played the old Croatian song 'Rise Up, My Lord!' seventeen times; Koki had counted because it was right under his window.

Half-drunk, half-uniformed creatures wandered around the town, and on Ante Starčević Square another rally was starting up, about the flattening of the Fiat. To avoid it they took a different road, around the Blok centre by the Emona super-market, past the Croatian National Theatre and the cathedral. As God was their witness they had no other intention but to go to the Tufna bar and get drunk legally, but some higher force got in the way.

They were passing by the match factory when the owner of the off-licence on the corner rushed out carrying a flag. He climbed into a car in which three other men were waiting with more flags, and the car screamed off down the street with its siren on, tilting dangerously as it rounded the corner.

The door of the off-licence was locked, but the window was open a crack because of the heat, and some crates of wine were within easy reach. Greg noticed this, and Bili made a step with his hands for Luka, who was the lightest of them, to stretch his arm through the window and reach for three two-litre bottles of white wine. He opened the bottles with his Swiss army knife and they drank, while Bili told them how he had ended his military service. It turned out that he had deserted:

'Fuck, man, I served my time. Nineteen days' leave, or rather fifteen, plus seven for good behaviour – I should have been out by the 24th, but the day before, the shithead captain calls me and says: "Bilek, tomorrow you post the guard." Not a word about leaving! Oh, I forgot I gave blood three times, that's six more days. What a fuckin' faggot! His dear Slovenian sergeant goes AWOL seven days before, he doesn't dare report him, so now it's down to me. I say nothing about leaving but I can see the kid doesn't know his arse from a hole in the ground. "Okay, Comrade Captain, no problem," I say. Then I pack my things and here I am, my darlings. They're so fucked out there they'll never notice old Domagoj Bilek's missing!'

He ended his story about his exit from the military machine by tipping a stream of wine down his throat. The drink quickly got the better of him, and he leaned over Luka trying to pour the rest of the bottle over his shoulder. Then he was overcome by romantic memories of the night before.

'Do you know what I told her? "Bea, my darling," I said, "if you don't pick this flower it will die." Those are the words of our great poet Dobriša Cesarić, if I'm not mistaken.'

He went off to take a piss with Cesarić still in the picture.

> *'Run on, little stream, pass me by*
> *What signifies the little drop which is I?*
> *See a little fruit tree after rain*
> *Drops still come down — again and again . . .'*

He shook his tool in disgust at Greg and Luka for still being sober. 'Why don't you drink with me? Why? Dogs.' He ended his speech, and collapsed unconscious on the steps of the off-licence.

'What's his problem?' Luka asked. He hadn't expected Bili to pass out so soon; he had planned to drown his sorrows slowly and savour them with his friends.

'It's a generation thing,' Greg explained. He was speaking thickly too, having drunk too much red wine earlier at Koki's. 'It's your problem as well, you know. The country's in shit, up to its neck in it, all thanks to demagogy.'

Greg developed his theory in a quiet, didactic tone, as he always did when he was really drunk: 'Take this kid.' He pointed to the slumped corpse of his brother on the steps below them. 'Take a good look at him and his bullshit. Runs every day, sweats like a horse in the gym — he looks more like a horse than a human being! Then all of a sudden, boom! First little problem and he gets pissed and destroys everything he's been building up to. He has no self-respect. And you know what the main problem is here?'

'No.' Luka sighed, although he knew this story down to its smallest detail, and that the main problem had to do with angles.

'It's the angle!' declared Greg. 'Take you, Luka. Fuck it, man, you're okay, you know what life's about. Maybe you're not aware of it, but it takes some people years to work it out. If someone looked at you from the wrong angle, they might say, "What's wrong with him?" Because sometimes you can be a real bastard. See what I mean? Life's like that. You see the bad side, you change the angle. Duck and dive. Keep moving, man! That thing with you and Maria, it's crap. You're a jerk, you know that? You don't know how lucky you are to have her. She's a first-class girl, and you argue about crap...'

Greg was gradually losing his thread, and his listener was losing patience. He was getting on Luka's nerves, going through his ganglia directly to his brain cells. The problem with people who earn good money, have proper jobs and get on well with their women is that they think it gives them the right to hand out advice to others.

'Women', Greg went on, 'are gorgeous. Life makes practically no sense without them. Take me, for instance. I carry my Katarina around with me like this.' He clasped his hands together in prayer and held them to his face.

Greg was done; it did Luka's head in when he offered himself up as a model of constancy like this. He had known him and Katarina for years. Greg had gone to Germany to make a little money, but landed a good job and stayed on for three years instead of three months, so Bili and Luka had had to guard his golden girl like Rottweilers. Bili would have been screwed if his officers had discovered how many times he had dashed off to Zagreb to keep Katarina on track, and Luka had run up heart-breaking telephone bills with her and grown little round calluses on his ears from the handset.

Then Greg started on about the wedding. Five minutes more of this and Luka was ready to go nuts.

Suddenly they heard the sound of sirens, and two old police Zastava 128s, symbols of the rule of terror and the police state, converged on them from both ends of the street, catching them red-handed at the scene of the crime.

Since the change of regime Greg had had no cause to complain about his relationship with the police, since his uncle, formerly a petty criminal, had recently become a big shot in the Croatian anti-terrorist unit; he wasn't really the biggest, but his ruined, thuggish face was forever on television now.

'This is no time to panic,' Greg said. 'We'll explain that we were thirsty, tell them to find the owner of the shop, and we'll settle up with him tomorrow.'

The cars swung to a halt, sirens on, lights rotating, and five cops leapt out, fully armed and looking mean, although it was clear from their white socks and black sharp-tipped shoes that they were merely Rambo-like reservists.

The three friends sat on the steps, lit up by the lights.

'Put your hands up, bandits!' shouted the smallest cop, a nasty-looking dwarf. The others walked five paces forwards with their Kalashnikovs raised; at this distance it was obvious that they had had a few. Greg and Luka had no choice but to put their hands up, and they each raised one of Bili's. The poor guy was barely conscious and looked around him vacantly, his eyes half-closed in the blue light of the cars.

'Get up, animals!' shrieked the pint-sized maniac, pointing his rifle first at Luka, then at Greg. His hands were shaking dangerously.

'Put away your rifle, my friend, we're not armed,' Greg said affably, as though offering to buy him a beer in a bar.

They got up slowly, and the rifle pointed at Bili. 'What's up with him?' the little cop asked unpleasantly.

'Oh, you know how it is.' Greg shrugged his shoulders, and tried to pull Bili up.

Somehow it all ended in a scuffle. Big Bili stuck his elbow out and banged the little cop's head, which clanged like an old metal dustbin. The little cop slapped him two supersonic backhands, after which Bili kicked him in the stomach and laid him out on the asphalt. At this point, another cop took out his baton. The third cop tried to restrain him, but Bili was too drunk to care and knocked them both down.

The fracas looked more like a summer harvest than a real fight, and since all five cops seemed to be in a mood to do Bili some real damage, Luka grabbed him round the waist to hold him back. 'Cool it, ape-brain! It's me, Luka!' he said. This calmed Bili down a bit, and the pressure on his stomach made him throw up all over the little cop, who was still rolling about on the pavement.

After this the cops clapped handcuffs on the three of them, and really laid into them.

A big cop, evidently the patrol leader, whacked Luka a few times in the face and stomach with his baton, then bent over, whacked him a few more times on his back, kicked his arse and tried to shove him into the car.

He didn't succeed immediately, and Luka met the car door frame a few times. Greg met it more than a few times, and when they ended up on the back seat together he looked like a different man. The cops went on stamping on Bili, thumping him with their rifle butts for a while, then they threw him into another car, and they all sped off to police headquarters, taking the bottles with the last remaining drops in them as evidence of their crime.

'You've cocked it up this time,' muttered Greg darkly through his split lips. 'My uncle will screw your mothers for this. He's in the Special Police.'

'We'll rip the skin off your back, and your uncle's too!' the driver said, turning round and taking his hands off the wheel, almost crashing the car into a lamp-post.

'Mind your driving – you at the back, shut up!' snapped the fifth cop, who was the most sober of them.

They soon arrived at the police station.

Luka experienced a moment of stage fright as they led him into the building, for the first time in his life in handcuffs, but the duty officer at reception greeted them like long-lost relatives. He was eating a pizza and reading the *Liberal Weekly*. He looked like a serious type, probably from the reserve squad; in fact the whole police station was packed with reserve cops, as though a state of emergency had been declared.

Chairs were put out for the three of them. The duty officer peered at them. 'What fair wind blows you here, my friends?' he said, throwing a chunk of pizza down his throat.

'They broke into the off-licence by the match factory, got

drunk, and started a fight,' the little cop explained. 'They were seen by the nightwatchman at the factory. He reported them to us and we picked them up. These are the bottles of stolen wine.'

'Lies have short legs — I thought yours were short because your mother had sex with a dachshund!' Bili said through gritted teeth, and the little cop stuck his baton in Bili's eye. He sat sobbing on his chair. He was covered in blood and vomit and had evidently pissed himself when they beat him up. He had numerous bumps on his head, and bruises from where they had massaged his scalp.

The wise-looking duty officer, obviously recently recruited, put away his newspaper and nodded. 'So who are you, a gang or what?' he said at last in a bored tone.

'We are the nephews of Mate Karoglan,' declared Greg, wiping his nose with his sleeve.

'I'm delighted to hear it, Karo's nephews,' said the duty officer. 'Where are your papers?'

'Here they are. Bilek, Mijatović, Bilek,' the big cop said obligingly. 'Doesn't say anything here about Karo being their uncle.'

'We'll have to keep them in for the night then. He's out on night patrol and won't be in till morning,' the duty officer said. 'We're a bit short of space, they'll just have to put up with it.'

The cops took their details, removed their cuffs, and handed them over to a podgy turnkey who led them down to the cells.

'When I lock you in with those Chetniks you'll see your god,' he warned, throwing them into separate cells.

Luka wasn't impressed by his: bare concrete, no windows, and the so-called Chetnik curled up on a concrete bench. He was a thin, stunted kid of about seventeen, with a smashed face.

The podgy one slammed shut the door and switched off the light, but in the light from outside Luka could see his cell mate still curled up silently on his bench. The room stank of shit and piss, and there was no toilet in sight. Luka's beaten body cooled and began to ache — stomach, head, back, legs — he never knew there were so many bits to it.

Around eleven they heard a sputter of machine-gun fire and sporadic gunshots, then silence. The little Chetnik began to fidget.

'What's up?' Luka asked.

'Fuck my arse, whenever there's shooting I get beaten up.'

'You're a bit young for the barricades, aren't you?'

'What barricades? They picked me up from a field. They took me off my tractor.'

'Where are you from?' Luka asked.

'From Šodolovci,' the kid said.

After that they said nothing for a while. Luka thought about Maria, and wondered what she would do if she knew he was in the nick. Jump for joy for the first hour probably, then cry her eyes out. She had a good heart.

'What are you in for?' the kid asked.

'I raped a nun,' Luka replied.

The cell was shit, all concrete, with a few flattened turds and bloodstains on the floor. He had the chance to observe it more closely when they came in to collect Dule (that was the kid's name). Three men came dressed in camouflage outfits and covered in mud, looking as if they had just risen from the grave. They immediately laid into the kid, kicking and punching him.

'Okay, Chetnik, you're fucked!' they said, leading him out.

The door closed, leaving Luka in the dark until morning. Then a regular cop in a blue uniform turned up and took him out to the corridor.

'Let's go, bandit, we'll see what we're to do with you.'

They threw him into the same room as Bili and Greg, with a table, a telephone, four chairs and lots of blood on the floor.

'What's the matter, run out of tampons?' Bili asked one of the previous night's cops. The cop raised his baton and was about to lay into him again when they heard Karo's hoarse voice bellowing in the corridor: 'Of course they're my nephews, what else would they be, cunt?'

He came crashing into the room, looking like a rhinoceros in his camouflage outfit, with a knife, a pistol, a baton and a collection of other tools at his belt. He stared at the trio, and finally recognized Bili and Greg.

'Is that you, Gogo?' he asked Bili.

'No, it's you,' the other replied; he was in a bad way.

'When did they let you out of the army?'

'Yesterday.'

'Why didn't you stop by and say hello? What are you looking at, cunts? Fuck off!' he shouted at the other two cops, who withdrew looking disappointed.

Karo pulled up a chair and sat astride it. In less than a year he had acquired all the tricks of a cop and over twenty kilos in weight.

'Sorry, boys, I'm bushed. We wasted the whole night

chasing round the barricades in Bijelo Brdo. What kind of shit are you up for this time?'

'Hail fellow well met, the kid just came back from the army. We wanted to celebrate a bit, and those drunken louts got heavy,' Greg explained.

Karo tutted and shook his fat head. 'And where did you find this long-haired specimen?' He pointed at Luka.

'An old friend, since nursery school.'

'Never met him before,' Karo said.

'The pleasure's mine,' Luka said politely.

Karo gave him a weary, menacing look.

'What are you, a smartarse hip fucker?'

'Not quite,' Luka replied modestly.

'Come on, yes you are, I can tell.' Karo banged the table with his baton, making the telephone jump up and start ringing. 'You can't fuck with the police, son.'

'Excuse me,' Luka said, 'I don't think I—'

'You don't think anything.'

Grabbing the phone, Karo bawled out the duty officer and the patrol leader. Then he led the boys out to reception, where they were handed back their documents and keys and Luka's Swiss army knife. After this Karo packed them all into his car; he was among the first to have the popular chessboard on his number plate.

'Here, keep these in memory of your uncle who saved you from the shit,' Karo said, throwing some papers on the back seat. 'If it wasn't for me those jerks would have charged you with robbery, plus two burglaries from last month.'

'I only came back yesterday,' Bili said, as proof of his innocence.

'Yeah, and you'd have sat in the can for a few weeks till they checked your story,' Karo said, speeding up. 'I'll drop you off at my place, I'm half asleep.'

'You're doing well, Uncle, if I were you, I wouldn't be able to sleep a wink,' Bili remarked sarcastically.

'Cut the crap, Gogo,' raged Karo. 'You're boozing and messing around while I'm saving Croatia and wearing my nerves to shreds on the barricades.'

'And paid a bomb for it too, I bet,' Greg put in, covering for his brother.

'I'm paid shit, don't you know there's a war on?' Karo shouted, turning up a radio news report on troop movements in Slovenia. 'Do you realize the army was shooting at our people last night outside the downtown garrison? Seventeen wounded! You didn't know that either?'

Karo was well supplied with fresh information, from all sides.

'I'm telling you, boys, it's time you got yourselves sorted. I need skilled people like you in my unit.'

'Go to bed, Uncle, I just came back from the army, I don't want to wear a uniform again,' Bili said.

But Karo persisted in an avuncular tone: 'Stop it, Gogo, if everybody went on like that, the Chetniks would smash us! I could get killed any day, and what would happen to Božica and the kid? Okay, you don't give a damn. But some day you'll remember that Uncle was good enough to pull you out of shit, you and your pansy friends.'

The car had stopped in front of Karo's house, and the three of them climbed out. It was a nice old house covered in ivy, with a garden and trees at the back; Karo was fighting for the right things, no doubt about it.

'Hey, thanks for the lift,' Greg said sardonically.

'No problem, any time,' his uncle replied. 'If you need anything, just call.'

'You can send a Black Maria for us next time,' Bili said. 'You know where to find us.'

But Karo was already driving his car into the garage and didn't hear.

'He used to be a real dosser,' said Greg, observing the modest features of his uncle's property in this elite area of town. 'When Ma was alive he used to invite himself over every other day to scrounge meals off her.'

Bili spat, and Luka suddenly threw up all over the ivy-covered wall.

'That's good, let it go, my son,' Greg said. 'Look at us — they've wiped us out.'

'Let's go to the Big Moustache's for a meat pie,' Bili suggested.

Luka looked blankly at him. 'Do you want me to puke my eyes out too?'

'No, you can have a nice bowl of yoghurt,' Bili said, and they all turned towards the Castle area.

At the Big Moustache's Albanian pastry shop they ordered two pies, as greasy as Bili's jokes, and a plain yoghurt for Luka. It was just after five in the morning, so the Big Moustache himself wasn't there, just an apprentice whispering apprehensively with his two Albanian pals, who had just deserted the army but still had their uniforms on. They were sizing up the boys and their bruises. Luka cursed the morning in Albanian, and they greeted him in the same old way. Then the three of them went out with their breakfast, and gave the full support of their backs to the eastern wall of the shop, watching the sun come up. It came up crookedly and made Luka vomit up his yoghurt. Now he had nothing left in his stomach but nausea.

'Listen, you'd better lie down and recover for the wedding,' Greg said. 'It's going to be on Saturday, if there aren't too many funerals.'

'I wouldn't miss it for the world,' Luka said. 'Fucking good morning to you.'

Not wanting to have to tell his old man that he got his bruises playing basketball — not really wanting to see his old man at all in fact — Luka went down to lick his wounds in the basement storeroom he had set up as his gym.

He followed the war in Slovenia and as the army was getting its arse kicked harder and harder, his swellings went down and his bruises changed colour, from purplish-red through blue-green to yellow and brown. In Slovenia it looked as if it was all over. But around Osijek the tension was building, and he could hear shooting. At first it sounded like a farewell party, then a wedding, then a New Year celebration, then it thundered on through the night like Midnight Mass.

6

AVE MARIA

Luka was woken early next morning by a light glaring into his eyes – the reflection from the mirror perhaps, or some other polished surface. Bili had a key to the gym; he was probably playing one of his army pranks.

'Stop mucking around, I'm awake!' Luka pleaded, but the light didn't move, so he threw his pillow at it.

It wasn't Bili, it was Maria. She was sitting on the bench, and the rays of sunlight flashed from the mirror she shone in his face. She turned the mirror away and the light glinted through her hair, which hung down over her face almost covering it. Luka could only see her red lips, patient and calm. She swept up his pillow in a circular movement and gently returned it.

'About time too,' she said.

He sat up in the bed. His long hair was greasy and dishevelled and fell over his face; he was neglecting himself these days.

He crawled to the rusty sink, threw off his pyjama top, turned the tap and waited for the sink to fill, then dunked his head in the water. One hit and he was awake. He washed, pulled his hair back in its ponytail, then dried his face with the cleaner side of his pyjama top.

'Ave Maria,' he said at last, sitting opposite her on the bench. She didn't reply.

She was wearing a short black lycra dress, without a bra (she didn't need one). That night he had dreamt of his girl who brought him the light, and across town she kept vigil all night in her room, through the shooting. Her eyes were hollow with tiredness and misty with tears. She was crying, but she was there.

Luka realized Bili must have sent her. Good old Bili, half orang-utan, half fairy godmother. His friend.

'They ironed you flat,' she said, touching the cut on his lip. 'Does it hurt?' She kissed him slowly, carefully, while her hands stroked his neck, his shoulders, his chest, along his ribs and below; he didn't know how many organs he had and how long it would take.

Her legs were dark, as if the sun was shining between them. Her soft thighs wrapped themselves around his waist, the bridge lifted, something slapped and he was inside. Her dress rode up to her neck, over her head and flew to the far corner of the room. She covered him with her hair and moved slowly, saying soft incoherent words in a voice as dark as red wine, disappearing and coming back, taking him far away to a drunken place from which he never wanted to return.

She clung to him, kissing him, moving faster and faster, opening herself to him, finally coming with a deep gasp to that shuddering beyond all shudderings that begins as silent liberating laughter, and reverberates through the body as skins lock and nuzzle together in the stickiness.

Afterwards he lay on the bed with his head on her small breasts, her hair spread out over him like threads of silk. He said nothing, not wanting to spoil it, and she was silent too, yet her voice rang in his heart. He didn't understand what the voice was telling him, but everything was clear. They were about to build their house of cards all over again and enjoy the game until the next storm; maybe it didn't make much sense, but the rest hardly made any more.

Soon he left her to get some sleep, and went upstairs to call Bili. He found the wedding invitations in the flat. No one was at home. He dialled Bili's number and Greg picked up the phone.

'Hi, Luka, my brother's in the shower, he just came back from the gym.'

'How are your bruises, any better?'

'Yes, thanks,' Greg said.

Then there was the sharp slap of a wet towel and Bili grabbed the receiver. 'What's up, sweetheart?' he laughed.

'I'm calling to thank you for all the little things that make a man's life beautiful, with the emphasis on this last one. Maria says thank you as well.'

'So give her one for me, only she came for the key herself, it was nothing to do with me.'

'So much the better.'

'Be at the tram depot at half five tomorrow, okay? We're meeting there before we go to the church.'

7

A CARVED WOODEN DONKEY

It had poured with rain the night before the wedding, but by midday everything was dry. Maria had slept over at Luka's place and had to go home to change, so he walked her there. The afternoon passed in the stillness of the Lord, with no sound but the chirping of a lonely cricket. She lived in an area of small family houses, with little gardens crowded with pine trees and roses. There was a cat, a dog and a canary in every house. It was a carefully tended idyll. Nobody seemed to be at home, apart from the menacing shadow of her brother lurking in the background; he vanished into the garden the minute they arrived, but Luka still felt the burden of his presence.

'So where are your parents?' he asked when she came down in a new skirt.

'Upstairs. They're boycotting you.'

'Great,' he said. 'Let's go.'

The festive mood at the tram depot was already spreading far and wide, and even at this distance the tram-workers' brass band could be heard running through their chosen repertoire of Christmas carols – at the beginning of July. Maria smiled happily; she had ten good reasons to be happy, and it had been dawn before they got to sleep.

A spruced-up tram stood parked in the shade of the poplars, surrounded by twenty or thirty men in dark suits, among them Greg's father who was supervising operations.

'Welcome, Luka, Gogo was looking for you a moment ago,' cried Bilek senior, hurrying up to greet them.

They kissed each other twice in the old Catholic way, then Luka gave him one kiss more to make it Orthodox, and the old man did another to neutralize it.

'This is Maria,' Luka said at last.

Old Bilek stepped back to take a better look at her. 'So you and Greg have fixed yourselves up, what are we going to do with Gogo?'

'Give him time, Uncle Bostian, he'll find someone,' Luka said placidly as old Bilek handed them glasses from the loaded table.

'Luka, Maria, cheers!'

'Cheers, Uncle Bostian!' They clinked glasses.

The old man downed his in one gulp. 'Never leave her full and never leave her empty.' He winked.

Old Bilek was a veteran of agricultural aviation, and in the best traditions of avio-alcoholism he never flew sober; he had had a few scrapes, but nothing too serious.

The band stopped for a rest. Stipe and Jure gave them beer, after which they played the popular Dalmatian song 'Mount Marian' to show their gratitude.

Bili turned up from somewhere in a suit and looked approvingly at Maria in her skirt; she looked good in it.

'I'm glad you're riding together again,' he said, pointing to the tram on the opposite track; it was stuffed with food, with drink in the fridge and everything laid on as though for the

Olympic Games. Attached to it was the trailer for the musicians.

Luka had borrowed a pair of trousers from his father because he didn't want to ruin his own, and there was a big gap between his stomach and the zip.

'Give me something to fill this void,' he said to Bili.

Bili fetched two bottles of beer. Luka poured the remains of some grappa into his and they laid bets to see who could finish theirs first. Luka won the first round; during his army days he had held the record not only in his unit but in the entire garrison, with a winning time of nine seconds. He won the second round, and would have won the third too if Maria hadn't taken his hand.

'You won't last two hours this way,' she warned him.

She was right, he felt dizzy already, but his trousers fitted him perfectly.

'I've a few things to sort out. We'll be off as soon as the bridal couple arrive,' Bili said, putting his empty glass on the ground and hurrying off.

Luka squatted down to get a better view of Maria's legs, with their lean calves and smooth fine ankles; no tram-conductor ever had legs like that. She squatted down with him, and they kissed for a while among the piles of rusting tram-tracks and cubed granite cobbles with grass sprouting through them.

The tram-drivers continued their ear-splitting performance. Just then they heard the ridiculous klaxon of Greg's VW, and the elder Bilek boy appeared with his fiancée. She was dressed all in white and was followed by her parents and her two sisters. Her parents seemed slightly confused by the ceremony, but it wasn't every day you pushed your daughter into the arms of an eligible guy like Greg. Greg's father did his best to charm them with his easygoing manner, and soon everyone had climbed aboard the tram.

As they dusted along the half-empty former YPA Boulevard, the band played the tune that roused them every year for the First of May celebrations, and Stipe moved around serving juice and beer to the thirsty guests; the seats had been rearranged and they had put in a table and cleared a space in the middle, through which he pulled the crate behind him. The function was also honoured by the presence of fat Karo and his fat wife, and they all felt much safer with him sitting there at the head of the table in full combat uniform.

All of a sudden Luka felt the urge to toast the happy couple. Standing up, he grabbed one of the ceiling straps and shouted, 'Hey, let's hope it lasts, Greg!'

'Let's hope so!' Greg shouted back.

The tram stopped in front of the Peter and Paul parish church, which the people of Osijek in a fit of provincial megalomania had named their cathedral, and the band stopped their racket to rest their chests and lubricate their throats.

In the church a strange wedding march was being played, but at least it wasn't 'The Internationale'. As the main forces concentrated around the altar, Maria and Luka sat on a pew at the back, enjoying the shade. She was enjoying the ceremony. Luka tried to get to grips with the idea; he thought he could probably stand about two days a week in a happy marriage.

The ceremony was drawing to a close and Maria was getting twitchy. 'See how nice it is, why don't you come to church with me sometimes?'

Luka choked and jumped up from his seat. He didn't want to disrupt the liturgy so he said nothing. There were all sorts in his family, but no Catholics. His father was a stunted Orthodox, his mother a deformed Protestant or something. No one hassled him about religion, except Maria.

'Let's go outside, it'll be over soon,' she said a bit later, as the ceremony stretched on like a pig's intestines.

Kids were waiting outside, ready to ambush the best man for money to buy ice creams. After that there was a lot of unhygienic kissing, then they all drove off again, this time to the registry office.

Maria wanted to stay outside, but Luka dragged her in and it wasn't so bad; the registrar was Greg and Katarina's old primary-school teacher, and she got so carried away with her wise advice that everyone was soon cracking up with laughter.

Gathering up the musicians proved a bigger headache, because they had crawled round all the restaurants and cafés by the church after Stipe and Jure refused to give them any more to drink. Fortunately, because of their instruments they were easy to spot, and they were hauled away and pushed in to the trailer. The old maestros were insulted and refused to play without more drink, but when they got it their music wasn't worth listening to anyway.

Karo requested that they throw the tram turntable towards the police station, so he could check on his boys. Outside the building he produced his pistol and fired a few shots in the air. This brought out some cops who felt obliged to see what the matter was, but when they saw it was their boss they greeted him politely and went back inside.

At the turntable by Green Field the music was finally beaten. Greg thanked the musicians for their services, and a group of the most sober ones got out at the depot, while the more serious cases were left lying in the trailer.

'I thought they'd have lasted longer,' Luka observed, checking with Greg to make sure none of them had died.

'Sodding pensioners, give them five beers and you can throw them away,' Greg grumbled, turning an old grey man on his stomach. 'Still, it's only to be expected. At seven we'll collect Mile's gypsy band from the station.'

'We can't go to the station without music,' Luka protested. So he, Bili, Karo and a few more of the drunken guests charged on to the trailer, where they armed themselves with the abandoned instruments and produced a noise that gave them great personal pleasure; some were holding the instruments for the first time in their lives, but most managed to blow into the right holes.

At the railway station the cops were already harassing Mile and his gypsies, but Karo soon rushed out of the tram to sort them out. By now he was roaring drunk and his big Herzegovinan gypsy soul woke up. Hugging and kissing the bewildered musicians with their tambourines, he declared that he was the biggest gypsy of them all, and that nobody understood them as he did: 'I'm honest, I defend you from the Chetniks, I negotiate with them for you, I listen to their songs all night on my walkie-talkie. So you'll have to listen to them and sing them too! Come on, Mile, sing! Let it rip!'

Mile and his group kicked off with a bilingual Serbo-Croatian patriotic song. Most of the people around Karo joined in with Croatian words, but he sang the Serbian version, and with the help of his gun he made the others join him. 'You see, you do know the words! Anyone who doesn't can learn them from me and not be ashamed when the Chetniks come! Greg, my son, live a hundred years!'

Then he sprawled out on the conductor's seat and fired his pistol out of the window. They were approaching the downtown garrison now, and his wife had to calm him down because the army had been traumatized enough by their defeats in Slovenia and the slightest thing made them jump.

'Stop that noise at once, do you hear, Mate? Are you sick?' she said.

'I've never felt healthier in my life!' he bellowed, then turned to Jure and aimed the pistol at his head, 'Gimme a beer!'

Jure passed him a beer with one hand, and with the other he removed the pistol. Cheated and disarmed, Karo pulled another gun from his pocket, a revolver this time, and continued speaking with it aimed it out of the window at the garrison.

'You sing "Rise Up, My Lord" blah-blah-blah, but when it's time for you to rise up, you can't be found! There's just old Mate Karoglan and his orchestra standing between you and those Chetniks out there, you faggots!' Then he sat down at the table to eat.

No one paid him any attention. The gypsies played their old town and old country folk music and teased the bridal couple, and a more stable atmosphere set in.

It was dark by the time the tram rounded the park by the Health Centre and stopped to let the men water the sides.

'Only fifteen minutes now, don't get lost, you drunken bastards, just wet the lamp-posts!' Bili shouted into the darkness.

Luka emptied his reservoir against the nearest tree and returned to the tram. An academic quarter of an hour passed, and still it didn't move. Then the baker's van arrived and Stipe and Jure pulled out several trays filled with roasted lambs.

'Come on, kids, hold out your hands!'

The trays were hot, and Stipe and Jure salivated like dogs as they carried them on to the tram.

Soon the other guests emerged from the darkness. 'This park's full of perverts,' said Maria, breathless after her short run.

Bili and Luka discreetly counted the guests who were hurrying to the sound of the tram bell like Pavlov's dogs.

'Your uncle's missing,' Luka observed.

'Your aunt as well,' smiled Maria, 'I saw them.'

'Perverts,' Bili said distractedly.

On the trailer the gypsies played a bouncy melody while the guests on the tram started consuming the meat. Bili was consumed with worry about his uncle now, and went off in search of him. Luka joined him, and they called into the darkness. Finally they heard a sound like a herd of elephants pounding through the jungle, and Karo appeared in all his glory with his uniform unbuttoned and his wife by his side.

'We said just fifteen minutes, Uncle!' Bili said reproachfully.

'Fifteen minutes wasn't enough, my son, I'm not that old yet!' Karo winked at his wife.

'What's wrong, Aunt, can't you find a better time for your marital duties?'

'I'm telling you, Domagoj, if he didn't have to piss he'd never remember,' complained his aunt. 'He fucks more with those Chetniks than he does with me.'

'Don't you talk like that, Božica, it's what I do for a living.' Karo soothed his wife as they made their way back to the tram.

In their absence people had devoured almost all of the lamb. It was the best lamb, from the island of Pag. This and the freshly-baked pitta bread and good Dalmatian wine had lifted the party spirit almost to the point of ecstasy, when Stipe slowly rose to his feet and calmly, without staggering, grabbed hold of one of the ceiling straps to make a toast:

'Our beautiful Greg! From my earliest days I have been in the habit of running a mile at the mere mention of marriage, like when someone mentions cancer or some other fatal disease. Later, when I realized more clearly what the word meant, it was still difficult for me to comprehend why two young people who love each other should want to ruin their lives in this way. However, you soon realize there's no other way, so fuck it, though personally I wouldn't have thought there was any need for it yet.' He stared at Katarina's stomach, which showed no signs of bulging. Then he coughed and resumed: 'But let me give you a few tips anyway, as an older man. We all know that Kate and Greg here love each other like two turtle doves. But for your marriage to work that's not enough. Greg, you have to turn into a donkey; be full of patience, put up with things, and don't give up even if you're dying. And you, dear Kate, must treat this donkey properly; you must feed him and water him so he can pull well, and push too by Christ, for the good of everyone. If you see he's dying, take some of the weight off him. If he kicks, kick him back.' He paused. 'And finally, in memory of my words, Jure and I wish to present you with this de luxe carved wooden donkey. To the happy couple!'

Everyone raised their glasses and cheered. After this Greg's old man stood up, and leaning against Katarina's father he delivered himself a touching fatherly speech of which little could be understood because it was in Slovenian. Then the toasts and speeches came fast and furious.

The lamb was too salty. Luka drank more wine and felt very tired.

8

MORE IMPORTANT THAN LIFE

Luka was woken late the next afternoon by the persistent ringing of the telephone. He was lying on the floor of the sitting room with the furniture dancing around him in a circle, and a waterfall roaring in his ears. Maria's voice on the telephone also sounded a bit hoarse and hung-over.

'Are you feeling any better?' she asked.

'How can I tell? How was I?'

'Don't you know? You got dead drunk and sang a load of Chetnik songs. You burned the flag, the whole show.'

'No kidding.'

'Okay, you didn't. Listen, I'm leaving today.'

'Yeah, right.'

'I mean it. I'm staying with my aunt in Germany for a couple of months until things sort themselves out.'

'Yeah, right,' Luka said again, wondering how things could possibly sort themselves out in such a short time.

'Is that all you've got to say?' She could hardly believe it, having hoped for a hysterical outburst.

'What else do you want me to say? I'm drunk. I'll see you off at the station.'

'Be there at five,' she said, putting down the telephone, and that was that.

*

The day was horribly hot. Luka felt cold and sweaty, as he always did after too much wine. He arrived at the station before Maria and bought two cans of tonic water from an Albanian in a kiosk, then put his arse on the asphalt and waited.

Crowds of cops moved lazily around the police station opposite. Getting in and out of their cars, revving their engines, putting their sunglasses on, taking them off again and looking at themselves in the darkened windows of the building. Never in his life had Luka seen such a bunch of narcissistic pigs.

His beloved came stepping over the yellow paving stones of the square with her rucksack on her back and a bandanna in her hair, just like in the good old days when they had hitch-hiked and inter-railed around Europe. She took the rucksack off, sat down next to him, and silently took one of the cans.

Everything reminded him of Spain in 1989. They were sitting in a godforsaken Spanish village, filthy from the cheap trains, drinking a sobering drink with quinine in it and watching the cops hanging around outside the police station a few hundred metres away. The heat was maddening and the drink evaporated instantly through their pores, and it seemed that no power on earth could induce them to make a single unnecessary movement.

All at once the police station blew up. Luka and Maria sat rooted to the spot as pieces of it fell from the sky, along with the remains of the cops and several unlucky bystanders. Basque business probably. They had slept the night in the train station, and the next day they had left for France. Maria drank her tonic and watched the cops.

'Do you remember Spain?' she said.

'Uh-uh,' he replied.

'Do you think it'll happen here?'

'I haven't a clue.'

'So will you get on the first train and get out, like you did in Spain, citizen of the world?' She didn't say it aggressively, it just sounded sad and a little pathetic, seeing as she was the one leaving.

He said nothing.

'You want to know if he's at least a little bit sorry that I'm going?' she asked the can, as if there were a ghost in there who knew the answer.

But the ghost didn't say a word.

'I don't know,' Luka replied for it. 'I wouldn't say so. It's so stupid.'

What was stupid was that her folks were packing her off, away from the shit, and most of the shit was him. He didn't go to church or eat ox on the spit on 30 May to celebrate the Day of the Croatian State – what future could they possibly have together?

Like parents the world over, they had a foolproof scheme for their children's future. They had always seen Maria's thing with Luka as a passing hormone imbalance and teenage folly, and now things were slowly turning their way.

'Dad and Marian have both enlisted,' she announced self-importantly.

So now they were laying down their lives for their country.

Luka considered this for a moment, and summed up his thoughts in a single word: 'Idiots,' he said.

'Maybe some things are more important to them than their lives.'

'I suppose they'll tell you what those are when they're dead,' he said.

And then to his surprise she didn't talk about ideals or big words, too big for his small soul. He had no ideals anyway, the word was always connected in his mind with cheap Czech ping-pong balls and floor polish; he just had a few healthy ambitions – to work less, get drunk sometimes, eat well and that fourth thing he had with her.

They walked to the platform. The train was already waiting. He felt a pang of regret as he watched her take off her rucksack again.

'Listen, when all this is over we'll go to Spain,' he told her.
'What for?'
'To see if they built a new police station for those cops.'
'Is that all?'
'And to drink sangria. Then we'll go to the South Pole and have our picture taken with a penguin.'
'Yeah, on inter-rail,' she said.
'Listen.' He peered into the empty can. 'I was bullshitting earlier about you leaving. I wish you weren't. I feel sorry for myself.'

But she just sealed his lips with one of her glamorous kisses, then without saying a word she turned and put her rucksack into a compartment. He didn't want to look at her through the window, and all of a sudden his nose started running, his eyes were wet, and he felt the urge to go home;

an unbearable, inexplicable urge, like the physical urge to piss.

Outside the police station he passed a group of cops dressed in American uniforms, hanging around the flower urns, smoking, eating sandwiches, cleaning their weapons and talking. They didn't look like cops, they looked like a foreign army in foreign uniforms. Most of them were Luka's age, some were even younger, and the urge to go home became so strong that he wasn't sure he would be able to hold it in until he got there.

9

ONE OF THE BETTER
BIRTHDAY PARTIES

Maria's departure coincided with the start of the worst period in Luka's life.

The town was hit by one of those unbearable heatwaves from the Panonian plains that spare no one and during which you would gladly jump off the top of a building or shoot yourself in the head just for the cooling draught.

At this time the skirmishes around the village of Tenja to the east were becoming more fierce, with shootings and explosions all night long and army convoys leaving town in the morning to pick up the dead and wounded.

The people of Osijek coped with all this thanks to their highly-developed capacity for double-thinking. They knew in their balls that Croatia would win, but they bought up every can of food in the shops just to be on the safe side.

Luka laid in vast reserves of beer, and Bili came round and they would drink together and curse the authorities, the army, the police, politicians, women and everything else.

A fortnight after Maria left, he got a letter from her. It was written on the till roll of the supermarket where her aunt worked and where she had a job stacking cans. It began 'Dear Luka', and it ended 'Love you' with a lipstick stain for a signature. In between she wrote about her cousins, the supermarket, the town's beautiful Gothic cathedral, German boors and Deutschmarks.

He read her letter fifty times a day, imagining some horrible ginger-haired Kraut coming on to her with a pale moustache, pale eyelashes and tight, stone-washed jeans tucked into high trainers, and the image was so vivid he thought he was losing his mind.

Bili came round and they sat in front of the building with their beer and went through their news. Or rather Bili went through the news from town, and Luka would cry into his beer over Maria.

'Hey, Greg called from Thailand,' Bili interrupted.

'And? What's his news?'

'He's got diarrhoea, they both ate some rubbish over there. Some honeymoon,' Bili said, opening his beer with his teeth, though he knew this grated on Luka's nerves.

'How many times do I have to tell you not to use your teeth?'

'Millions of times, mate.'

'So?'

'So what? You want me to open it with your teeth instead?'

'What's wrong with the opener?'

'It's unhygienic.'

'You know what? I don't see you for two days, and in two seconds you're getting on my tits.'

'I'll go then.'

'Don't go, please. I'm scared stiff when you're not around. I'd die without you.'

'You've gone fucking crazy, Luka. Two weeks without her and you're pissing your brains out.'

'Fuck it, you're still on the bromide from the army!'

'What a blessing!'

'I mean it, don't mention her or Germany, and we'll get along fine.'

'She doesn't write or what?'

'Bili!'

'Just wondering.'

'Stop wondering.'

They said nothing for a while, then Bili started on Luka's third most hated subject.

'The Croatian Guards have got their new uniforms.'

'Oh, really.'

'From Germany.'

Luka cursed; he was sick of Germany. Bili stood up to take a leak under the big plane tree. He kissed it. 'Hey, the lungs of our town.' Then he opened his flies and watered it – to make it big, he said. 'All right, Luka, I'm going now.' He waved.

'Thanks.' Luka waved back.

The lift was out of action as usual, so he walked up to the flat. In the fridge he found the remains of his father's sandwich; it seemed his old man had at last found a woman who knew her way round the kitchen.

He dialled the number in Germany Maria had given him, then went for a piss knowing it would take a while to connect.

It was dark outside now, and the guns were roaring like crazy; the day had been too hot for a quiet night. All the lights in the flat were off, and he sat by the telephone with his mouth full waiting for the connection. Finally he got through.

She answered in German.

'*Ja, ja,* it's me, *meine Liebe.*'

'Thank God, Luka, I thought you got hit.'

'I'm not in the flat, there's been shelling all day so I'm in the cellar.'

'Jesus, how do you go to the toilet?'

'No problem, your arse goes tight.'

'What's that sound outside, shooting?'

'No, it's the TV with the sound turned up.'

'What's the matter, are you drunk?'

'Like a pig. For days. I haven't come to my senses since you left.'

'Don't do this to me, Luka.'

'Only kidding. I got your bill from the supermarket, so I'm celebrating.'

'You mean my letter? Write me one.'

'I wrote you a song instead.'

'Have you got it with you?'

'I've got it in my head.'

'Let me hear it.'

'Okay:

> *You left this town*
> *Till things calmed down*
> *Auntie got you a job*
> *Stacking cans in her shop*
> *The Balkan streets are dark*
> *All night the dogs bark*
> *Maria, Maria, Mari-ah!'*

There was a pause as he took another bite of his sandwich and chewed.

He heard her take a deep breath. 'Is that song about us?' she said.

'It's the truth about us.' He took another bite.

'Are you eating?'

'Yeah.'

'Typical.'

'People have to eat.'

'Not while they're on the phone they don't.'

'So what do you eat over there?'

'Plastic and broken glass. I've lost two kilos.'

'Great, you could lose some weight.'

'Get lost! Listen, don't cheat on me, okay?'

'I couldn't even if I wanted to. There's only Bili and me left here.'

'Don't let him touch you.'

'Don't let any of those Krauts touch you.'

'Even if they have a new BMW and a swimming pool?'

'Especially not them.'

'I can't be like that, Luka, when all's said and done they're our friends.'

'Friends, shit. They send us tinned meat and uniforms and take our best skirt. They ate shit in two wars, and now they look at us like we're animals in the zoo!'

'It's all right, Luka, I only wanted to wind you up. Do you really think I'd go to bed with someone who eats popcorn with sugar?'

'Do they do that too?'

'I'm telling you, this is a nation of perverts.'

'How do you know if you haven't slept with them?'

'You're cracking up, Luka. You'd better lie down.'

'Don't be angry. I've had this funny feeling ever since I got your letter.'

'Just for the record, no one's screwing me here apart from the warehouse manageress.'

'What can I do? I'm jealous as a dog.'

'It doesn't matter. I loved you calling me. Your song's great.'

'It's yours. I'll call you same time tomorrow. Sweet dreams.'

'Take care, Luka.'

She hung up and he sat in the dark, then took another piss and went down to his gym. Outside, the street was filled with the noise of squealing tyres and car horns. This was the Croatian Guards fooling around with their confiscated cars. Luka had his own personal jerk, who passed the building at regular two-hourly intervals and honked for two minutes before leaving.

He lay on the carpet in the dark, drinking. Beer dripped on to his chest, his hair, his ears. He didn't care.

At the beginning of August, just before Luka's twenty-third birthday, the fun finally seemed to be over. After a quarter of a century of surgical practice, Luka's next-door neighbour, Dr Mitrović, vomited for the first time when he smelt the stench from two refrigerated lorries bearing to the mortuary the mangled corpses of the Croatian unit killed during the fall of Dalj.

The story of these unpleasant by-products of the fight for freedom had a terrifying effect on the town, which until two years before had been sleepier than Sleeping Beauty's castle, and crowds of people publicly and in broad daylight took to their heels and got away as fast and as far as possible.

Maria's second letter arrived on Luka's birthday. Her aunt had taken her on a trip somewhere, and the envelope bore a postcard with a picture of a mountain and a bored-sounding message on the back.

As well as his letter from Maria he had a call from his mother, with whom he was in irregular telephone contact, inviting him to celebrate the twenty-third anniversary of their mutual project at ten that evening in the hospital, where she was on duty. No doubt she had made a cake with candles on it; she still treated Luka like a child, it probably helped delay the ageing process.

He was lying in the bath drinking beer from one bottle and washing his hair from another, when the telephone rang. He jumped out of the water without drying himself, grabbed the phone and returned to the bath. It was Maria.

'Happy birthday!'

'Thanks, baby.'

'Pissed again?'

'Just a bit melancholy.'

'And you never get over it.'

'Whereas you're conquering the peaks, of course. Have you conquered any Krauts yet?'

'You're a pain in the arse,' she said, and the line went dead.

His toenails had softened in the water, soon he would be able to cut them; they were very long. A moment later the telephone rang again. He dried his hands so as not to get electrocuted.

'Yes?'

'We were cut off.'

'Piss off, Maria. I don't feel like talking. Hang up again, I don't care.'

'*What's wrong with you? What's happened to you?*' she screamed down the line at him.

'Nothing's happened, I'm just having a bath, listen.' He splashed the water with his free hand.

Her voice changed suddenly. 'What d'you want? Do you want me to come back?'

'No way, you have to make lots of money for Spain.'

'Be serious, Luka, it's important.'

'It's not important at all, you're better off where you are. Marry some rich old Kraut and don't come back to this hell-hole.'

'You drunken monkey, you imagine I keep running into millionaires in my supermarket? Get sorted, I'd like to hear you normal for once!'

'Then call another day.'

'You can't think how terrible it is for me to hear you like this.'

'So hang up.'

She hung up. He continued with his pedicure, then the telephone rang again.

'Fuck off!' he yelled.

'What's wrong with you, Luka? Fucked up your birthday too?' Bili asked in a surprised voice.

'I was talking to Maria.'

'And she hung up on you?'

'What else could she do?'

'Man, you're in trouble. But I've got something for that. Stay where you are, I'll pick you up at eight.'

Bili drove up in Greg's VW dressed in jeans and an old American M-65 army-jacket; his hair had grown a bit too.

'Many happy returns. Happy birthday.' He was carrying something wrapped in a little blanket.

'What's that?'

'A souvenir from the army.'

Inside there was a YPA M-70 assault rifle, the type Luka had used during his military service. 'What am I supposed to do with this?' he said.

'We're going out for a night's target practice.'

'Eh?'

'Grab that crate of empties and we'll be off.'

They put the wrapped gun in the boot of the car, Luka brought out the empties and some full bottles, and Bili started the engine. The town was deserted and in darkness; there was no police patrol on the bridge. Bili drove up the road to Bilje village under the starless sky, and on to the dirt track leading to the place on the old Drava Lake where they had picnicked earlier that summer. They stopped at the shore, lighting the water with their headlamps, and threw the bottles into the lake, where they glowed like Christmas decorations.

'That's the spot,' Bili said, handing Luka the gun.

Sliding a luminous bullet into the barrel, Luka shot at one of the bottles, and the glass top shattered and sank to the bottom. He and Bili sat on the bank drinking beer and shooting at the bottles. The night was very still, with no sounds but their lonely gunshots and the poplars rustling in the breeze. They stopped shooting and listened to the crickets in the grass singing in harmony with the bullfrogs from the irrigation ditch, just like the Serbs and Croats used to long ago. Then they drank up the beer and sank the last of the bottles. It was quite a decent birthday party, one of the better ones. They used up the remaining bullets by firing them into the sky, making a din as if a flaming squadron of bees was eating a hole in it. Then Luka took the gun apart and cleaned it, and the smell of the smoking barrel and the traces of powder under his fingernails reminded him of his army days; it hadn't been such a bad time really. He stuck the rod in the sand by the lake and twisted it a few times to clean it, and the metal was shiny again. Then slowly, ceremoniously, he reassembled it. After that Bili drove him to the hospital.

Even at that time of night the place was heaving with Croatian Guards and police, walking around with their guns and talking to the nuns and nurses. Luka nodded to the security guard whom he knew, and walked coolly past the nurse at the reception desk, who was talking on the telephone and didn't look up.

His mother was no longer a ward sister but she still had her old office, which was where he found her.

'Ciao, Luka,' she said; for some reason she always addressed him this way.

'God bless you, Mum,' he said, looking at the mud and rubbish on the floor. 'It was cleaner when you were in charge.'

'Yes, they come straight from the trenches and we've no time to clean up. Wait, I'll get your cake, it's in the fridge.'

She brought out a cake, or something rather less than a quarter of a cake. 'Dr Mitrović is on duty, I offered him some,' she explained.

'I can't believe he guzzled almost all of it,' Luka said, staring at the little piece left.

'It wasn't him, we had a bit of trouble a few minutes ago,' his mother said. 'They brought in this wounded fellow full of holes, and four of them, muddy as pigs, followed him into the operating theatre to keep an eye on Dr Mitrović. But there was nothing he could do, the poor chap was riddled with lead, so we covered him up and sent him down to the morgue. Dr Mitrović had to chase the four of them out and they practically beat him up, if I hadn't called the emergency staff God knows what would have happened. Later we brought them in here to calm them down and Dr Mitrović explained about antisepsis, and I offered them some cake. What can you do, Luka, war is a terrible thing.'

Luka couldn't imagine Dr Mitrović chasing anyone anywhere; he was the most peace-loving man in the world and lived only for his work, his plastic gloves and his green operating gown. On the two occasions he had come to Luka's place for lunch, he had washed his hands at great length in some very complicated way, and talked of nothing but his aquarium, which Luka occasionally looked after for him when he was away.

Luka ate his cake – his mother had made a good job of it – and they talked a bit about this and that, mainly Catholics. Catholics were her pet obsession: she had a sort of merciful contempt for them, regarding them much as she did her patients. Luka had never been able to work out why Calvinism was so *über*; he always thought Catholics had more fun, with their decorated churches, their funny liturgies and all their countless feast days with excessive quantities of alcohol, but he was in no mood to discuss this with his mother now. She was busy anyway, so he went.

Outside, the Guards were drinking, arguing and singing, and the nurse at the reception desk was still on the telephone as he walked out.

The Sjenjak estate was in darkness, and the shadows of his building were darker than the night, like the legs of a chair turned upside-down on a table after closing time. Guards from a drunken patrol were shouting at people to turn their lights off. Ignoring them, Luka slipped in unnoticed.

It was a quiet night, so he decided to sleep upstairs in the flat. He had reached the landing when he heard the telephone start ringing inside. Hurrying through the door, he picked it up. An unknown voice swore obscenely at his Chetnik mother and hung up. A moment later the same person rang back with the same message, but this time didn't hang up.

'Listen to me, fuckface,' Luka said in a rage, 'I'll bet you don't even get a hard-on with women, you faggot!'

Then someone with a Bosnian accent came on and raved about slitting throats and gouging out eyes. He said he'd wipe them all out.

'Praise Allah, my friend, but there is a catch — we are hardly ever at home, so you must tell us when you plan to come and we'll have the coffee and plum brandy waiting,' Luka said, imitating the man's Bosnian accent.

'We'll string you up by your bollocks, Chetnik!'

'Okay, my friend, just don't take your shoes off at the front door!'

In the background he could hear a drunk guy with a Zagreb accent yelling, 'We'll pluck your eyes out, Chetnik!' Then the familiar voice of Maria's brother came on the line. Their folks had certainly not bothered about their names; Maria and Marian, no imagination required.

'Happy birthday, little Chetnik, I fuck your Serbian mother.'

'Hi, snotty kid,' Luka said calmly, sticking to his Sunday manners.

'Hey, we just had a few drinks.'

'Then put your finger down your throat, not down the phone.'

'Fuck your sister, why don't you join us?'

'I don't drink with faggots, and regarding sisters, I've already done yours about five hundred times.'

'You son of a bitch, when I get you I'll skin you alive and cut your fingers off!'

'I don't fuck with my fingers like you, didn't Maria tell you?'

Marian swore at him a bit more, and finally slammed the receiver down. Luka had had many such calls from kids in the reserve units, acting like Ninja heroes down at the community centre and running off home as soon as the shooting started.

10

OLD TATTOOS AND NEW SHAMPOOS

Next morning Luka ran into Mrs Bakarić outside the door to his gym. Mrs Bakarić was the unpleasant widow of a volunteer who had died during the winter of 1942 at Stalingrad. She hated everything that moved within a radius of ten kilometres, and from her flat on the ground floor she monitored the activities of the kids in the playground, the courting couples in the hallways, even the poor vagrants fishing old newspapers out of the rubbish bins.

Luka had no idea what she might want from him, but he didn't have to wait long to find out.

'Luka, Crisis HQ has given orders that all basements and hallways are to be cleared and made ready as shelters in case of air raids. So if you don't mind . . .'

Luka couldn't believe his ears. She was telling him to move his gym, despite the contract he had signed with the house committee and the advance rent he had paid for the next five years. He happened to know that the money had already been spent to mend the intercom and paint the banisters and the lift. He was furious.

'My gym won't be open for your inspection until the year 1995, dear lady. If you have any problems with that, I suggest you talk to the president of our house committee, Dr Nikola

Mitrović, who lives on the sixth floor. He has a copy of the contract, if you need to take a closer look at it.'

Mrs Bakarić stood there opening and closing her ill-fitting dentures, spitting saliva and squeaking as if she had a scrap-metal machine in her head. It was a disgusting sight for so early in the morning and, ignoring her moans, Luka gently pushed her away from the door and locked himself inside the gym. He lay down on the bed, listening to her sniffing around the rest of the basement and the boiler room. She was in the habit of doing this for hours, but would go into hiding the minute she heard the familiar klaxon of Greg's VW as Bili drove up for the next beer session.

When Luka heard his characteristic knock at the door that morning he responded by hurling an empty bottle at it. There was a smash. Bili unlocked the door and Luka threw a full bottle at him. Bili opened the bottle on the door, not wanting to irritate his friend by using his teeth.

'I expect you have toothache,' Luka said in a didactic tone.

'I just brushed them. Let's go.'

'Okay.'

Greg's car was still in one piece, although the way Bili drove it made it unlikely that it would stay that way; the Guards were requisitioning all the better cars in town, and most of the drivers were like Bili, crashing and killing themselves on every corner.

They drove around aimlessly for a while, until Bili finally drew up outside the café across from the Town Hall. Sitting at the tables was a crowd of familiar and unfamiliar faces, some in camouflage outfits, some in grey uniforms, and a few in black. Their weapons had been carelessly left on tables, or propped haphazardly against walls.

'What in hell's name are we doing here?' Luka asked.

'To see Bisa and Njaka. I hear they've signed up,' Bili said, parking the car in an empty space under a 'No Parking' sign.

It didn't take them long to pick out the shaven skulls of their friends in this scum of plankton and dandruff. Bisa and Njaka were sitting at a separate table, apart from the others, drinking beer with the air of proud losers. The rest were a sad and seedy crowd of predominantly middle-aged, idle louts and sacked workers. Not even the uniforms and weapons could lend them any kind of military respectability; they were a mob of unshaven, broken-toothed, long-haired pot bellies, who addressed one another as 'Brother', 'Pal' and 'Colleague', and began each sentence with the mantra 'Know what I mean?', which could mean anything, not that any of them knew or meant anything.

Most of the crowd was concerned with how to get rid of their old tattoos from the Yugoslav People's Army. Many wore gloves, bandages or long sleeves, and the most extreme cases had even peeled off bits of skin, or changed the embarrassing Yugoslav Army initials JPA into DONA.

In this classy environment Njaka and Bisa could have effortlessly claimed any social group as their own — aristocracy, circus artists, intelligentsia — but it didn't seem to amuse them very much. Bisa was dressed all in black as usual, plus a belt with a knife and grenades. She wore her own boots. Njaka was almost unrecognizable in his camouflage get-up.

'I like your disguise, old boy,' Luka said as they sat down

at their table. Bisa's AK-47 lay beside her, painted deep black. Bili locked it and turned it away from himself.

They didn't seem too happy to see Bili and Luka, but they never looked that happy anyway; Bisa's old man was Muslim, and Njaka's was Russian, so it couldn't have been easy for them to play their roles as Croatian defenders.

'Looks good on me, huh?' Njaka said, showing off his uniform.

'A bullet in the head looks good too, but no one's wearing that,' Bili remarked. 'Where are the waiters?'

'None left, they've all been made captains and majors. Just go in and help yourself.' Bisa jerked her shoulder towards the entrance to the café like a hospitable hostess, and Bili went in.

'It's not a bad life.' Njaka was making an effort to open up new horizons for Luka. 'They give you all the ammunition you want, and you get to meet Germans, Poles, English, even Russians! It's great!'

'The cream of Europe,' Luka said. 'Is there any money in it?'

'Yeah,' said Bisa. 'The pay lasts five days, like a period, then I can fuck myself.'

The joke fell flat as everyone knew that Bisa did it on the rag, but Luka managed a grin. He found it funny that Bisa, who a couple of months ago hadn't known the difference between a Serb marching song and Ravel's *Bolero*, was now prepared to pull the trigger for the Croat paramilitaries. But what the hell, these were only small transformations; no one could see the full picture yet.

Bili came back with two beers, and they were quietly picking the labels off the bottles when a man turned up and bellowed, 'Unit on duty, shift your arses on the double!'

Several people jumped up from their drinks and went off, tightening their belts. One looked sadly back at his empty place, then came back and drank a beer he had left on the table. 'It may be my last,' he said, flashing a toothless smile at Bisa.

The toothless one left, and Bisa and Njaka threw accusing looks at Bili and Luka. 'Those Zagreb idiots are coming here to fight, and you're bumming around town in your car.'

Bili and Luka went quiet and watched Bisa arranging the beer labels on the table; if they had wanted to join the Guards they would have been there before her.

Anyone who has grown tall and beautiful drinking Osijek beer knows that with the right rearrangement of the message on the label, you can get a certain four-letter word for a part of the female anatomy. Bisa had made this word, and drew Bili and Luka's attention to it. Bili looked and sadly shook his head, while Luka stared at the café window above Njaka's head and gently urged Bisa to change her shampoo as the one she was using had brainwashed her. Then the two of them stood up and said goodbye.

'Take care, kids, I don't want to see your photos on the obituary page,' Bili said.

They drove more erratically than ever down Old Republic Street. Then Bili deposited Luka outside his building, and careered off.

11

SPIRITUAL INTOXICATION

Soon after that day Bili took Luka to watch the show outside the cathedral for the Feast of Our Lady. These were difficult times for the town. The YPA had barricaded itself into the suburban barracks and polygon C, and mortars started shyly dropping on various quarters of the city. One night sandbags appeared, and barricades constructed from old rail-sleepers. The Croats' chances weren't looking good on the other fronts, and this was the start of a major religious revival unseen since the golden days of the Counter-Reformation. Every day massive religious rallies took place, and at night, instead of the old witch-hunts, determined individuals would plant mines around Serb buildings and monuments. Anyone who cared for themselves sported a rosary around their neck, and those in uniforms hung them on their epaulettes. Most of these rosaries were the cheapest kind, made of transparent red glass, and were obviously very new. It looked just like some new fashion, like the one for break-dancing or the hula-hoop, and Luka had an allergy to such things.

That morning Bili parked the car some distance from Ante Starčević Square. They were walking completely sober towards it through quiet Šamačka Street, when they were accosted by a middle-aged drunk outside the butcher's pop-

ularly known as 'The Elephant', on the corner of Strossmayer
Street.

'Guys, help me home, will you, I can't walk 'cause of my
heart.'

He lived in a squalid hovel propping up the remaining wall
of the old brewery.

'Thanks, pal,' he said to the wall, wobbling like the
character with typhoid from the war film *The River Sutjeska*.

As Luka and Bili turned back, another fat monkey came up
and threw his arms around them. 'Hey, brothers!' he shouted.
Another drunk. He handed them an almost full bottle of
brandy, while his companion vomited into the red bin hanging
from the lamp-post and swore at its Bolshevik mother. Then
the two drunks embraced and staggered off down the street
together.

All around the square they saw the same thing: everyone
was drunk to the gills, and this spiritual intoxication was their
one connection to Our Lady.

The procession was enormous, miles long; you couldn't see
the beginning or end of it. Everyone carried candles, some
carried two or three; some of the candles were the size of
baseball bats, and in the place of honour walked the courageous Croatian defenders, washed and shaved and respectably
dressed in clean uniforms for the occasion.

Luka and Bili lurked behind a group of bystanders. As they
finished off their bottle of brandy the atmosphere became
more bearable. The sky was blue and festive, friendly flags
flapped victoriously in the breeze, men in uniforms smiled
innocently at the nuns, and the patriotic war songs sounded a
lot less loud, tuneful even. Marchers and spectators alike were

practically having orgasms on all the love, patriotism, goodwill and unconfined joy. Even the long-haired nutcase shouting, 'Hang the Serbs!' seemed benign and friendly to Luka.

This was his hometown, he had rolled on this square drunk as a pig with his old high-school friends when they were the first, the biggest and the best, the core of the future intelligentsia, and of course the world existed only to be changed by them.

Then someone shoved a narrow bottle of Badel brandy into their hands. They sipped it, knowing its powerful effects, which could knock the shit out of a man when he was least expecting it. Suddenly they found themselves in the crowd, which was grabbing candles sold by Bižo, skilfully disguised as a friend of Croatian democracy with the help of a rosary casually thrown round his neck.

Luka saw Bižo's astonishment when he spotted them. 'Fucking mother of Jesus, what are you two doing here?' he said, forgetting himself for a moment. But Bili was already handing him some money. 'Give us six and stop moaning,' he said.

'Hey, come back later when I shut up shop!' Bižo shouted, up to his neck in business.

Bili and Luka pushed through to the tram-stop. They lit their candles there because the crucifix was crowded with people, and then sat down outside the Slavonia clothes shop and quietly sorted out their impressions. Compared to this bedlam, the downtown Pentecostalists were just a cheap puppet show.

All around, the crowds were beating their breasts and asking to talk to Our Lady, and for a moment Luka had a

vision that God Himself was on the line. There was a
crackling and buzzing in his ears, and he was flooded with
waves of religious ecstasy. Then Bili led him towards the friar,
who was coming out of the Capucin monastery dressed in the
brown cassock of the Little Brothers; he was wearing the same
sandals as Luka, which must surely mean something. They
kneeled before him and kissed the cord around his waist. The
friar blessed them and passed on. The crowd followed suit,
and Luka saw among them his old school maths teacher with
the Einstein hair and chicken brain, who had seldom succeeded in converting his pupils to his unorthodox doctrines
about the use of classical formulae. It was impossible to count
the number of those who had seen the apparition of Our
Lady; a few women became hysterical and practically drowned
in their tears. Bili and Luka decided to stand to one side, and
the crowd fell before the friar as he pushed on down the
street, blessing them with his hands and feet, until he finally
turned the corner by the Yugoplastika department store.

It was there that they ran into Bižo again, standing on the
side of the street happily counting his profits. 'I've made the
killing of the century!' he told them, rubbing his hands. 'I sold
everything the boss had in the warehouse. Let's drink to it!'

In the desolate Rendezvous bar at the end of Šamaćka
Street Bižo bought them beers.

The bar used to be a meeting-place for hookers and
soldiers, but since the blockade of the garrison the soldiers
had had to toss off in the toilets and the hookers had moved
on.

'Everyone's gone crazy,' Bižo said. 'I took more money
today than I did in two months selling ice creams.'

'People could certainly use something to cool them off,' Luka said, rolling the bottle between his hands.

It had been another hot Panonian morning, and now it was a disgustingly sweaty afternoon. Droning squadrons of repulsive metallic green flies danced in a circle in the middle of the room, shagging on the wing, far from the reach of mundane politics. They doubtless came from the loos, whose stench rose up from the cellar below. The friends scratched themselves, leaving dark semi-circles of half-eaten skin under their fingernails. This merely made the itching worse, and they soon tired of the beer and chat and left Bižo for home.

Nothing good awaited Luka there, just the broken lift and a few million stairs he hadn't the strength to climb. He felt like weeping, cursing, grabbing the first thing harder than concrete that came to hand and with six or seven punches demolishing the entire building to its foundations, then finishing off the rest of the world with a few more energetic blows; but this was harder to achieve than it seemed.

By the time he reached the second floor he was feeling a bit calmer. On the fourth floor he heard mumbling and heavy breathing, and on the sixth he met the sad figure of his neighbour, Dr Mitrović, dragging two heavy suitcases out of his flat as he prepared to take off for the Montenegrin seaside; he went there every summer, but this time he was evidently going for longer.

'Hi, Luka, I'm glad you're here; I was looking for you. I wanted to leave you the keys. I can't take any more, I'm leaving for Kotor.'

'Fine, Uncle Nikola, shall I feed the fish for you?'

'No need, I've thrown them down the toilet. Thanks anyway. Say goodbye to your dad for me. Take care, bye.'

He left, and Luka stood on the landing playing with the keys. Then the telephone started ringing in the doctor's empty flat.

It rang importantly, as though there were a fire somewhere, or someone was drowning. The keys itched in Luka's hands. The telephone went on ringing. He unlocked the door and went in.

On the other end of the line an unusually fine, calm voice enquired why he had not left yet, and politely advised him to hide before it was too late. The voice belonged either to a gay man or a cultured lady, both of them rare birds in Osijek.

'Why the hurry?' Luka replied, doing his best to make his voice sound polite.

'Because you are in grave danger,' the voice replied. 'I'm calling on behalf of a good friend of yours who very much wants you to keep out of this. Your friends haven't forgotten you, but you also have enemies. I'm not one of those who are threatening you, I'm begging you to leave. We can't help you in any other way, but we don't want anything to happen to you. I also know that your telephone is being tapped. You mustn't risk more problems. Understand me, please. Is there anywhere you can go?'

Persuasion had never fallen more kindly or more gently on Luka's ears. Like a balm for his soul.

'Thank you for your concern, dear lady, you really shouldn't have troubled yourself. I shall remember your kindness to my dying day,' he said, and the person hung up.

He hung around the flat for a while. Most of the furniture was still there. Dr Mitrović had taken with him his TV, stereo, video recorder and a few other things, but he had left the telephone, maybe because of the bad memories associated with it. Luka pulled the cable from the wall so as not to put any more good people to the trouble of calling, seeing as its owner probably wouldn't be returning in a hurry.

12

MEDIEVAL GHOSTS AND OBITUARY NOTICES

The army was reported to have brought in reservists from Serbia, but all they could think of doing was to blockade themselves in their barracks, bombarding every corner of the town in their attempt to break out. The sandpits in the children's playgrounds hadn't a grain of sand left in them, all of it was taken to make sandbags against the mortar attacks and air raids, and God knows where they got hold of the museum-piece anti-aircraft guns arranged tastefully on lorries on the street corners. The civilians didn't feel much safer with all the guards and cops around the place though, because those in uniforms generally joined up only to save their precious arses, and the small fry found comfort in tidying up their basement storerooms and polishing their hoarded cans of food.

Luka was most affected by Dr Mitrović's departure as chair of the house committee, because Mrs Bakarić instantly started the process of electing a new chair who would refurbish his gym for the needs of the civilian population, even though there were four other basement rooms that could as easily be used.

Luckily for Luka the new chair was Žunić the architect, a frothy intellectual who hadn't the balls to tell him anything

directly but communicated by hints and written notices. Old
Mrs Bakarić, on the other hand, rode her hobby horse flat out
to the limit and spread her network of spies around the
building. Two days after Dr Mitrović left, she invited her
cousins over, refugees from Dalj, and moved them into his
old flat. The children had been wisely packed off to Poreč, on
the Istrian coast, and their father was out most of the time
trying to 'find something in Zagreb'. Since Luka didn't fancy
his new neighbours very much, he moved himself down to the
basement and only went upstairs for a shit. Luka's old man
was out practically all the time now, protecting the various
cultural monuments that had started cropping up all over
town; it seemed any shack older than a hundred years was a
cultural monument these days.

In Luka's gym, he and Bili drank beer and watched
television until it came out of their ears. Croatian television
had a new, round-the-clock programme, *The War for Freedom*,
for the senile, the illiterate and the rest, with Tomislav Ivčić
singing his mega-hit 'Stop The War!' (the logical continuation
to last season's 'To War, To War!'). This was accompanied
by pictures of guards crawling in the mud through the
coppices around Zagreb, or skipping in four lines and singing
about throwing the Serbian warlord Martić out of Croatia. In
the intervals they served warmed-up reports from all the
million crisis zones around the Republic; the war was
merciless.

People's loathing for the Serbs and the Federal Army had
already exhausted the existing fund of insults, and Croatian
TV struggled hard for words to do justice to the indescribable
crimes of the Bolshevik–Serb–Chetnik–Yugo Army. Each

morning would bring up some foaming fresh neologism, but by midday the enemy would have committed so many more atrocities that the newsreaders could only sob, blow their noses, and tearfully repeat the shabby dirges and insults from the day before.

Then there was TV Belgrade, with its dozy phrases about the weak being expelled from their firesides, which might have made the uninitiated think the conflict was taking place some-time in the Middle Ages. Along with this they mumbled on about the fighting morale and organizational strength of the army, as though all that was needed was a few ears pulled and arses kicked to put things right. It seemed to Luka as if Belgrade were in some other galaxy, whose radio signals took light years to reach his television set.

But the truth was all around, and he had only to look outside the door of his building to see it. Pinned to the trees and lamp-posts of the neighbourhood, the faces of known and unknown heroes peered out from black-framed obituary notices. Some of the photos had been taken only a month or so before, and were still displayed in the window of the high-street photographer. There were smiling high-school prom photos, fresh army photos, photos taken from driving licences and from the student index. But what they all showed without exception was that none of them had been told that bullets had the habit of travelling in both directions.

13

GENERAL ALERT TAKES OVER

In the evening hours, when the melodious hoot of the General Alert sounded over the radio, the neighbours would rush down to the boiler room in the basement to watch TV, and Luka would spend time there examining the reactions of the two different audiences, Serbs and Croats, to the same situation.

Half the faces he was seeing for the first or second time, and those who weren't strangers to him he knew mainly from complaints to his father about his loud music and parties, or by their dirty looks whenever he ignored them on the stairs. None of this bothered his old man, but it now stood between Luka and a pleasurable meeting with his neigbours, so he preferred to stay next door in his gym.

During the first evening of shelling and fireworks they all sat on the stairs formally dressed in their pyjamas and nightgowns boosting up their last reserves of courage. No one bothered to drag themselves all the way down to the shelter; they knew it would soon be over.

When it turned out that the shit was likely to take a bit longer, they rummaged around their storerooms for something to put under their backsides, and Luka came in to find them sitting around on improvised chairs staring stupidly at one another.

In the background someone had switched on the radio, which was issuing an interminable list of instructions in case of air, or heart or nervous attack, but nobody was paying any attention. It was an ethnically polarized crowd, which made it hard to find any neutral topic of conversation, but when old Weigel from the fifth floor started cursing the army the atmosphere immediately grew more convivial. Everyone had something to say on the subject, and old Caktaš from the third floor outdid them all with a lot of inspiring swear words in his Dalmatian dialect. Later on the group started smoking and Luka went outside to stand by the entrance with a bottle of beer in his hand, to enjoy his heroic solitude and the magic of the nocturnal bombardment.

Extravagant machine-gun fire reverberated from the direction of Tenja and the downtown garrison; the army evidently had plenty of ammunition. The blackout in the area was total, thickened by the shadows of the tall buildings, and only the cigarette smoke and fragments of conversation percolated through the bars of the basement windows.

Mrs Bakarić put her Pekinese face round the door, monitoring the situation. 'It seems to be calming down a bit, eh, Luka?' she said.

Just then the first shell hit the back of the building with a deafening crash, and was followed by a second one further up by the front of the building, which made a real mess of the row of cars parked there. Luka hurried down to the boiler room past some women who were hurling a choice selection of curses at Mrs Bakarić. 'That witch'll get the planes on us!' one of them said.

After that two more mortars hit the building, and they

could clearly hear the rubble sliding down the walls and thudding on to the concrete. The women started wailing, and their menfolk calmed them down with curses and fretted about their bangers parked in the firing line. Žunić the architect, proud owner of a brand-new Toyota, bloodthirstily declared that for every dent in his car he would kill one Serb, and the other car-lovers started throwing out higher and higher numbers.

A few days later there was a putsch in Russia. This gave the basement crowd pause for thought. Everyone was scared shitless and was as polite as if it were New Year's Eve, assailed on all sides by ghosts with big moustaches and shiny boots. But the putsch soon collapsed, Gorbachev came back from the Crimea happy as a virgin after intercourse, and in the basement things went back to normal.

That morning the radio played the General Alert three times in the space of two hours, and Luka's old man returned early from work with his Protection of Monuments armband. He wasn't happy wearing this; an armband was an armband even without the swastika or the Star of David. He looked tired and didn't feel like going to the shelter, but when the planes started flying overhead they both hurried down. They were the last to arrive, and found their anxious neighbours already at their posts.

The old ladies frantically swallowed the last of their trophy sedatives, which Mrs Kuna had rescued from Dr Mitrović's flat. Luka's father placidly munched a sandwich.

'It's all right for some, eating away as if nothing was happening,' old Mrs Bakarić remarked pointedly.

Luka's old man gracefully batted this back. 'You're wrong,

dear neigbour, just because you're bored stiff doesn't mean the rest of us aren't doing anything. I'm busier than ever. At the Institute we're on our feet all night long; this is my first meal in twenty-four hours.'

Everyone looked at him like a young falcon. Like a fucking hero.

'Have you anything for me to drink with this sandwich?' He turned to his son.

'Just the beer.'

Luka expected an expression of disgust from his old man, who didn't tolerate alcohol, drugs, smoking or any other vices.

'You'd better give us some then, what can I do?'

Luka handed him his open bottle, and old Weigel sneakily asked if it was cold. Luka didn't reply.

'Ah, there's no better drink than cold beer.' Weigel sighed.

Without saying a word, Luka went out to his gym and returned dragging a crate behind him. Weigel had clearly lost every trace of self-respect; it was written all over his forehead that he would give his arse for a beer.

'This is so you won't swear in my presence any more,' Luka said, handing him a bottle.

Weigel nodded and downed half of it in one gulp, then started talking in a voice full of sorrow about his disillusion-ment with the human race. 'For years we live side by side in this building, and some people I'm seeing now for the first time. It took war to bring us all together.'

'Big deal! We could have done without this war,' chipped in Mrs Weigel, reaching into the crate and helping herself. She opened the bottle with a key like a practised beer drinker, and gulped down half the bottle as her husband had done; you could see what kept their marriage together.

'It makes you wonder, doesn't it?' Mr Weigel said. 'This time last year we were at the seaside in Opatija, and now...'

'What's there to wonder about?' snapped Mrs Weigel. 'You'd wonder at anything!'

'Your wife has a very sharp tongue,' commented Luka's old man, finishing off his sandwich.

Mrs Weigel downed the rest of her bottle flirtatiously and waved off the suggestion. 'What do you mean, "wife"? I'm a widow, dear neighbour, a widow!' She then confided her anguish to the assembled crowd, but her words were largely unnoticed because they were more interested in what was happening on the screen.

Luka stood up and walked to the window. His old man was now boring the neighbours with his thoughts on life. Mrs Weigel was piously nodding her head and every so often pointing an accusing finger at her husband, who sighed and threw his bottle from hand to hand and waved aside her threats. Like many asthmatic people, Mr Weigel had trained himself not to worry, and would spend days walking around the estate wheezing and spluttering in a pair of old jogging bottoms with his socks falling down; his wife treated him like some old pet she hadn't the heart to take to the vet to be put down.

Luka looked through the bars of the window at the remaining bit of sky, covered in a trail of smoke from God knows where. The bombardment continued, further away now. Slipping unnoticed to his gym, he spent the rest of the afternoon going through his old photos and school memorabilia.

All his notes from those years fitted into two thick notebooks, like a sort of unwritten diary made up of cartoons, caricatures of the teachers, accounts of card-parties and mysterious codes that used to make him laugh for hours, and which now looked like something he had no right to see. A few literature lessons had made their way into the notebooks, plus some sociology, maths and physics, all jumbled together because he had never felt the slightest inclination to listen to anything his teachers had to say.

The main feature of these notebooks was their idiocy. He sighed and hurled them at the wall, where they spewed out the photo of his class prom. The happy crowd in the picture looked like frozen fish on a slab. He spent a long time looking for himself, but his class had mainly girls. Four years had passed since they had left, and most of them he hadn't seen since, but he knew beyond all doubt what had happened to these girls. The pretty ones gave up studying, shagged someone and got married, and the ugly ones ended up at university. This was the fate of the girls from his classy two-hundred-year-old gymnasium.

When speaking of this school people never failed to mention that two Nobel Prizewinners had once been pupils there, but strangely enough no one ever heard the prizewinners bragging about the place. One of them had visited for the bicentennial celebrations, a feeble, nerdy type in fusty clothes, looking just like a Nobel Prizewinner is supposed to look. The pissed pupils had gawped at him as he was helped along

the red carpet by two spotty hackers, the best the school had
to offer, and regular as a train timetable, a short article had
appeared on the penultimate page of the local newspaper
about his visit. The piece included the usual spelling mistakes
in his name and was marked by the supreme indifference of
the illiterate provincial towards long-gone greatness. Had Jesus
of Nazareth come down for them in Osijek, they would have
calmly nailed him back on the cross and gone back to their
beer, their fish paprikash and tambourines.

Luka's wild cult of the individual was striking even among
his traditionally antisocial countrymen. He didn't care about
99 per cent of the things that ate people alive here; such as
why the matches of the first-division football club were less
well-attended than others; why the players had beer bellies; or
why the rowing club had no money for oars, let alone new
boats. He used up all his energy in the gym or jogging, and
sometimes Maria used to join him and they would end up
going off to the woods, or for midnight swims in the river
Drava. But now Maria was far away, further away than ever
before, and it was less painful to drown in the beer and
memories. Evening would come, darkness would fall, and with
it the darkness in his head.

14

BORN LEADER OF A MASS-SUICIDE CULT

Next day Luka went for a walk to the town centre, drawn there by dramatic reports of the destruction the night before.

What had been destroyed was the monument to the victims of fascism, a huge bronze sculpture of an unfortunate couple with their hands handcuffed together. Now all that remained was the massive marble base, freshly graffitied with several Ustashe slogans appropriated from the quisling times of the Independent State of Croatia. The man, a giant with a bare, buffalo-like chest, had been taken all the way up to the chemist on the corner, and the woman lay on the other side of the street, opposite the tennis courts.

Luka knew some guys for whom this would mean the realization of all their childhood dreams, who dreamt of plastic explosives while playing with their modelling clay, and who in their vulnerable teens had caused quite a stir by blowing up the offices of the Serbian newspaper *Politika*; he wondered where their pyrotechnic appetite would end.

A strange type with a camera was moving around the debris under the monument and snapping away, so he hurried off.

The streets were already filling with promenaders. There was no shooting because some negotiations were going on. Luka had no idea what these negotiations were about, but he soon noticed the white jeeps of the EU observers, then the observers themselves, standing outside the buildings of the Croatian Democratic Union across from the post office. They were observing the tyres of their vehicles, scowling and knitting their brows at the state of their cars, untroubled by the destroyed monument, the smashed windows and the demolished roofs of the buildings.

Luka went down to Starčević Square, where he found the cathedral untouched. Guards sat at the tables of the Psunj Hotel, less drunk than usual. Trams buzzed round the square, and he could see almost no sign of war, apart from the fact that everyone was behaving as though Nothing Was Happening, like when people are being recorded on television and pretending not to know it.

Everything was brave somehow: the breeze was brave, the sun shone bravely in the sky, and Ivčić's song about stopping the war rang out bravely from the cafés where the guards sat bravely drinking away their modest salaries. Clinging to all this was the thick veneer of patriotism, and every so often trucks full of guards would rush along the one-way street in both directions, singing war hits from the crazy 40s.

Luka returned home by tram. The negotiations fell through as usual, and that evening the Yugoslav Army took Baranja, pushing the modest Croatian police forces to the village of Podravlje.

After the fall of Baranja, crowds of refugees poured into the town, some from Baranja, some from Vukovar, some from the surrounding villages. Every day there would be new peace negotiations and ceasefires, and every night would bring more grenades, mines and conflagrations. The basement club in

Luka's building was thinned by a half, and everyone who had anywhere to escape to got out. Furthest of all went the Weigels, to stay with their daughter in Australia, and Mrs Bakarić handed the keys of their flat to her friend from Vukovar, a large truculent woman with two kids. Darko was four and Ivana was six, and they brought a little liveliness into the deathly atmosphere of the basement. But there was a lot of sorrow in their liveliness.

They talked mainly of their dad, who had stayed to kill Chetniks and would call for them in seven days after he had thrown the bandits into the Danube. The kids repeated this more and more loudly and persistently with each day that passed.

Everyone's nerves were frayed, so Luka gave them his old felt-tips and crayons to do some drawing. When he saw their pictures he was seriously worried. Their dad was always enormous, taller than their house, with a Kalashnikov in one hand and a flag bigger than himself in the other; take away the old man and there wouldn't be much left of the picture. The tanks Darko drew were in many ways more accurate than Luka remembered from his days in the army. The kid knew more about weapons than was decent for someone of his age; if the UNICEF people had seen his pictures they might have put them on one of their Christmas cards. Luka had never cared much for kids, but these he felt close to, and he wanted them to accept him.

During the evening bombardments he taught them to tell the time, play cards, tie their shoelaces and use a tin-opener, but he never managed to prise them away from their Vukovar war film for more than a couple of seconds before some higher force drew them back to the television, or to the evening prayer circle for Croatia, Mum and Dad, for their uncle and other hunters of the bearded prey.

Bili was even more allergic to children than Luka was, and it seemed to be mutual. Ivana somehow discovered that he was Slovenian, and coolly informed him that Slovenians were cunts.

'How come, Ivana?' asked Bili.

'Because they fucked off and left us to bite the dust,' she replied.

'Who told you that?'

'My dad.'

'Didn't Dad say we were going to win?' Darko said apprehensively.

'Yes, Darko, we'll win, but we all have to die first,' Bili explained patiently. 'That's how it goes.'

Another time there was a conversation about Serbs.

'Do you know who the Serbs are, Ivana?' Bili asked.

'Yes I do. It's what the Chetniks call themselves, we used to call them that before.'

'Did you know Luka's a Serb?'

'No he's not, he's good,' Ivana said through abraded milk teeth, and Luka felt glad he was good, but also guilty about being a Serb. Ivana watched him through half-closed eyes, looking to find the traces of the monstrosity they were talking about on television and at home, but she couldn't, so she calmed down.

The shooting intensified. Bursts of machine-gun fire from Tenja mingled with mortar explosions from Baranja, and Luka's father was coming home from work more and more exhausted and irritable. His endless hours on call for the Protection of Monuments made no sense; who cared about monuments, with scores of people dying and hundreds wounded? But someone in Zagreb was watching like a hawk to make sure everything was in its place, especially the team in charge of preserving monuments.

That morning the old man was furious because he had discovered that his overtime was to be taxed, which meant he wouldn't be paid for all his hours of duty, and instead of the biggest paycheque in his life he would receive the usual pittance. Žunić the architect did his best to console him, saying war was war and every dinar was needed for the defence of the country. Then he changed tack and started talking about the dead and wounded, until Luka's old man threw up his hands in despair.

This was the secret of Žunić's greatness. He was a great town planner, a great humanist, a great communist and worker-manager, and now he had turned into a great democrat, a great Croat and a great Catholic. The roles changed, but Žunić remained great. Way back when Luka was shitting in nappies, Žunić was bullshitting away in conferences, commissions and committees. At the first dawn of pre-election fever he ditched all his set-piece phrases about medium-term plans, prospects and agenda, and had shone for a while in one of the borough's more strident opposition parties, expert and irreplaceable in any position he chose for himself, more convertible than the Swiss franc.

By some strange freak of nature it happened that at the first democratic elections his coalition gained even fewer votes than the communists, so he disappeared from the political scene for a while, and now he was starting again from scratch as chair of the house committee. He stopped at nothing, organizing his followers into day- and night-shifts, stacking five layers of sandbags outside each window in the basement, and taking strict care that no outsider stole a grain. In the basement, the radio and television were on night and day and candles burned constantly for the brave Croatian defenders. Žunić and the old women made themselves a pleasant corner for their prayers, and every hour he would repeat the long-forgotten words with them. And just as nobody in the socialist work-brigades used to shout 'Long live brotherhood and unity!' more loudly than Žunić, his voice was now the loudest to be heard at prayer.

A person of inexhaustible energy, Žunić surrendered himself to everything with inordinate passion and enthusiasm, and in the spirit of the dialectic he would end up by turning everything into a joke that only he could find his way around. He was cut out to lead some mass-suicide cult. In the catacomb-like early Christian environment of the basement, Luka felt more and more like an outsider, until dusk came and Bili would turn up and they would sit in the gym drinking beer and following the prayers next door with loud belches, which drew the understandable fury of the old women and the chair of the house committee. But Luka knew the battle was lost, and that sooner or later he would have to leave.

By September the shooting was going on night and day. The basement crowd was once again reduced by a half, and Ivana and Darko's father finally showed up to take them away. He didn't take them to Vukovar, however, but to Zagreb, because something had gone wrong with throwing the Chetniks into the Danube. Unshaven for a fortnight, his gut full of beer, Luka said goodbye to the children, and Ivana tied around his wrist a chessboard-sign amulet, which she had woven for him to remember her by.

Their dad was just another balding, broken-toothed, pot-bellied man in a dirty, creased uniform, who didn't remotely resemble the superman in the children's pictures. Loading them into a confiscated Mercedes, he tore off with them in a cloud of dust, leaving behind in the basement just ten old men and women led by chairman Žunić, who had meanwhile passed through yet another of his transformations, this one with a near-fatal outcome.

At the end of another long day, one of his young colleagues had turned up dressed in a Guard's uniform and had requisitioned his new Toyota for government needs. Žunić couldn't believe it. He accepted that such things happened to others, but why him, who had given so unstintingly of himself? The blow was terrible and unexpected and he went into a state of mourning, sitting in silence for hours at a time and rousing himself only in the evening to listen for the hoot of his beloved car as the drunken warrior returned from the field of honour. At these moments he would sigh deeply and move the beads of his rosary in devout prayer for his unpaid-for car and the life of his young colleague at the wheel. Each night he would creep out to the parking lot in the neighbouring estate, and each morning he would ramble incoherently about dents and scratches to the paintwork.

The night he discovered a broken headlamp some hidden talent awoke in him and, without any previous criminal experience, he smashed the window with a brick, fiddled with some cables and started the engine, setting off the alarm as the shelling intensified. Then he stepped on the accelerator and drove at full speed – a hundred kilometres an hour – into the tree in front of the building. The crash woke everyone in the basement. They hurried out to the street thinking that at the very least a plane had come down, but instead they found Žunić sobbing like a baby, picking green leaves off the roof of his wrecked car.

He suffered no injuries, but something in him was broken that night, and he threw away his rosary, stopped praying and no longer led the discussion around the TV set. When Luka found him weeping over an old Toyota catalogue, he knew the man had had it.

15

LEAVING HOME

On the morning of the 13th, Bili turned up with truly bad news. Karo had told him in confidence that as from Monday the military would be forbidden to leave town without a permit from HQ. It was then Bili finally decided they must get out. His iron uncle had softened considerably due to the numerous nightmares that had been haunting him since July, including a friendly gunshot wound in the back, and he had achieved a more mature philosophical approach to questions of life and death. So when Bili asked for a permit for him and his Serbian friend, he didn't bat an eyelid but just sat down and typed it himself.

On that morning of the 13th, Bili found Luka in the worst possible mood. They were downing their last bottles of beer and reading comics under the wall of sandbags piled up by the entrance, not wanting to disturb Luka's old man who was sleeping in the gym while a mortar raid was going on. Most of the mortars the army was firing were several years older than Luka, and only every second one would blow up, with a lot more whistling than exploding.

After one of these whistles a fat 120-calibre shell hit the wall of sandbags and poked out half a metre above Bili's head. Bili examined it and came to the conclusion that it had not gone off.

'Fuck it, it'll be ugly when they finish getting rid of their vintage stuff. I hope I'm not here,' he said.

'Hope on,' Luka said. 'The beer's all gone.'

'Ugh, I could have used another.'

'Don't worry, we're off to the supermarket.'

'Don't risk your head, Luka,' Bili warned.

Ignoring him, Luka strode to the gate.

He told himself he would go out after the next close detonation, as if this offered him some protection, and after three mortars had exploded on the flat roof of the nearby kindergarten, he set out. He was passing the kindergarten when another faulty mortar dropped gently into the empty sandpit and bounced off the concrete bottom, forcing him to hurry his step. The supermarket had officially been closed all morning, and most of the windows were smashed. Avoiding the stones and rubble littering the ground and the jagged bits of glass bristling from the frame, he climbed in. The floor between the shelves was strewn with shards of broken glass. He looked around wondering where to start the shopping of his dreams, then collected a trolley and pushed it up the aisle with the glass crunching under the wheels. He passed the racks in a consumerist frenzy, grabbing everything that came to hand until he had filled up three trolleys. Then he went to the manager's office to rest.

The windows of the office had been nailed up with planks, and the air was stuffy and smelt of mouse shit. He felt thirsty. Taking a bottle of red wine from one of his trolleys, he poured half of it on the floor, filled the rest with Coca-Cola and drank to the bottom. The spilt wine trickled to the door and down a couple of steps, which made him laugh. Then he felt hungry, so he went to the delicatessen counter, picked a big cheap salami and chopped a juicy piece from the middle; cheap salami from the middle was always best. Since there was no fresh bread he filled up on crackers, which made him thirsty again. Once more he went through the same routine with the wine, but this time he drank a bit less. After that he returned to the office and tried to call Maria. He picked out various wrong numbers. Sharp Kraut voices answered, and he swore at them down the receiver and called her name. After eleven tries he got her aunt, who told him Maria wasn't there. He hung up and, sick of it all, started throwing wine bottles at the ceiling until there were none left in the crate. Bits of broken glass fell down on him, but he was too drunk to notice.

He pushed a full trolley across the kindergarten playground, oblivious to the fact that the bombing was over and people were peering out at him from the door of the building.

'Are you crazy? Fuck you, they'll pick me up for this too!' said Bili, who was waiting for him in the doorway, edgy after his long absence.

'Did I complain when you stitched me up outside the off-licence?' said Luka, setting off back to the supermarket for another trolley. But when he got there he found it full of people grabbing everything they could lay hands on, so he picked up a box of chocolates and left.

'Now we'll have to find a place for all this,' Bili grumbled, looking at the beer, wine and delicatessen treats.

He quickly worked out the most practical solution. Picking up the trolley between them, they dragged it up to the sixth floor, sweating and panting all the way. Then Luka emptied everything on to the sofa, and while Bili sat in front of the television with a well-deserved bottle of beer, he wheeled the trolley to the balcony, tipped it over the railings and watched it disintegrate with a crash on the concrete of the parking lot.

He stood looking out over the estate. From Tenja and Jug in the south, columns of smoke rose into the still air. From Bosutsko to the east, detonations could be heard like invisible giant carpet beaters shooting out the dust from the primeval plain, and from Baranja came the answering boom of heavy-calibre mortars.

Around the estate he could see ant-like people dragging things out of the supermarket, and the occasional guy from Civil Defence, whose appearance spelt an end to the shelling. These types were mainly the offspring of the better-off families, whose parents had got them into Civil Defence so they wouldn't catch anything worse. They were given anti-quated weapons and guarded Croatia from a safe distance in their neatly-ironed salamander uniforms, polished boots and Raybans, with the inevitable arosaries round their necks. At the first sign of attack they would run to the shelters with the rest of the population to keep their blood pressure down and their spirits up.

Inside the flat, Bili had discovered that the TV was broken: a shell fragment had gone through the set and landed in the wall. This was the last straw. Going out to the balcony he told Luka it was time to move on and ordered him to pack. Luka put a few of his favourite things in a kitbag, and it ended up weighing over twenty kilos. Telling his old man he was leaving would be even heavier; he could hardly get across to him even the most unimportant things.

Their parting turned out to be pretty stupid. They had to hurry because a raid on the downtown garrison was starting, and the old man was worried about his ward sister, who was on duty at the hospital.

'Listen, Luka,' he kept saying. 'Listen.' But he didn't know what to say.

Luka listened, but all he could hear were explosions and bursts of machine-gun fire.

'I'm listening,' he said. His dad wanted to tell him something, God knows what, and he didn't know where to start.

'Have you money?'

'Yes I have,' Luka said. He had three thousand Deutschmarks, which he had been saving up to buy a van. The band had been going to pick up something second-hand in Germany, drive it around Europe and sell it again somewhere; it seemed pretty stupid now.

'That's all right then.' His dad shrugged. 'Call me when you're settled.'

'And what will you do?' Luka asked.

'Nothing. I have to stay. I've nowhere to go.'

'Because of your nurse?'

'Yes, it's serious this time.'

'Can't she have an abortion?'

'It's not that, I want to marry her.'

'Who's the lucky girl? Do I know her?'

'No you don't, she works in internal medicine.'

'Is she young?'

'1956.'

'Good vintage, eh?'

'Not bad.'

'One of ours?'

'What kind of question is that, Luka?'

'Well, is she?'

'Yes, she is.'

'How many months?'

'Four.'

'You'd both better pack your bags then, old man.'

'I have to stay here, Luka. I've nowhere to go.'

'Fuck it,' Luka said, turning his head away.

'Listen, Luka,' his dad said again. 'Listen.' And again he didn't know what to say.

Conversations with his old man always ended the same way they started.

'I have to go,' he said. 'She'll be worrying.'

'Safe journey,' said Luka.

'Safe journey to you too, son, take care.'

They kissed three times, and his father turned to go. He took a couple of steps and turned back.

'Luka?'

'Yes?'

'I want to tell you something important.'

Luka couldn't believe his ears. His dad never told him important things, he had always preferred to keep them to himself.

'Are you sure?' Luka asked him.

'Yes, I'm sure.' He sighed deeply. 'Don't hate people, Luka. Don't ever hate anyone.'

'Why not?' Luka looked blankly at him. It seemed to him at that moment as if the old man had never in his whole life understood anything.

'I don't know why, but it's important.'

'You're a fool, Dad, you know that.'

'Maybe I am,' his old man said.

Then he went to work, and that was how they parted.

After the first fierce detonations close to the garrison, mortars were fired from the direction of Tenja; Baranja was still quiet, only shooting when they felt like it. The mortars fell fairly accurately and soon the electricity went off, the radio and TV fell silent, and even the well-practised prayer circle stopped functioning.

The flock in the shelter herded tight together as a multitude of explosions reverberated through the buildings. Luka stared at the hands of his watch, glowing feebly but still circling. The passing seconds turned to minutes, each one different; each one bringing something new. The first brought the flash of an explosion. The next brought the crash. In the third, someone turned on their mattress. In the fourth, the blood started pounding in Luka's ears. The seconds and minutes stretched into long columns of hours, marching with a roar over the injured contours of his brain.

The damned in the basement finally succeeded in falling asleep, their faces shining unhealthily in the occasional magnesium flashes of the flares and mortars, like the faces of unwrapped mummies in an empty tomb.

It was three a.m. when Luka, looking at this array of the living dead, escaped from the stuffy air of the basement into the corridor. Candle flames were still flickering. His feet crunched sand that had trickled out of one of the sandbags and had been spread along the corridor by the basement people's feet. Walking up the stairs to the landing he trod on a cat, which ran off with a scream that took at least three years off his life. Taking its place on the stairs, he banged the back of his head several times on the wall to wake himself up, then stood for a moment staring at the ceiling and the dancing reflection of the flames. The smell of burning pricked his nostrils; someone's shop, or house or car was burning down, but he didn't care.

He waited for morning in a state of resigned, relaxed fatigue, as though he had just recovered from a major illness. In the basement someone turned on the radio and he felt better. The morning's stretching, yawning and coughing began. The old women hissed, belched and hiccoughed, old bones groaned, slippers shuffled across the concrete floor in a well-choreographed return to the flats. Then the door of the shelter creaked and Bili appeared, opening his mouth in a wide hippopotamus yawn; Luka hadn't seen him arrive. He was followed out by Mrs Bakarić with her messy, rat-like physiognomy; they didn't exchange a word, but Luka felt more cheerful as he realized this was the last time he would be seeing her. The rest of the neighbours followed her out in a straggling column. They ignored him; he had no idea how long this boycott would last, or even when it had started, but it already seemed quite natural.

Bili sat down beside him on the stairs with a bottle of Coke and a box of biscuits. He was wearing a second-hand

Croatian Special Forces camouflage uniform, and had brought Luka the black issue. Funny disguises, like fuck.

'Our train leaves in half an hour, I hope the car wasn't burnt out in the night.'

They ate and drank in silence. Their army kitbags were waiting for them in the gym, and Greg's car was standing under the plane tree ready to go.

They sped through the barricaded town towards the railway station. Bili parked some way off in the street formerly named after the venerable father of Serbian letters, Vuk Karadžić; the street had received innumerable hits because the police head-quarters was there, and all the buildings had their windows nailed up with boards and piled high with sandbags. They jumped out of the car. Bili didn't bother locking it, and left the keys inside. 'My old man will come and pick it up later,' he explained.

Then they slung their kitbags on their shoulders and walked along the middle of the street, avoiding the debris from the collapsed façades that threatened to fall on their heads.

It was early morning. The concrete smelt like morning gymnastics on the day Luka finished his army service. After twenty years pressing their native concrete with their arses and brushing it with their trainers, they were finally pounding along it in military boots, probably for the last time too.

The street was as empty as a graveyard, with no sign of the crowds of cops usually hanging around outside the police station. Most of them were busy at the garrison at the other end of town, and only one police car went by.

When they reached the station they found their express

train waiting for them on the tracks, so they got on and sat by the window, putting their bags next to them on the seats. While they were waiting for the conductor to appear, more passengers arrived loaded with things for the long stay away from home. Irons, saucepans, sets of glasses and other evidence of refugee foolishness shone in the morning sun, and there was much pushing and shoving as everyone tried to get on board, having heard on the grapevine that the train would be leaving on time.

The conductor put his head round the door. He had been drunk since six that morning, and hassled them for not buying their tickets at the station, until Bili shut him up with a look and he went off forgetting to take the money they offered him.

It was time to start on this five-and-a-half-hour journey, which for Luka lasted a lifetime.

PART TWO

ESCAPE

16

PLAYING THE OLD SOLDIER

The carriage was full of fat old women, whimpering kids and half-crazed young mothers holding crying babies on their knees and thinking of their uniformed husbands in trenches and coffins, all that shit. The thick smell of female sweat, urine and hysteria was like the smell of a gynaecologist's waiting room, but after the train moved out from the station someone unexpectedly opened the window, sparing them the stink of an unforgettable five hours. The atmosphere became more cordial, even intimate, and they all dived into politics at every level. Bit by bit everyone was chewing away at the same words, from the mustachioed mouths of the old women to the dribbling lips of kids who had just learnt to talk, and the carriage became a big parliament on the subject of war, the Bolshevik Yugo Army, imbecile Serbo-Chetnik scum and sleepy civilized Europe.

Luka tried to sleep through it. He put his sunglasses on and dozed until the little front-line town of Koprivnica, where for some reason the train stopped for a whole hour.

Bili went to take a piss, and came back with a perfectly rational explanation: Croatian guards and police had stopped an army transport train from Slovenia, and its escort commandos had threatened to blow it sky-high if they didn't let them through with their inventory intact. They had argued about it for a while, until two low-flying MiG planes swept low over the station, and from then on everything went according to the timetable.

At Koprivnica two old women got on who fell instantly in love with Bili and Luka, and demanded to sit next to the two brave Croatian defenders. The boys gave them their seats like gentlemen, while the grannies loudly recalled their precious memories of the old Ustashe army, and what fine, courageous boys they had been, just like these two. This entertainment went on for some time, until a Guards military police patrol showed up. The patrol consisted of three spotty whipper-snappers in brand-new uniforms, armed with brand-new Kalashnikovs. They came in making a lot of noise. Standing up solemnly, Bili removed their caps from their heads and pointed at the kitbags on the seats, then at the last issue of the *Voice of Slavonia*, which contained a large obituary on the penultimate page.

'Boys, before you in our bags lie the remains of five brave volunteers from Zagreb, who gave their lives defending Slavonia. The least they deserve is that you stand to attention and honour them with a minute's silence.'

At these words, half the carriage stood up with pain in their eyes. Luka stared absent-mindedly out of the window.

'What's with him?' asked one of the cops suspiciously.

Bili put a hand over the cop's mouth, but it was too late. Turning to him, Luka threw him a vacant look. 'Am I crazy, Domagoj? Is that what you were going to tell him? Am I crazy, or what?'

'No I wasn't, Luka. On my dead mother's body, I swear I didn't tell him anything. Ask him yourself.'

'What did he tell you?' Luka jumped on the policeman, who grew confused.

'He didn't tell me anything. I just asked if you were all right...'

'He asked me if I was all right? Like fuck he did. I can't stand any more, Domagoj!' Luka stuttered, his mouth distorted, his face wet, his red eyes surveying the carriage as he tried to explain his tragedy to the unthinking civilians.

Bili hugged him to his chest and whispered to him to cut the crap, but Luka was in full flow. 'It's all right for me, I'm okay, but they're not okay. It's all right for you, you don't know what it was like. I was scooping them up with my bare hands ... It was dark ... With these hands I scooped them up ... All five of them – Čoki and Breg and Dižo and Bager, and that little one, what was he called?' He turned to Bili, who was patting his shoulder trying to quieten him down.

'Biba,' Bili said sadly. 'Pinocchio we used to call him, because he was so small...'

Remembering Biba, Luka could bear no more and the tears poured down. 'That's it, Pinocchio. God, he was always laughing, everything was a joke to him ... They ran them over with their tank. I came back that night to collect the bodies...'

At this tragic story, many of the ladies burst into tears. The young policemen were also moved and wanted to leave them in peace. But there was no stopping Luka now.

'Hey, Domagoj, show them the papers. Screw it, guys, they

give you five papers and say, "This is Čoki, this is Breg, this is Dižo, this is Lag— Bager, and this is little Biba, Pinocchio. Take these bags, give them to their families and tell them they sacrificed their lives for the motherland." I can't handle it, Domagoj, I can't!'

For a moment it seemed as if Luka might pass out, but the cops held his arms and he calmed down, though his face was still red and blurred with tears.

'Thanks, you're good, you're doing your job. Just tell me how to do mine. They give me their papers and say, "There's Greg— Breg in that bag." There's less of him than there is of Biba, and he used to weigh … How much, Bili? You tell them.'

'A hundred and thirty kilos.' Bili nodded sadly. 'A hundred and thirty, boneless. Six foot ten, he was. We were always kidding him about it, but he never got angry. Fuck it, what a guy he was!'

Luka fell into despondency again. One of the older ladies fainted with sadness, and the policemen wept tears of vengeful rage at the deaths of so many good men.

'See, Domagoj, they were good, I swear on my mother … My friends, I'm crying like a girl because they … they'd all be alive today if it wasn't for that bastard …'

'Žunić,' Bili put in calmly. 'Major Žunić.'

'No! He's not a major!' Luka shouted, 'he's a major bastard! He was a captain in the Yugo Army and changed his uniform, the motherfucker! He sent them there. "Go ahead," he said, "it's all clear." They didn't stand a chance. And he was promoted to major!'

The young mothers were becoming hysterical now. The cops were speechless and breathing heavily.

'But I tell you one thing, my friends, he won't be a major when we get back from Zagreb. My pal and I will see to that. We'd have done it earlier, but first we had to tell their families. God, I can't...' Luka's tears welled up again. 'I can't do it to his mother. She brought him to me and said, "Take care of him, Max, he's still a child, but his grandfather was an Ustashe heart and soul." Now I have to go to them. They must be told. His mum Fanika, and Čoki's wife Dea. Kill me, Domagoj, I haven't the heart to do it.'

The young cops shook their fists and gnashed their teeth, and Luka pulled himself together and delivered another short speech before they left. 'Look here, boys, let me tell you and anyone else who's listening. When we stopped today at Koprivnica and let that transport train through, I thought I'd go crazy. My heart was breaking. They're killing our people, and you're letting them through. If you had turned up then with your guns, I'd have grabbed 'em from you and killed every last one of them. You have weapons and you let them through, because you don't know what they're doing to us every day! I'm telling you, don't let any more transports through! Lie down on the tracks, let them kill you all if they want to, but show them they can't pass through our beautiful...!'

Luka's speech was interrupted by scattered applause from those present, then a choir of female voices started singing 'Our Beautiful Country', the Croatian national anthem. The guards were set on fire by this story and swore solemnly that they would blow up the next enemy transport train, with their bare hands if necessary.

In fact they were so enraged and taken with this show that instead of getting off at Zagreb they disembarked at Dugo Selo, got drunk in the station bar and smashed it up. In the military surgery, where they were taken to have their wounds stitched up, they harassed some army pensioners waiting for their blood pressure to be taken, and accused them of ordering some young Croatian volunteers to be sent to their deaths, and as a result of their claim the War Veterans Association informed the foreign and local opposition press in order to blow up the misunderstanding.

Luka used the short trip to Zagreb to describe to a couple of caring old ladies how Čoki had been unfit for military service because of his bad eyesight, but had voluntarily signed up nevertheless; how, two days before his death, Dižo had stolen a whole truckload of ammunition and equipment from under the Chetniks' noses; and how Bager had for a bet resisted an enemy battalion attack for half an hour all on his own, while the others went off to lunch. Bili was meanwhile making his protest against the obituaries in the *Voice of Slavonia* by drawing beards and fur caps on them, and publicly announcing that he would kill at least one Chetnik for each of his friends. The two of them were soon so popular that they received over fifteen offers of accommodation that night, and the two women from Koprivnica even offered to collect money for the dead soldiers' families.

Fortunately they reached Zagreb just as the whole thing was threatening to reach the opposition media. Bidding a touching farewell to the rest of the passengers, they picked up

their bags and headed for Koki's Zagreb residence five minutes' walk from the station in legendary Dorđićeva Street,
right next to the lair of the Zagreb police.

Koki had his family's revolutionary past to thank for this
prestigious location; in 1945 his partisan grandfather had
forcefully evicted an Ustashe sniper from the second-floor
window and, charmed by the memory, had decided to keep
the apartment on.

During their walk from the station, Bili and Luka were
irritated by the idyllic tranquillity of peaceful Zagreb, which
had preserved the contours and manners of a real town
despite the tons of shells pouring down on Osijek, Vukovar,
Karlovac, Zadar and masses of nameless villages. Wherever
they looked they saw unbroken windows, sandbags tastefully
arranged like a tourist attraction, and well-behaved school-
boys in clean new uniforms and neatly tied shoelaces, combed
and pressed by the motherland and sent out to play. Nowhere could people be seen rushing into shelters. The trams
trundled along the street as normal; Luka even saw an
inspector arguing with a good-looking girl he had caught
without a ticket, and he was struck by the strangeness of the
sight.

As they climbed the spiral staircase to Koki's flat he
remembered the night in November 1990 when a crowd of
them had met here after a Ramones concert and trashed the
place. They rang repeatedly at the door before Koki finally
came down to answer it. He saw his friends in their uniforms,
and Luka could see it stuck in his throat; Bili obviously hadn't
told him they were coming, and they hadn't seen or heard
from him in over two months.

He pulled himself together quickly, and let them in with something like excitement.

'Look at you in your uniforms, I thought you were...'

'The military police?' Bili laughed heartily, wanting to tease Koki about volunteer units and the general mobilization. Luka had already exhausted his hero act, and in the spirit of his newly acquired veteran logic he merely enquired if the bathroom was free. Koki helplessly waved him on.

Taking one of the towels and Koki's shaving kit Luka looked in the mirror, and for the first time in a fortnight he saw his face. His beard wasn't so much a beard, rather a bunch of eyelashes sprouting from his cheeks. These he could easily shave off. The bewilderment in his eyes would be harder to remove.

17

A FRAME FOR A SMILE

It was an old-fashioned bathroom, high-ceilinged and rather cold for the end of summer, but the pressure in the taps was okay. Luka stepped into the tub, stood under the shower washing his hair, and let the water bring him back to life. His hair was covered in lather when the door opened and someone came in.

'Hey, I'm in here!' he said, washing the soap from his eyes.

'It's you I want,' said a voice he recognized as Maria's.

Opening his eyes he saw her by the bath, dressed in a bathrobe. She let the robe slip to the floor. She had nothing on underneath. In fact she had everything underneath but clothes, and Luka found her more beautiful than ever. She stepped into the tub and joined him under the hot flood of water. The water and lather made her body miraculously soft and firm at the same time, as slippery inside as out. The drops gathered on her eyelashes like tears, but it was her lips he concentrated on: soft and red like blood, making the most beautiful frame for her smile. This was possibly Luka's last thought before the bathroom filled with steam and the windows fogged up. His look grew foggy and so did his consciousness. Every image and sensation melted away, and in the intoxication the first shapes to reappear were her face, her neck, her breasts.

They lay in the bath with their bodies overlapping and the water overflowing on the floor. Maria stretched a slim leg, which was still shaking a little, and lazily put out her fingers to turn off the taps. The water dripped a bit more.

'After us the deluge,' she said pensively, clasping his neck.

'What the fuck are you doing in there, you'll ruin my parquet!' Koki whined desperately outside.

His voice trembled with sorrow, and Luka took an innocent delight in his misery: he couldn't stand guys whose hearts beat for order, discipline and private property. With creeps like that friendship was always in the balance; they measure everything, how much to take, how much to give. They have a box for everything, even their own dick, and Koki was on the way to becoming one of them, sorting his life out and not giving a damn for anyone else; he just wanted a full water tank and a dry floor.

Maria finally pulled the plug of the bathtub. Her move was complicated and irresistible, and Luka pulled her to him again. After that they dried the floor with her bathrobe. It absorbed most of what had slopped over the bath. They wrung it out together without a word, and Maria kept laughing. Sometimes it was just perfect with her; life seemed like one big juicy kiss when that smile floated over her lips and she wasn't talking about things she knew fuck all about. All the happy, lost hours of boring lectures spent in the park or riding their bikes, all the quarrels and reconciliations, all the gigs and moonlit meetings, all the things he could have had with some other girl but had only had with her – he could see all this in her smile. It erased all the bad things for a moment – long enough to make Luka smile too, but too short to make him forget what was going on outside.

War was raging, and Koki was having kittens about his floor. In fact there was nothing really wrong with the floor apart from a few stains because it wasn't varnished; Koki's unhappiness clearly stemmed from something else.

Fed up with all the talk, Maria marched off and came back with a five-hundred-Deutschmark note, which she laid on the table.

'There, take that for the floor and the distress caused,' she said.

Koki looked embarrassed.

'That's overdoing it a bit, Maria,' Bili said from the settee.

'So what do you know about floors?' Koki burst out.

'I wasn't talking about floors,' Bili said quietly.

Koki went quiet too. Picking up the money he handed it back to Maria. 'I'm sorry, I didn't mean it, take it back.'

Maria hugged him and kissed his cheek. 'Keep it anyway, I didn't buy you a present.'

They're still friends, Luka thought.

He spent the rest of the afternoon with Bili and Maria, moving from the settee to the armchair and back again, walking barefoot around the flat. Bea was busy in the kitchen, and Koki was swotting in the spare room. All summer he had failed to pass a single exam, and he was mad as a dog; that university seemed to produce broken people, rather than help them mend others.

For dinner Bea had cooked one of her pizzas; it seemed to be the only meal in her repertoire, and she was good at it.

They drank Coke with red wine and watched the news on Croatian TV. There was a report from the front showing some heroic defenders who had managed to escape from Kostajnica. They made a good show in front of the cameras, but they looked a bit pissed off; at least Luka thought so, although he said nothing.

When the news finally ended he felt a bit sick, so he went out with Maria. All the street lights were on. The pavements were wet from the evening downpour and covered with green leaves, which were falling early from the plane trees that autumn. After all the weeks of curfew, Luka found it strange to see the orange glow of the lights lurking from the puddles and the wet car windscreens. The town was clean, and Maria's hand was cold and wet in his as she told him she couldn't take any more: the news was horrible, she hadn't known what to expect when she came back, and things seemed so dozy and hopeless. As they walked across the park to Jelačić Square she described some German programme she had seen about the children of Vukovar, and how they had no fruit or milk. Luka was only half-listening; he was remembering those Vukovar children Ivana and Darko. He remembered them reluctantly and clearly, but he didn't want to say anything to spoil that night, so he kissed Maria's mouth to quieten it, without passion or desire other than the desire to stop her talking. She sensed this, looking at him with lost, wide-open eyes, wanting him to kiss her for real. He did so, and they found themselves kissing in the middle of the street.

She didn't want to go to the square for some reason, but Luka urged her on. They found crowds of people there, most of them with the forlorn, anxious look that marked them out as refugees. Luka found fragments of his own puzzle in their eyes; they still didn't understand where they were and what had happened to them, the fuck up had been too fast. The day before they had been people. Now they were standing in the middle of the capital of their motherland with a lot of unspoken questions in their heads, and instead of feeling warm and at home, everything was cold and senseless and washed out as a marble tomb.

The square was bright with candles, and old women like the ones in Luka's basement were praying and piously intoning the names of various unknown European towns – Brussels, Bonn, The Hague – like a sort of witches' incantation. Flapping lazily from the surrounding buildings were freshly ironed chessboard flags. The refugees had quickly tired of these; what the fuck do you need a flag for if you have no home to put it on?

Around the tram-stop, the newspaper-sellers were yelling sensational headlines from the *Liberal Weekly* and the *Globe*. The noise mingled with the depressing din from the square. On the right side of the fountain, kids with shaven heads were having fun setting fire to the Yugoslav Federation flag, reviving the good old tradition of burning the occupier's emblems on this square. On the steps to the left of the fountain sprawled drunk and drugged hippies and pacifists, lost, sad-looking types with narrow shoulders and wide pupils and peace signs on their banners, who seemed completely out of place here and did nothing to alter Luka's mood of indifference.

They turned down Vlaška Street, past the flag-seller and the men selling 'Clean Croatian Air' cans and T-shirts with

'Thank God I'm a Croat' on the front; both were heavy with irony and long past their sell-by dates. Then it started to rain again.

The Albanian foreign-currency traders ran for cover under the roof of the town café. Luka and Maria went on walking until the rain became too heavy, then they sheltered under the porch of a clockmaker's shop. The rain was pouring down now. He put his arms around her, and they stood looking at the cheap watches in the shop window. Then she said, 'I bought you a present for your birthday, can I give it to you now?'

'Yes, you can,' he said, surprised; his birthday fell on a day when everyone was at the seaside, or he was at the seaside, and normally he never got any presents.

She took a box from the pocket of her wide silk gypsy skirt and put it in his hand. He opened it without taking his arm from her shoulders. Inside was a handsome black watch, better than his old Swatch. He thanked her. 'So what can I give you?'

'Now you've got a new one you can give me your old one,' she said.

He unstrapped the Swatch and gave it to her, together with the woven bracelet with the chessboard pattern that Ivana had given him. Maria looked at it warily. First the uniform, now this. 'What's happening?' she asked him at last.

'Just a cover, to get me through,' he said.

'I thought so.' She looked disappointed. 'It would look good on you.'

'A bullet in the head looks good too.'

'You fooled Koki.'

'And you too.'

'A bit.'

'There's nothing like that going on, Maria.'

'Why not?'

'Only a dead Serb makes a good Croat.'

'Where did you learn that?'

'At university.'

The rain cooled the asphalt, the watches in the shop ticked away. Luka sat down on the steps. Maria sat on his knee looking out at the rain, and his fingers slid over the silk of her skirt. Everything was wordlessly breaking up between them. It was like the time several years before when he had met another girl after a quarrel with Maria. He spent a couple of hours with her, walking through the park in the polar cold of February. They barely exchanged more than a dozen simple words, and it was all a bit silly, really. He had walked her home but they couldn't part, just stood there in front of her building until darkness fell, which it did quickly. He didn't even notice when she left, and he never got to tell her how he had felt with her. Next day he didn't see her, and later he heard that her father had died and she had gone to live abroad. He couldn't remember her name, or even if she had told him her name, and he almost forgot her face, remembering in a dream the snow, the park, the grey sky, a mountain of clouds, and the heavy persistent silence of this girl who went without saying goodbye. And now the silence seemed to be descending between him and Maria.

He loved her body, her eyes, her smile, her voice, her walk, herself. But he couldn't come to terms with the rest; her parents, her brother, her girlfriends, and all the rubbish

Marxism called superstructure: her God and her Jesus, the Church and the motherland. She believed in cheap things. If Luka had been some big name's son, maybe he would have had a better opinion of Jesus; as it was, he thought of him as just the first in a long line of big men's sons who go around bragging and playing the hero, and when they blow it Father pulls strings, forgives them and sets them at His right side.

There was also that stupid stuff with her folks and her brother, although that didn't bother him nearly as much as the fact that Maria understood perfectly well what he was talking about, but hadn't the strength or the will to accept it. What was the point of dragging her around with him? Wouldn't it make more sense to leave her in her mental cradle and look out for himself?

The rain had stopped and was dripping from the rickety porch above them as people continued their nocturnal mingling on the street.

She gave him her hand to pull him up, and they walked on through a network of streets congested with cars ending up in the park again. The benches were still wet, so they sat on the back of one quietly observing the passers-by. A few drops fell on Luka's neck from one of the tall trees above, and he pulled up the collar of his jacket. A few kids of fifteen or sixteen were necking by the tram-stop. A group of giants in camouflage uniforms stepped up noiselessly from the direction of the station and said a few brief words to the loving couples, who immediately stopped kissing. The others burst out laughing, then they all rushed on to a tram and the men in uniforms disappeared from sight.

'That's the Croat Defence Force,' Maria said. 'They've set up their headquarters in the Ante Starčević building.'

Luka said nothing. He looked at her again and they kissed for a while, then she said it wasn't such a good idea doing it on the street, so they headed back to Koki's building. They started up the stairs, groping each other in the arches and on the stairs and landings, and arrived a good hour later at the door of the flat.

The others had been drinking wine and watching members of parliament making frothy speeches on Croatian TV, and they were all pretty drunk by the time Maria and Luka walked in.

Maria went off to her room to fetch some Bart Simpson pyjamas she wanted to show Luka. Koki and Bea were sitting on the sofa together. Bili had taken Koki's dusty guitar from the cupboard and was tuning it. The President of the Croatian Republic flashed across the screen, and Bili struck a ceremonial fanfare. The strains of the Croatian national anthem rang out, and Bili and Luka started yelling the words of the Italian partisan song 'Bella Ciao'. This got on Koki's nerves so much that he turned up the volume of the President's speech, which was about every foot, inch and millimetre of Croatian soil, and would probably go on for hours. Bili and Luka sang even louder, but nobody else joined in. When they finished, Koki didn't remonstrate with them, just expressed his surprise that they were in such a good mood considering they had come from a bombarded town.

'I realize we must be making you a bit uptight, but we have no reason to be in a bad mood,' Bili replied.

'Could you kindly shit less?' Koki said quietly.

'What language, Koki, you always used to be such a nice-mannered boy,' Luka reproved him.

'From a good partisan family too.' Bili revived some common memories. 'My grandfather was shot by partisans. I had no one to teach me manners.'

'That's plain to see,' Bea said curtly.

Bili looked at her in astonishment, then pointed up at the white square on the wall where a picture of Koki's grandfather with Marshal Tito, his Commander-in-Chief, used to hang.

'Hey, Bea, the picture's not there any more. Did you take it down?'

Koki opened his mouth to say something, but Bea got in first. 'You'd better keep your mouth shut, Domagoj, unless you want to screw things up.' Her voice was cold and full of contempt, but Bili couldn't have cared less.

'Come on, why haven't you put *your* grandfather's portrait up instead, since you think everything should be the way *you* like it?' he insisted.

During the Second World War, Bea's grandfather had been a big noise in the quisling government of the Independent State of Croatia, and his CV boasted of several thousand civilian corpses. Bea didn't like him mentioned, even if it was no longer a disgrace.

At that moment Maria came in wearing her new pyjamas, and asked the irascible party what the fuck was going on. Bea opened her mouth to say something, but Koki told her to shut up. He told them both to shut up, and did so a bit too sharply; even Luka was annoyed and felt like handing him his change in smacks. An inarticulate tension built up. Koki told everyone to give it a rest, then took Luka's and Bili's bags and threw them in the corridor.

'This way, friends, party's over.'

Bili didn't say a word. Standing up, he put the guitar down, threw Koki a look of clownish respect and went out without saying goodbye. Maria stood there in her funny children's pyjamas, which looked so sweet on her. She had no idea what was going on.

Luka waved her goodbye and swept past Koki, who was standing in the middle of the room like a life-sized monument to himself. The President of the Republic followed everything from the small screen and seemed happy with what he saw.

Luka's bag felt as if it were full of feathers as he went downstairs, leaving one of many places he would never visit again. On the street he shouted to Bili, who stopped and waited.

'I went a bit too far this time,' he said, when Luka caught up with him.

As they walked on down the street they heard Maria shouting at them to wait. She was still in her pyjama top, but she had put her skirt and trainers on.

'Hurry up, sweetie, or we'll never get out of here,' Bili urged.

'If you think anyone else will join you, Domagoj, you're crazy!' she told him angrily.

The pavement was clogged with parked cars, and the friends had to dodge around them as they made their way down the street, two boys with army kitbags slung over their shoulders and a girl in a pyjama top and gypsy skirt, like characters from a drunken fairy tale.

Maria walked between them, lecturing them in a self-righteous tone. 'Fuck you and your wine, you could at least have left as friends!'

Luka gave her a warning whack on the bottom, but Bili said sombrely, 'The kid surprised me pleasantly, I must say. I never thought he'd have the balls.' He thought for a bit, then added, more to himself: 'If I punched him it wouldn't do him any good, he was always an idiot. I told him a million times, "You find another one, I'll find another one, let Bea go fuck herself if no one else is to hand." But oh no. I swear on my mother, I don't care about her, I just don't like him screwing her to spite me.'

They had reached the park again. Luka and Maria sat on the bench and Bili gave them his bag. He was already very drunk, but he needed a few more.

'I'm going to the off-licence, make sure the girl doesn't freeze.'

The night was not warm. Luka took his thick red jumper from his bag and gave it to her, and she put it on over her pyjama top. Then she drew her feet under her skirt and rested her chin on her knees. He hugged her, and they watched a refugee family approach with three crying children. Their hair was sticky and their gait was unsteady, and it was clear that the purpose of their walk was to forget.

If it wasn't for the war, none of them would be in this deserted park with the early fallen leaves and the orange reflections of the street lights in the puddles, and Luka wouldn't have a hand grenade in his pocket. But fortunately there was a war on, and everything had its logic; the grenade was a present from his friend, and now they were sitting quietly waiting for him to come back with his drink.

Time passed, and still Bili didn't show up. Luka wasn't worried. Bili never blew things. Well, not irreparably.

The darkness was all around now, lit by glittering lights. It was Luka's last night in Croatia, and he didn't want to talk; he would remember it better afterwards without talk. Maria felt the same way. He laid his head on her shoulder and wrapped a piece of her hair around his fingers. The refugee family had gone, and they were alone in the world. He looked up at her face. She was his best girlfriend. Gently she caressed his hair. 'Sleep,' she said.

18

BUDAPEST
Fuck the Solar System

When Luka woke at half past six the next morning the first idiots were already going to work, but there was no sign of Bili. The only thing he could imagine was that he had got pig drunk the night before and forgotten who he was or where he was going.

Led by some sure instinct, he found him on a patch of grass a hundred metres from the station, looking like a heap of meat. Luka rolled him on to his back, and he smiled at him with hungover eyes and deadly breath. 'Great you came. I'd never have made it on my own.'

Since Bili was in no state to move unassisted, Luka took both their bags to the station and left Maria there to look after them, then bought two tickets for Budapest to save trouble later on with the conductor. When he went back for Bili he found him staggering up.

The three of them descended the steps to the shabby underpass, decorated with graffiti of lascivious and patriotic content, and smelling like people did nothing but shit and piss down there. They hadn't walked more than a few steps when Bili threw up. It was a long process, and he did not do it politely in a corner but right in the middle of the tunnel, to the quiet horror of those who walked by. Luka climbed the steps to the platform with the bags, then went back for Bili, and he and Maria pushed him into an empty compartment. Then they stood on the platform together to kill the fifteen minutes before the train left.

Exhausted by her struggles with Bili, Maria leaned against the concrete support of the roof staring at Luka out of the corner of her eye. The September morning was cold and lit with the diagonal rays of the sun. Her face was pale. He tried to push her hair from her eyes, but she shook it down again.

Then he kissed her, and there was nothing there any more; the kiss came out like an exit stamp in a passport.

'How far will you go with Bili?'

'To Budapest.'

'And then?'

'You know.'

'I hope you drop dead,' she said, moving away from the pillar.

He didn't try to stop her. 'God willing I'll do that,' he said as she ran down into the underpass.

For a while he stood there waiting for her to come back. But she didn't. He went to the station bar to get something to eat, but seeing the wilting sandwiches and the charred remains of the cremated chicken in the window he realized he wasn't that hungry and returned to the compartment with a few cans of Schweppes.

Bili was fast asleep in a pool of sick, making no sound. The compartment had been smelly even before he got in, and Luka opened the window to at least dilute the smell of vomit. Then he stretched out across three seats, drinking his Schweppes and glancing every so often at his new watch. In the end he took it off and stood up to peer through the window. A big bull of a man in a red cap waved his flag and the engine pushed the carriages along. Soon the station was behind them and they were passing through the scorched suburbs.

He closed his eyes and tried to sleep, and when he opened them they were met by a boring fertile landscape of corn, sunflowers and telegraph posts. The motherland. A cracked plate of land on which the fools had been slaughtering each other for thousands of years over the sovereign right to be buried in it.

Some brainy person said that wars would disappear when the causes for them disappear, which is only a more delicate way of saying never, never, never. The wheels clattered along the tracks. A couple of stations passed by which God had forgotten to cross off the timetable; even in the bright sunshine they looked dark and deserted. Then more corn, sunflowers, pumpkins and sky, dead and transparent as a glass bell, until they reached Koprivnica, where they had to go through the same shit all over again with the military transport trains and the army throwing a fit about their bits and pieces, although they finally got through it all as before, without shots being fired.

As they approached the Hungarian border the tracks ran through swamps and willow groves. Bili slowly came to his senses, and by the time they reached the border he was sitting in an upright position.

The border-control was simplicity itself. Two Hungarian passport officers with Lech Wałesa moustaches got on, glanced at their passports and asked them to empty their bags. They were still suspicious even when they found nothing, but they stamped their passports and Bili instantly fell asleep. Luka stared through the dirty window at the Hungarian telegraph posts and wheat fields, and the sad Hungarian stations with their incomprehensible mile-long names and tons of dots and dashes and syllables. Finally he too went to sleep, and when he woke they were in a dirty workers' suburb of Budapest. It wasn't clear if anyone worked here in fact, since over half the factory chimneys seemed to be idle. Then they passed a characterless building caked in grime from years of past industrial production, and he knew South station must be close.

Bili woke up sober and in a foul mood. They went into the corridor with their bags, and some Asians – Mongols or Chinese – poked their heads out of the next compartment and asked if this was Budapest. They replied that it was, but they went on travelling for a good five minutes more, moving slowly through layers of dark brown buildings. Something was clearly wrong with the place; it was midday, but it was obvious that the sun didn't shine here as it ought to.

South station's white marble floors and colourful indigenous crowds placed an additional burden on the friends' fragile refugee state of mind. Hardly any of the aborigines here spoke a foreign language, and it was impossible for foreigners to know where anything was. After a great deal of unnecessary talk they finally found a kindly old woman who directed them to the ticket office to buy their tickets for Munich and Belgrade. They stood in their respective queues. Luka got his first, since there was less demand for tickets to Belgrade. They charged him in Deutschmarks and gave him change in forints, at some disgraceful exchange rate that he would have felt cheated by if he had been in a better psychological state; as it was, he was indifferent to a few Deutschmarks.

Bili left his queue with a ticket for the 16.10 express, and they realized they would have time to eat something. The station restaurant was well-appointed, and the waiter, although unshaven and untidy, was very helpful, and his light brown eyes seemed to comprehend everyone's sorrow. Bili tried to speak German to him, but he knew no foreign language and explained the menu to them in friendly sign language. Bili finally threw up his hands and the man brought them mushroom soup and chunks of fried cheese coated in bread-crumbs. The rest of the meal was good except for the cabbage salad, which had a ridiculous amount of sugar on it as things always do in Hungary, but neither of them felt like complaining.

Sitting at the table next to theirs was a crowd of Krauts with white eyebrows, eyelashes and moustaches, who embod-ied all of Luka's worst nightmares. They had ginger ponytails, and they wore tight stonewashed jeans tucked into high trainers, and sleeveless T-shirts that exposed their freckled shoulders, and they made him want to puke. They snottily sipped their pissy Hungarian beer and told noisy jokes. These were neo-Krauts, loud and arrogant, like Yugoslav tourists on a pre-war trade-union trip to Budapest, with the only difference that the Germans didn't smash beer bottles or leave the waiters lavish tips. The jolliest of the group approached Luka and Bili, pointed at their jackets and bags and asked them in German if they were travelling to Yugoslavia. Bili replied that they had just come from there. The guy probably thought they were German volunteers. Bili waved him off.

He and Luka had eaten and paid and were getting ready to leave when the character came back again and asked if they would join him for a beer. Fortunately Bili had just been fed. Getting up close to the man's freckled face he said something short and to the point, and the Kraut evaporated into thin air.

The entire company, all six of them, stared at Luka and Bili as they left the restaurant with their bags on their shoulders. They walked on without stopping or looking back, until they reached the top of the stairs leading to the basement. There Bili stopped, swept the station with a look, and uttered a mighty curse that encompassed fucking Europe, the planet, the solar system and the galaxy. And splitting the last atoms of his defiant hangover, he prepared to put his tail between his legs and set off for Germany to earn money as a bouncer in some club, making executive decisions about which Kraut to let in and which to keep out.

As they came down the stairs and watched the crowds milling under their feet, they wondered how there could be all these people on the globe who didn't give a damn about the war in Yugoslavia; if there was any pain on their faces it wasn't because of the war, but because they had toothache or piles, or because there was no seaside in Hungary.

In an old street by the station they found a cheap shop with a good stock of Hungarian drink. Bili took a couple of bottles of red, and Luka bought two small bottles of apricot brandy. They dipped the bottles in the nearby fountain to cool, then drank a bottle of wine and one of the brandies.

After this Bili made himself throw up in the fountain so as not to travel drunk.

It was time for him to go now, so they dragged themselves to the station and Bili somehow found his express train for Munich. He became terribly emotional as he said goodbye to Luka. Then he pushed a bit of paper with his address into his pocket. They kissed, and Luka waved drunkenly as his last friend left for his new life. Another painful parting since morning; it was all making him a bit tired.

He returned to their place by the fountain, put on his sunglasses, and smiled benignly at the world around him. There were long-haired Euro-youths in tattered clothes, and masses of people with yellow skin and slit eyes. All the slit-eyes of Budapest swam into his field of vision, then darkness came down.

19

BELGRADE
Six Times Faster than Light

When Luka awoke, the darkness was all around, lit by a few stars and street lights and other nocturnal decorations. Around him on the steps of the fountain the *jeunesse dorée* were asleep in their sleeping bags. Jumping up to catch a cab for East station, he fell into an old green Lada, uttered the magic words to the driver and they drove through Budapest's night fireworks of neon signs and traffic lights.

The driver was a soothing fellow and didn't open his mouth, just shook Luka out at East station, took his five hundred forints and disappeared into the night. Luka lugged his bag to the platform where the carriages for Belgrade should have been standing. They weren't, so he moved on to the waiting room.

The waiting room at East station was something else. In fact the whole of East station was like one big waiting room, where newcomers from the East spent time acclimatizing to the town and learning a few words of Hungarian before crawling round the squares or the underground stations, depending on the time of year. Before Luka's eyes a tribe of Russians some fifty strong lay on pieces of cardboard on the asphalt. They weren't going anywhere, they were just sleeping, as if they had been born there and had no intention of ever leaving. He stumbled over a fat Russian in a track suit, slippers and a dirty, slightly too short vest that exposed his hairless belly, moving rythmically up and down as he slept on. There were lots of Russians at East station — no one was chasing them there; they were simply hanging out with their Vostok sports bags and their beer bottles, most of them as empty as their souls. These offspring of the glorious heroes who had fucked up Hitler and Napoleon now sat around the waiting room like tree stumps, scared of Hungarian railmen.

Luka began to feel terribly bad. He had the urge to write a letter home, although he had no one at home to write to, no one to tell he was doing fine. Sure, everything was fine. Besides, where would he find an envelope and stamp at ten o'clock at night? And with whose hand would he write that everything was fine, in this place that was more like a shithole than a train station, stinking of piss and old Slavonic curses? So he gave up on the idea.

Before long a voice trumpeted a message over the loudspeaker, in which the only word he could make out was Belgrade. This was his signal to leave the wretched waiting room.

When the train finally arrived on the tracks it looked almost clean. He climbed into an empty compartment. A minute later a huge-headed Hungarian with the state coat of arms on his T-shirt jumped aboard carrying an enormous ghetto blaster with hundreds of little lights winking on and off to the merciless beat of Hungarian heavy metal. He was followed by a polite old lady carrying innumerable bags and cases. The Hungarian produced a pair of headphones and plugged them in, presumably unwilling to share his divine

music with others, and Luka felt almost ready to fall in love
with him.

After the train had left the station, two unshaven types
came in without saying anything and occupied two empty
seats. They didn't have to say anything, Luka knew unmistak-
ably that they were his countrymen. They were about thirty,
but being unshaven made them look younger. The older of
the two seemed a little slow-witted, and held a loaf of bread
under his arm throughout the journey. The other man kept
trying to open a bottle of cheap wine with a key, so in the
end Luka handed him his Swiss army knife, which was how
he attracted his attention.

The Hungarian writhed and shook his head to the sounds
of his silent music. The old lady kept a watchful eye on
everything. The lights dimmed and the compartment grew
cosy, and they travelled on through the night in silence.

There was trouble at the border because Yugoslav customs
officials discovered that the old woman had a Russian passport
and ordered her to open one of her bags. She did so to reveal
piles of needles, buttons, sewing-threads and other strategic
materials, and since the other bags revealed more of the same,
the officers asked her in jocular tones to accompany them for
a more detailed search. She had to carry all the bags herself,
and the train finally left without her, but at least customs had
successfully bagged another smuggler. These men were draco-
nian: ten trucks loaded with Kalashnikovs could pass under
their noses, but not an old woman with her needles and
thread. Luka still had his hand grenade in his pocket; he was
back in his country again.

The Hungarian got off in Subotica, and the two unshaven

ones in Novi Sad, and Luka travelled on alone with an unobstructed view of the fields of wild and harvested corn and the day breaking over Yugoslavia, or what was left of it.

Belgrade station was heaving with people. An elderly porter offered to carry his bag, cabbies vied to give him a lift. Confused by the warmth of their welcome, he took his bag to the cloakroom. The man behind the desk peered at his ID, saw he was from Osijek and asked him how things were there. Telling him to mind his own business, Luka walked off up the hill to Zeleni Venac and the central Kalemegdan area of town.

Knez Mihajlova Street was packed with people. It was Monday morning, and everyone was going to work. Each face he passed was a shock. He wished it would rain – a real downpour that would drive everyone away to the underpasses and side streets.

He ended up at the ancient fortress, now the home of the military museum. Staring at the antiquated weapons displayed outside, calm and superior in September sun and January frosts alike, he felt almost envious of all this green-painted metal that had survived so many wars and outlived those who had made and used it and would outlive him too, if what he was doing now could be called living.

He sat on the ramparts and drank the rest of his apricot brandy, and as he looked out over the glittering glass cages of New Belgrade and the mouth of the river Sava flowing into the Danube, he flowed with it, and a thousand black bats flew into his head as he slept soundly until midday.

It was already afternoon when he stood up to leave. The alcohol had evaporated from his body, and he couldn't understand why the little stone church had failed to ring the hour.

As he walked through the park he peered at the people playing tennis and basketball in the Red Star sports ground, and wondered where he should go next. The only person he knew in the city was his old army friend Siniša Živković. They had been inseparable in the canteen and on the parade ground. The last time they spoke was when Siniša called to ask if he was all right after the controversial TV broadcast of the Army Intelligence footage starring Croatian minister Špegelj, in the role of arms smuggler for his government. Siniša's was his only address in Belgrade, so he decided to go there.

He came out of the park, had a bit of a wash at the drinking fountain on Knez Mihajlova and wet his hair, then walked on to the monument with the horse, where he happened on one of those celebrations of Something Important.

It was a serious gathering, with no loud speeches, and everyone wore solemn, formal expressions. Luka learned from someone in the crowd that they were there to honour the death of Đorđe Božović Giška. The name meant nothing to him, so he pushed closer to find out.

Candles burnt on the pedestal of the horse, and men in faded green uniforms stood motionless around it. They had even laid flowers. There was no priest, but a character in a black beret was explaining to the crowd who the dead man was and his place in Serbia's rich tradition of unsolved murders.

On the pedestal of the monument they had stuck a big

picture of the martyr in his uniform. At least he got his monument for a few days; others were buried with bulldozers, or their remains were squeezed with tweezers into matchboxes.

Every few seconds the people Giška had imagined himself fighting for would come up to the monument and stand there for a while, then hurry back across the square and jump on buses like ordinary mortals returning from work.

Luka kept running through his mind the film about Siniša Živković, and wondering how he would find him. Siniša lived on Albanska Spomenica Street, in Palilula. He had arrived at Luka's barracks after a six-month stint at the reserve officers' school in Bileća, still with the rank of corporal, and still, after six months of boots, knapsacks, winter uniforms and a shaven head, the biggest greenhorn the unit had ever known.

Luka and his two other pals became corporals after their two-week basic training, in accordance with the good old Yugo infantry criteria that they could read and write and weren't Albanians. At Bileća Siniša had had to piss blood for half a year, marching and breaking his neck on the Herzego-vinan rocks, and covering all the infantry training from A to Z. He was booked for some disciplinary rubbish there and packed off to Luka's cowboy garrison, where 70 per cent of them spoke Albanian, washed their backsides with bottled water and made shit frescoes on the toilet walls. The few officers who were stuck there drank heavily and were mainly sergeant majors and second lieutenants on the verge of retirement, and other army dross. Siniša found himself in a collective he could have hardly dreamt of at Bileća. It was the end of the 80s, just after the Serbian nation had found its voice, and several sleeping soldiers were massacred in a dormitory at the Paraćin garrison. The corporals ostentatiously carried guns at their belts (although without ammunition), the privates were armed with dummy bullets, and security was tight as they tried unsuccessfully to track down the vandal who signed the walls 'Aziz Kelmendi', the Albanian soldier who had committed the Paraćin massacre.

During target practice from a moving tank, Luka and Siniša had to sit back to back, making sure no one turned round until the ammunition was finished, and searching them all before and after the shooting.

Despite this, the wily Šećiri somehow managed to smuggle out eleven bullets, enough to kill all the Serbs in his platoon twice over. Old Šećiri might have followed in Kelmendi's footsteps had Siniša not discovered the bullets at the foot of his bed, and he took great pleasure in stamping him flat. For this he got fifteen days in prison and a month's extra leave as a reward. Šećiri never returned from the hospital, supposing he ever got there. Siniša finished his military service with the rank of junior sergeant, but was never made an officer.

The building where Siniša lived was old, and reminded Luka a little of Koki's place in Zagreb; here too he rang for a long time before anyone appeared.

An eye peered warily at him through the spyhole, and an anxious female voice called out, 'Who is it?'

Siniša's mother didn't recognize him, having met him only once, in his uniform and with short hair.

'It's Luka Mijatović, Mrs Živković, Siniša's friend from the army, don't you remember me?'

'Of course I do, Luka, you were his only friend there,' Mrs Živković said, opening the door. 'He tried calling you, but you were never in. He was worried about you.'

Luka went into the front room. Mrs Živković seemed to be alone in the empty flat. Siniša had a father, two brothers and a twin sister, but there was just a woman's slipper and tracksuit top in the room.

Mrs Živković's voice hinted powerfully at some domestic catastrophe — a white laundry disaster maybe, or something worse, like a fireproof pot cracking during the making of jam, and Luka knew something truly terrible must have happened.

'It's all too much for me,' she said. 'The rod in the closet broke. God knows when, and now all the suits are creased. Heavens, what am I talking about? Would you like coffee?'

Luka accepted. The room he was sitting in smelt fresh and aired and there were no ashtrays around, although he knew for a fact that the males of the family smoked at least four packs a day.

She brought in coffee and sweet jam. He took a spoonful, then another, and a third, and had difficulty stopping. The last thing he had eaten was cheese with Bili at Budapest's South station.

Mrs Živković had three sons so she understood, and when she offered him some stuffed pickled cabbage left over from lunch, he couldn't refuse.

'Do you know the biggest lie a student can tell, Luka?' she said.

'I'm not hungry.' Luka smiled at her.

'That's right, now eat as much as you want. Milica and I are all alone here, we don't eat much.'

She brought in the cabbage rolls and Luka started eating as if he would never stop, consuming one after another and then half a loaf of bread as she told him about her boys, the mobilization and the reserve:

'First they send the papers for Vlada to go on military exercises – he's my eldest, he's studying to be a doctor. After that they call up Dragan, he's studying Mechanical Engineering. He comes back after three days, mad as a dog, grabs his passport and leaves for Czechoslovakia. Two days later Vlada returns. He thought they'd put him into the medical corps, but they made him train to be a tank driver. He almost went crazy. Now he's hiding out at his girlfriend's place while he finishes his studies at the hospital. Then he'll go abroad too. Miša, my husband, was on a business trip when his papers came. I refused to take them. God knows he's a sick man. Now they want to put him in charge of some platoon, as if they don't have more officers than they know what to do with already. Luckily Siniša didn't get called up – he had a bad character reference from Bileća and they never made him an officer. He wanted to volunteer, but Irena eventually got him to change his mind. Irena's his girlfriend, she used to visit him in the army, remember? So she talked some reason into him, and now they've gone to London for a bit to visit my aunt. She's lived there since 1950, she's married to an Englishman.'

Siniša's mother went on talking. Until the first ripples of nationalism in Croatia in 1969, she had lived with her husband in Osijek. But even then they had seen the writing on the wall, and Miša had taken her and the two children to Belgrade. Neither of them had a job there and they were subtenants in their flat, but they knew things would eventually get better.

'Luka, I used to get up at half past four in the morning, take the children to nursery, work from seven to three, then go on to my second job. Soon I had the twins, and it went on like that for three years until things became easier and we got the flat and the children grew up a bit. Never mind, it's not important, though I thought I'd go mad then. I'd cry and try not to let Miša see, but I haven't regretted coming here for one minute, because there were no more telephone threats or drunks singing Ustashe songs under my window. Understand, Luka, you have to protect your peace of mind, your dignity, then there's nothing you can't do.'

There was something kind and reassuring about Mrs Živković's voice, and Luka listened with an occasional yes and no, agreeing with everything but not really taking it in. He felt he didn't belong in this room, and that somehow he must get away.

He thought about Siniša, who knew about every kind of weapon but nothing about women, and allowed his mother and his girlfriend to make his decisions for him. What was the point of all that training? Where was the buffalo who ran across the training ground, jumping over obstacles with a heavy machine-gun tripod on his back and laughing like the devil? He had been the first to break into the dormitory full of sleeping Albanians, line them up with their equipment and read them selected passages of the mobilization manual. Luka could have cried when he remembered this, but Siniša's mother just went on:

'I know men and their troubles, Luka. My husband and my

three sons were in the army, I know how hard it must have been for you with those savages. It was hard for Siniša. Later he told me how he found the bullets on that madman. I thought I'd go mad myself when my child told me who he had to deal with, but I kept telling myself someone had to defend the country. Until this madness I thought it had to be like that. Then after Slovenia I realized there was nothing more we could do. We can't make them live with us if they don't want to. I don't want to see my sons killed, or you or anyone else, just because the politicians are too stupid to make a deal. You must hide somewhere safe until this is all over, Luka, so we have some people left at the end of it. My father had thirteen brothers and he knew only three of them, the rest were killed in three wars. They never married, they were almost children themselves. You understand, Luka – you're not children any more, you just look like children. My Siniša used to look at me like that. "You talk crap, Mother, but you're right," he said later, and he didn't go. I know him, when things are hard he always laughs and his language gets bad. He'd call me from the army and tell me soldiers' stories, just like Miša and Vlada and Dragan used to, and I'd say, "I know it's tough son, be patient, it'll pass." I know what it was like for him, he has no one to talk to except you, somebody had to watch those madmen with their heads full of their republics. My boy has completely different interests, he has nothing in common with people like that. Demote all the officers to the same rank, I say, and let the generals go to war. The ones who want to fight can fight. Let the peasants fight. My father was a peasant, he went to war, that's all he knew. But you're different, you're educated, you can find yourself a more civilized way to fight, not with force. Switch off, don't watch television, don't listen to the radio, don't read the papers, they're the ones who started this. See, I've put the TV away and I haven't read the papers for four months. I told Miša, it's the papers or me, and he did what I said. Everything was fine until this mobilization, now the family's split up and we're living in four corners of the earth waiting for it to pass.'

She finished. Luka's mother would say the same thing, most mothers would say the same thing if they were asked, but no one ever did ask them. They were the losers in all wars, they just produced the fighters; they gave birth to all the thieves and killers and criminals, and no mother would ever admit that her son was worthless. All mothers go silly when it comes to war, they all sing the same tune.

Amongst the photographs behind the glass-fronted case Luka could see one of him and Siniša in the army. Mrs Živković said his name a thousand times, warmly and solemnly, and kept telling him she understood. He didn't pay attention to her actual words, but he was glad someone was saying them. When she asked him who he was staying with in Belgrade, he invented some distant cousins.

'Will you be all right with them, Luka?'

'I'll be fine.'

'Listen, if you get fed up there you can always stay with us, we've plenty of room, see for yourself. Promise?'

'I promise, don't worry.'

'Have you got enough money?'

'Yes, I have.'

'And that's the second biggest student lie!'

'I know but it's true,' he said, pulling from his pocket his wallet full of Deutschmarks. 'I'm not a student now. Goodbye, Mrs Živković.'

As he was walking to the door she told him about some phantom bank that was offering astronomical interest rates, some 20 per cent a month, on foreign-currency investments. She gave him the bank's address, and he asked her to say hello to Siniša for him, then he went down to the street.

The sun was setting. People with umbrellas hurried past through the gas-polluted atmosphere – solid, energetic people with deadened nerve ends, who couldn't care less if they poked out someone's eyes with their umbrella spikes. It was a street war, and they were returning to their unbombed houses with the unbroken glass in the windows, coldly determined to survive, if not to win. This homecoming didn't fill their faces with joy – they probably saved that for Christmas and New Year – and as Luka scanned their metropolitan masks drugged by private worries he despised his pathetic need to find kinship in every face he passed.

To hell with it.

He was on November 29 Street now, big, grey and worn out as its name. It started to rain. Walking wet and aimless to the corner, he stopped outside the Balkan cinema, waded through a puddle of water that soaked his ankles, and went inside.

An action movie was showing, a sterile hodgepodge of naive violence. He bought a ticket, slunk to a seat in a corner of the auditorium and slept through two showings of the film. The cleaner woke him carefully in case he turned out to be a junkie, and fetched the projectionist to be on the safe side. When they realized he was only sleeping, they were politeness itself and didn't call the police or even ask him to buy another ticket, merely led him to the door to rejoin the nightlife of the metropolis.

It was past 10 o'clock, and people were thronging the bus stops. Luka went down into the underpass, and found it filled with vagrants shouting and begging for money from the queue at the pastry kiosk. He was leaving with three bread rolls when an old man with a wild, bohemian look and a mass of grey hair on his head and face came up and asked him for a loan of ten dinars, which evidence suggested he wouldn't be returning. Luka gave him twenty to get rid of him, but the old man seized his arm and told him the Moon was just a dead star, and that he was an important inventor who had just invented a space ship that flew at six times the speed of light. The man looked to Luka as if he probably kept himself warm at night with the science pages of a children's magazine. They sat down on the ground outside a music kiosk, and he went on with his story as though he had eaten one of the records in there. It became more unbelievable by the minute: 'I showed my invention to everyone! Do you think anyone was interested? In this country? You must be crazy! Or do you come from somewhere else? They laughed at me, but I've got it all in here!' He tapped his head respectfully.

Luka didn't doubt it. 'Who have you shown it to?' he asked, keeping the conversation going.

'Everyone, I told you! None of them wanted to know. The army screwed me the most. Now I'm making it myself. The Slovenians wouldn't send me the condensers, so I've ordered them from Japan...'

'Have you talked to Flash Gordon about it?'

The old man was all ears.

'He does things like that. Him and Doctor Zarkov.'

The man grew suspicious. 'Are you taking the piss, young man?'

'Not at all.'

'What about this Zarkov, then? Nick the project, split the money and leave me high and dry, would he?' he said loudly, addressing the passers-by. 'Piss off, the lot of you. Piss off!' he shouted triumphantly, disappearing along the underpass.

At that moment a skinny, short-haired girl detached herself from a group of people and came up to Luka.

'Fuck me, is it you?' said a familiar voice, and he recognized his old friend Krišna.

'I don't know,' he said, looking at her spiky hair. She hadn't bothered to shave her head in the capital, but in every other way she was the same old Krišna.

'So when the fuck did you arrive?'

In two sentences he had heard more obscenities from her than in all the years he had known her. She was obviously happy to see him, but he couldn't understand what all the fucking was for.

'This morning,' he said.

'Let's fuck off out of here, you can come to my place,' she said. 'Where's your luggage?'

'I left it at the station,' he told her, lifting his arse from the smooth marble of the floor.

'We'll have to move if we're to catch the last bus,' she said, stepping eagerly ahead.

As they walked along Nušić Street he could barely keep pace with her; he had never been in such a hurry. They went through another underpass, which was empty, then a third one full of gypsies, until they finally arrived at Zeleni Venac.

The bus had either not arrived or had just left, as happens when you burst a blood vessel trying to catch one. Waiting for the queue to form were half a dozen card-sharps, playing among themselves and yelling at the tops of their voices as though playing for big money. They were soon joined by an open, simple-looking youth evidently from the provinces.

'Fucking redneck,' Krišna said angrily, swinging left in her high Doc Martens. 'I can't stand seeing someone ripped off.'

Luka shrugged. He liked watching natural things like volcanoes, geysers, eagles, leopards stalking their prey. But the boy from the provinces was no fool. He watched the players unobtrusively, appearing to take no interest in their game, and they slowed down so he could see what was happening. Krišna could have learned a trick or two if she didn't turn away from such things.

Luka didn't see the end of the game because the number 75 bus drew up, and she pulled him on.

He sat down next to the window and nodded off almost immediately. Every few seconds his head would bang the window, but after a couple of nights sleeping in pigsties his body was unstoppably seeking what it needed, and when the bus reached the terminus half an hour later Krišna had a heavy sleeper on her hands.

They walked across an ill-lit patch of mud littered with diggers, earth-moving machines and building materials. A few cabins had been thrown up; it was clearly some sort of building site. Putting his hand on his heart Luka asked from the depths of it what this place was.

'Bežanija,' Krišna said. 'It looks even worse in daylight.'

'Bežanija,' repeated Luka. 'Refugees. What a name.'

She did not respond to his remark but strode on. They walked through the darkness for some time, and finally arrived at a lit-up estate. The buildings were new, and there were several shops and a mass of cars with Croatian number plates. Luka noticed a couple of plates from Osijek. The place didn't initially make a good impression, but he was tired, and Krišna jingled some keys to indicate that they had arrived.

The building was brand new, the paint by the entrance even seemed to be wet. Luka wanted to try out the new lift, but Krišna's flat was on the ground floor.

'Here we are,' she said, unlocking the door and switching on the light.

He stood in the front room for a long time, taking it in.

'Welcome to our refugee den, Luka,' she said.

It was unclear why the flat needed to be locked, since it looked as though it had been burgled several times already. There was no clutter, and almost nothing in it. The bedroom contained two metal camp beds and two lockers, evidently requisitioned from some barracks or army dump, with a small TV set on one of the lockers. In the kitchen there was a small fridge and cooker, and a plastic garden table and two chairs. There was another room, which was completely empty.

Krišna made coffee, but Luka didn't drink coffee and he was sleepy. She drank hers from a big mug and told him her story. Before leaving for the front line in Slavonia, her officer father had packed her and her mother off to stay with friends in Belgrade until the army found something better for them. Her mother had cracked up and returned to Osijek in July, and Krišna stayed. Then a couple of days ago her old man had turned up and moved her into this new flat without saying anything about her mother.

That was her side of the story, she didn't know that Luka was well aware of what had gone on.

Last May, just before the war, when he was working on the population census, her parents had caused him major head-aches. The first time he went round to the flat he found just her mother in, and she had put the three of them down as Croats. The documents were already at the registry office when old Miljković came by in his officer's uniform to check on the information his wife had given, and when he found out he went berserk and caused havoc in the place.

At the second count, his wife had described herself as Croatian and he asked to be registered as a Chetnik, and Luka had to inform him in his official capacity that this would be taken as an insult to public morality and would have to be disregarded in the final count. When they had to decide where to place 'the little one', who wasn't at home, the real ethnic conflict blew up at the Miljkovićs', and Luka had to leave in a hurry with his job unfinished. He handed their registration papers to another census officer with a stronger stomach, and he took in return an illiterate Albanian family of fourteen, plus a couple who wished to be registered as Martians. He didn't think he'd got the worst of the bargain, because war had started at the Miljkovićs' long before the clashes at the Plitivice Lakes and the village of Borovo.

Too exhausted to talk any more, Luka went next door and fell fully dressed on the bed Krišna had made up for him. He was sure he would drop off the moment he closed his eyes, but he was kept awake by the sound of a car engine being switched off outside. A young couple came home late from a party. A child sobbed and its mother consoled it. At last it became quiet, but still he couldn't sleep. The ticking of his new watch rang out in the empty room. He took it off and laid it on the window ledge. Then the drumming of the blood in his ears disturbed him, and the glass of the light bulb glowing in the darkness. The rest of the night he spent tossing and turning in bed, sweating like a marathon runner and listening to Krišna sobbing and hallucinating in her room. This stopped just before dawn, and he finally fell asleep.

He woke at eleven, more exhausted than when he had gone to bed. Krišna wasn't up yet. Not wanting to wake her, he dragged himself to the kitchen to look in the fridge. There was nothing there, so he went out to buy some things. The shopkeeper was a bald, thickset man who looked like an executioner on disability pay. Responding to Luka's 'Good morning' with a look of envious hatred, as though the morning were already over for him, he picked his teeth with the nail of his little finger, scratched his hairy stomach and totted up his profit on a couple of bottles of wine, some cheese and shampoo. Vowing not to set foot in the place again, Luka went to another shop across the road for eggs and pastries.

Krišna was still sleeping when he returned. Her face was pale and composed, and he wondered if the weird sounds last night had been a product of his imagination. He put the eggs on to fry, opened the wine and sat down on one of the chairs with an unobstructed view of the disgusting potholed building site outside, exposed in all its hideousness by the early afternoon light. He turned his attention from the view to breakfast, and soon the hostess looked in for a chat and morning coffee.

'You didn't have to cook, I could have taken you out to lunch,' she said, shuffling round the stove yawning and politely covering her mouth with her hand. 'I didn't get to sleep until three in the morning, I sleep terribly in this place.'

Luka looked at her legs under her checked shirt; lovely muscular legs, he felt guilty he hadn't noticed them before.

'You should get the flat doused, there may be underground water, I read about it somewhere,' he said.

'Maybe. I've got to go to town to sort out some things. Stay here, okay? I only have one key.'

'I need to go to the station for my bag. I've got everything in there, pants, hairdryer...' he said.

'I'll get it for you. Give me your ID and cloakroom ticket,' she suggested intelligently.

'You can't carry it on your own, it's too heavy.'

'I'm meeting a girlfriend, she can help me.'

'How can I refuse? Do I know her?'

'No, she's from Zagreb. I met her here a few days ago.'

'Small world, eh?' he said between a mouthful of food and another of wine.

'Her old man's an officer, we met at the Topčider club,' Krišna said getting up.

He went through his pockets for his ID and ticket. 'Here, take care of yourself,' he said.

Seeing her off like a caring mother he returned to his breakfast, then washed the frying pan in the bathroom sink and took a shower. The towels were military ones with a yellow stripe down the middle, and he found himself thinking again of his days in the army.

Lying down on Krišna's bed he switched on the TV. There was a comedy on, which emphasized the desolation of the room. He switched channels. Even at this early afternoon hour someone was crapping on about the political situation: an 'independent' intellectual on 'independent' television. Luka had the good fortune to switch on just as the man came to his main point, and offered the brilliant conclusion that there was no justification for violence. He switched off. He was sick of everything to do with violence, yet everyone seemed somehow connected with it: cops and mobs, intellectuals on television, shitheads and piss artists.

He belonged to none of these categories, and to none of the places he had fetched up in lately. The screen was empty, like the emptiness of this miserable room, but this emptiness was specific and limited and was as nothing compared to the emptiness he felt inside him.

He felt like a button with only one hole. He wanted to die and disappear, and this feeling was so powerful he felt the need to do nothing, and his internal nothingness would turn him inside out like a sock and swallow him up. But instead of dying he heard the key turn in the lock, and Krišna returned with her friend.

The friend was carrying the bag, and was at least six feet two. He stood up from the bed and took her bony, muscular hand, which crunched his in a friendly shake.

'Hi, I'm Biljana,' she said, kicking off her shoes. He took his bag with a grateful smile and went off into the room where he had spent the night, resolving not to come out until she had left, though she didn't look like the type to leave in a hurry.

As he was going through his bag he could clearly hear Biljana's voice thundering away next door. Dropping the bag on the floor, he tuned in to her stories about her pulling power in the underground, although it became clear that it was a club she was talking about.

'I'm standing there with my cousin and this guy ponces up. "I can't dance to this crap," I say. So then the guy invites us to a party. I mean I don't know him, my cousin doesn't know him, this is the only place she ever goes to. Anyway her boyfriend is *really* heavy, the wanker just stands there not saying a word, and the guy keeps pushing it. Really fancies himself, all dressed up like a monkey. "Piss up a rope," I say, so he shoves his fist in my face and goes back to his friends. I'm all dressed in my mini-skirt and heels, so I take my shoes off and catch the guy, right, and kick him in the head. *Mae geri*, two teeth out and half the club are patting me on the back. My cousin and gutless wonder-boy over there are shocked — "How could you pick a fight with them, they're Montenegrins! That's why we never take you anywhere, you're too wild." "What do you mean, wild?" I go. This town's wild, it's Kabul, Afghanistan. If I wasn't a karate black belt I'd get a Rottweiler. So anyway, then I meet these two other guys, they're not bad, a bit skinny, I need a basketball player or something...'

Luka listened to Biljana drone on in this vein for over two hours. He didn't hear a word from Krišna. Maybe she had been suffocated. He wondered how long it would go on.

Biljana's story moved to an account of all the men she'd got off with in Zagreb, then all the guys she fancied, including various singers and actors; he had to admit that at least she was apolitical.

Her voice was killing him, and he tried to switch off. He wished she would switch off, shut up and die, but wishing was no good. Finally the noise stopped. He waited until he heard the blessed click of the front door, then he went to the fridge for the wine and took it in to Krišna.

She was lying with her arms and legs spread in a star shape on the floor, gazing at the ceiling; she looked wiped out.

'It's all right, she's gone,' Luka said.

'She's not all right, she needs her fucking head examined, that woman. She could have gone on for another ten hours, and there was nothing I could say to stop her.'

'I don't expect anything you said would have interested her,' Luka observed.

'She has a great time, what can I do?'

'You can drink some of this wine with me.'

'No, I've got my period. If I drink red wine I'll leak.'

Luka accepted her excuse and drank on his own. Then she brought out cards and they played five thousands. It went on for hours, and by the time she got to five thousand he had reached just one. The marathon game had exhausted his brain, and he fell asleep as soon as he hit the bed.

PART THREE

THE FRONT

20

JOINING THE EXPERTS

Luka woke at seven, which for him was the dead of night. Tearing a piece of paper from a notebook he scribbled Krišna a note to say he was going to town to put his money in the bank. Then he went to the bus stop. He didn't have to wait long for a bus, but it took him a long time to get on. It was jam-packed with people, and it seemed as though they had all skipped brushing their teeth. They stood there belching, farting and sweating. Dolled-up girls rolled their eyes and shouted at dirty men rubbing their zips against their pulled-in backsides. Anxious school-kids snarled at authoritarian pensioners. Old men and women jumped over each other trying to get out, and every opening and closing of the door was accompanied by fruity curses and sneaky elbow jabs. Everyone was acting crazy and seemed to think all was as it should be. The antagonism had reached its climax by the time they finally reached the terminus at Zeleni Venac. In the underpass and on Srem Street Luka passed crowds of foreign-currency dealers and their punters milling about with gamblers and theirs, plus a few cops standing around for decoration. Up on Knez Mihajlova Street a crowd of colourful people hung around selling Chetnik memorabilia and assorted army caps, but nobody seemed to be getting rich quickly or having much fun.

The photograph of Giška was still stuck to the monument, but the flowers had withered, the candles had melted and the glory had ebbed away.

When Luka saw the queue in front of the bank that was reputed to pay astronomically for foreign investments, he nearly threw up. It wound out from the Ateks shopping centre and through the middle of the dirty little park in front of the National Theatre, without a beginning or end in sight. He walked closer trying to eavesdrop on what was going on. When he heard an old woman say she had been there since three a.m. he turned away.

He was sitting on the wall of flower urns in front of the Cinema Adriatica, wondering what he would do with the rest of the day and every other day in his life and knowing that everything would go on perfectly well without him, when someone slipped up behind him and asked him the time. He caught a glimpse of blue eyes, and instantly recognized his old friend Bižo. His question went unanswered, and they hugged and kissed ceremonially three times.

'It's a small world,' Bižo said as they sat in the Index café drinking Nikšić beer.

Luka examined Bižo's uniform – or rather bits and pieces of various uniforms – and he felt as if a bird was fluttering its wings in his chest, a dove or a cuckoo, or maybe a hawk.

'I arrived yesterday,' Luka said. 'Where were you? You left Osijek like a hit man.'

'It was time you left,' Bižo said. 'I knew you would.'

'How could you know, smartarse? I didn't know myself.'

'I know everything. You were seen four days ago in Zagreb, three days ago in Budapest, and yesterday here.'

Since Bižo knew everything, the subjects available for conversation were quickly exhausted and Luka sat drinking his beer in silence.

Bižo ordered two more.

'It's not a question of knowing where you've been, but of knowing where you're going,' he went on. 'You've fallen into bad company, Luka.'

Luka thought of Krišna; he couldn't imagine what made her so many enemies among her friends.

'Her dad's smuggling weapons, some to the Ustashe, some to us. Seven hundred Deutschmarks a gun. A hundred guns means a flat in Belgrade. I hear he has four bedrooms.'

'Two bedrooms,' Luka said, feeling rather downcast by the news.

'The old man's found his feet here,' Bižo said.

He looked like he did in the days when they were in the wholesale chocolate business together. He was committed and well-informed. He didn't complain any more. On his jumper, by his left shoulder, he wore a little Serbian tricolour badge.

'You look like you've gone a bit nuts,' Luka remarked.

'You have to go a bit nuts,' Bižo said. 'Man, they're shooting out there!'

'I know, I came yesterday.'

'I don't do shitwork, I only do good clean stuff!'

'What a slogan for a business card!' Luka said. 'I suppose you pay taxes too.'

'Dead fucking right I do.' Bižo pointed to his head, and Luka saw there were quite a few grey hairs there.

Bižo had done his national service in the navy, working as a tea-boy: a land-based sailor, a shithead. On their benders afterwards he used to boast of taking one hundred and forty days' leave, and holding a gun only when he had to take the oath. Luka, on the other hand, was a foot soldier who sucked more dust than a Hoover and always got hopelessly drunk on these benders; the only thing he had to boast of was the dozen Albanian swear words he had picked up in the cage he shared with those animals. When they were in business together, Bižo was like a needle and Luka was the thread, and he felt as if something similar was happening now.

'Call it the transformation of the ownership of production, call it privatization, call it whatever you like, but don't call it robbery! *Nullum crimen sine lege*, and that is the law,' Bižo said, pointing at the gun tucked into the belt beneath his jumper.

Then he recalled the vocation for which they had both studied at university, and how they used to sit in the student canteen together drinking beer just as they were now. Bižo had always had a better brain for the Latin frills, but it seemed as if a million years had passed since then.

'Just four months, Luka! Everything went to pot in four months!' Bižo said suddenly in a different tone. 'They fucked us up in less than a year, but we'll pay them back a hundred times, you'll see!'

'The ones who survive will,' Luka said. 'When are you going back there?'

'What's it to you? Don't you like me being here?' Bižo sounded nervous.

'No, I want to go back with you to join our lot.'

Bižo called the waiter for the bill, and they went outside. Shaking his head and smiling to himself Bižo sat on the edge of the fountain outside the Beogradski department store and put his hand under the spurt of water. A few small coins glittered at the bottom.

'You're the sixth person who's told me that in the last three days, and I'm still here on my own. What the hell is wrong with you people?'

'What isn't?' Luka said. 'We're all fucked up, nobody cares, we've lost our faith, it's all shit. Want more reasons?'

'What's faith got to do with it? You think the people who fire their guns into the air every Christmas have faith? And the people I used to sell candles to? This has nothing to do with faith!'

Bižo took his hand out of the water and blessed himself with three wet fingers, Orthodox-style, and Luka realized he was right. Despair was at the root of all this. He remembered the celebrations for Our Lady. He didn't believe in the magic power of despair then, and here he was now, falling into the same old shit. If you didn't feel it on your skin you'd live for a hundred years and still not understand what was happening.

He took Bižo's wet hand and pulled him up.

'We'll go to Krišna's and collect my stuff, she'll be happy to see you.'

'No she won't. Believe me, she finished with me long ago. You have three hours, I'll wait for you here.' And Bižo disappeared across the Square of the Republic.

The cafés around the square were busy, and the tables were full, mainly of young people. There were young people skiving from school and skiving from Croatia, and a few better-off pensioners, and everything was exactly the same as when he had arrived an hour ago, the difference being that now he knew where he was going. He went through the same process of catching a bus at Zeleni Venac, and finally arrived back at Krišna's.

She was still asleep when he unlocked the door and walked in. Taking his stuff from his kitbag he looked at it, transferred a few things into his first-aid bag, then put the rest back and stowed the bag under the bed. He still had time to take a shower.

When he came out of the bathroom Krišna was already awake. She was sitting in the kitchen with bare feet and wearing stripey pyjamas, drinking coffee from her big mug.

'You want coffee?' she called out, then saw him in his black trousers and boots. 'What's happening?' she asked, suspecting what the answer would be.

Luka wiped a non-existent speck of dust from his eye and a non-existent stain from his Doc Martens.

'I met Bižo, he told me to say hello.' His voice sounded hollow.

Krišna tilted her head; her hair was still flat from sleep.

'He said hello to me?' she said, more to herself. 'Like hell he did!'

Luka looked more closely at her.

'You're talking shit,' she said.

He slung his first-aid bag over his shoulder. It was time to be going.

'You're both talking shit. He said hello to me, yeah?' Her mug came down on the table too hard, and she was left holding only the handle.

'Listen, do you know what that idiot has been saying about my dad? Did he tell you that too?'

Luka shook his head non-committally, not wishing to pursue the subject.

'He tells everyone he meets. I just happened to hear it from some woman I met yesterday at lunch. She doesn't even know him — or my old man or me.'

Laying the handle of the mug on the table she dropped her head, gripped the bridge of her nose with her thumb and forefinger and closed her eyes, like Luka's professors used to during exams when they had heard enough bullshit from their students; afterwards they would presumably go home, pull down the blinds and spend the rest of the day in bed.

'Draw the curtains, sweetheart, go to bed for a while. Here's some money for you.'

'I don't want your money.'

'Well, I do. Go on, put it in that bank where everybody's investing their cash. Take it, I'm off.'

Krišna shrugged and went into the other room without saying anything. Her silence haunted him all the way to the bus. The crowd had thinned a bit, or maybe people were standing aside to make way for this half-uniformed young man. He didn't know.

He found Bižo sitting in the same position by the fountain with his hand in the water. When he saw Luka he stood up and embraced him ostentatiously.

'Give over, everyone's looking,' Luka said. But no one was looking; people were sick of heroes.

Parked on the corner of Francuska Street was an ugly painted Citroën BX with Vukovar number plates, and a guy with dark glasses at the wheel. His hand was hanging out of the window and tapping on the metal of the door. He seemed agitated.

'Dule, meet Luka. Luka, this is Dule Tomaić.'

Luka had met Dule before, during his night in the police cells, but he wouldn't have recognized him because the police had substantially altered his face.

'I know you. You're the one who raped a nun, right?' Dule waved, taking off his glasses.

'Right,' said Luka.

'So how did you get off?'

'She confessed she'd asked for it.'

'Nice one,' Dule said vaguely.

Luka climbed into the back and Bižo sat beside Dule as he drove off very fast through the congested Belgrade streets — courageously fast for a young man with no driver's licence.

'If only he knew his colours everything would be fine,' Bižo said, turning back to Luka as the car sped through a red light.

This motherly remark was met with silence. Dule speeded up, more red lights flashed by, and soon they were on the motorway. Luka put his feet up on the seat and enjoyed the virtuoso driving skills of this under-age champion. They were travelling at about one hundred and eighty kilometres an hour. The Citroën flew like Concord, overtaking police cars as if they were matchboxes. Luka slept for an hour and a half, and woke as they turned into a dusty country track.

'Sorry about the bumps, they haven't asphalted the short cuts yet,' Bižo said.

The track had been flattened by tank treads, but numerous ruts and potholes made the going hard. Dule stopped and raised the Citroën's hydraulic suspension, then continued his bone-shaking drive. The car filled with sweet Slavonian dust, and raised clouds of it on the track behind them.

'Another half an hour to base,' Bižo announced, turning back to Luka again.

Five minutes later they arrived at a barricade where they were stopped by seven or eight elderly rogues armed to the teeth. Their warlike faces were veiled in cobwebs, and they lifted their weapons high in the air as though desperate for some action. Dule handed the men some papers, and they let them through with regret in their eyes.

'Nothing's happened here for ages,' Dule explained. 'It's a dead sector.'

The track led through a village and became a road, but they encountered nobody there. After the village the road became a track once again. By the exit-barrier they passed three more middle-aged men sitting in the shade of a large tree playing with their weapons. They were all in charge, and the one who seemed most in charge saluted Dule by raising his gun in the air.

'What's new, mate?' Dule asked.

'I just got this pump-action shotgun. Do you want to see it?'

'Another time, we're in a hurry.'

'Drive slowly after the second kilometre, there's something for you to see there.'

Two kilometres on was a charred cornfield, then some deep trenches, and a few metres later they stopped beside a burnt-out tank minus its turret. Lying beside it on the road was an upended personnel carrier with a gaping hole in the bottom. On the field behind it, instead of a combine harvester, an olive-grey minelayer was at work planting olive-green disks in the earth. Standing in profile in the middle of the road was a middle-aged man with a moustache, evidently a conscript in the reserves; he was dressed in an army greatcoat, and looked like a Red Army soldier from some documentary film about the October Revolution.

'Have you a light, mate? Mine's dead,' he asked Bižo.

Bižo passed him a box of matches through the open window. 'What happened?'

The man lit his cigarette between closed palms. 'What can I tell you? The enemy came out yesterday morning with their tanks and troop carriers and cocked it up.'

'Were you here?'

'Hey, I'm just a sapper, we're laying mines today.'

'Were many of them killed?' Bižo enquired.

'Yep, three troop carriers burnt with all their crews on board. They tried to get through but landed in our bunker, we were firing at them from five metres. They're up there, by the turning.'

The man turned and blinked into the September sun shining through its steel of clouds. Dule waved and drove the car towards the famous turning.

Three BVP troop carriers loomed blackly in a sharp wedge formation, yawning wide open like caverns. Dule stopped to see where the crews had been barbecued, but saw only a carbonated hand poking through the ripped-off door of the nearest wreck.

'Maljutka missiles, right?' Bižo queried.

Luka shrugged. 'Don't ask me, I've only seen them in one piece.'

Further on, the road led past a jungle of unharvested corn where members of some tank unit who hadn't yet been given their positions lay around in the sun with their shirts open and their weapons beside them, throwing cans at one another. They paid little attention to the painted Citroën as it passed. Dule drove on through the sleepy cornfields and halted in front of a 'STOP' sign that had evidently been brought from somewhere and bolted to the side of the road.

'Here we are,' said Bižo, indicating to Luka that he should get out.

He did so, and saw glowing in the sun five or six metres from the car the needle-sharp cogwheels of some harrows poking out of the dust. If Dule hadn't stopped the car, they would have ripped all four tyres off the wheels.

'Fuck it, man, don't shoot, it's us!' Bižo yelled the password in the direction of a bushy cornfield. The harrows were jerked to one side by a rope, and as the car drove through, the barrier moved back slowly without the slightest noise from the cornfield. Luka was impressed.

'We have a couple of real experts here,' Bižo announced proudly as they approached the base.

It was just a village really, smaller than the first, well cared-for but equally deserted. Dule stopped the car outside a straw-thatched cottage with one window overlooking the street, and told them this was the end of their journey.

The cottage had belonged to Dule's late uncle, and was an old one-storey building, more of a shack really, of a kind that no longer exists and is unlike those being built in the villages now, which tend to be inspired by *Dallas* or *Dynasty*. People inherit these properties from spinster aunts or hermit uncles who wash twice a year without soap, and the inheritance generally brings more grief than joy because they are cold even in summer, it's impossible to get rid of the dust, the floors crack even when no one walks on them, and an average-sized person has to crane their neck when walking through the door. Luka knew such houses because his Hungarian grandmother used to live in one, and he would spend summers with her as a kid, preying on frogs and grass snakes in the ditches.

She had had a summer kitchen with an earthen floor, and as he walked into the yard now he could almost smell her good food cooking, and imagine her bobbing up with her Mongolian cheekbones and her Slav accent, which would drive Hungarians from the mother country wild. But nothing bobbed up. Instead he saw a dark-haired girl with slim arms and a good arse hanging out washing on a line stretched between two posts. She saw them and waved to Bižo.

'Go through to the kitchen, I've just cooked lunch,' she said, and Luka saw she had good tits as well.

'My sister,' Dule said.

Luka peered around the yard, and realized that it was crammed with electrical goods.

'Our shop,' Bižo explained. Then he went into the kitchen with Dule, leaving Luka to wander around the yard, stagnating under the weight of its television aerials, cookers, refrigerators and other household items, neatly stacked and covered with tarpaulin. What with all this stuff looted from the war and Dule's big-arsed sister it seemed as if Bižo had acquired a solid starting point for the twenty-first century, and the whole project suddenly made sense to Luka.

He found them waiting for him at the table with a dark-haired little boy who was devouring bread and jam. Pointing to the boy, Bižo picked him up by the shoulders, put him on his knee and rubbed his bearded cheek against his turned-up nose. The kid came out with a stream of bird-like squeaks and spluttered with laughter. Bižo put him back on his chair. 'Gugi, this is Luka,' he said. 'He's new here.'

Paying Luka no attention, the kid went back to his bread and jam.

'He's deaf as a post,' Bižo explained. 'Someone left him on the doorstep two weeks ago, maybe they'll come back for him.'

'He's a great kid,' the hostess said, handing them their soup. 'He eats everything, he's quiet as a mouse, doesn't cry, doesn't wake in the night, doesn't whinge – not like some.' She leaned over Bižo, and the way they looked at each other told Luka everything he needed to know about them and what would happen next, with lots of meals and children and nights spent together.

'He looks like he's yours,' he said, taking a spoonful of soup. Bižo choked, and Dule and his sister laughed, more at Bižo's reaction than at Luka's remark.

'What is it, Bogdan, don't you like your soup?' she said, then turned to Luka. 'Hi, I'm Bosa.'

'Luka,' he said, saluting her.

'Your hair looks terrible, I'll cut it for you after lunch if you like, we can't have you looking like Conan the Barbarian.'

'If you cut hair like you make soup, you'd better not,' Luka said.

'So you don't like my soup either? Eat grass then!' Bosa said angrily.

At that moment a tall, well-built man appeared at the door and stumbled into the room.

'What's up, Bosa? Are they annoying you?' he said.

'They're full of crap, Doctor. They just came. You tell them what kind of cook I am.'

'The most beautiful in the village,' the man said tactfully, avoiding a direct answer for fear of causing more offence.

The man Bosa called Doctor was a sturdy, angular, clumsy character. His long bony face looked rather like the tower of a Romanesque cathedral, his completely bald skull the dome on top; even the few hairs around his ears had been shaved. It was hard to guess how old he was, forty or fifty maybe. He had sunken cheeks and deep-set eyes shadowed by thick eyebrows, which gave him a sombre, ascetic look. At second glance he seemed more approachable, with smile lines around the corners of his mouth and long, horse-like teeth slightly corroded but still capable of chewing tough food. Yet his smile was bitter, as if to say, 'Shut up, we know everything,' and it seemed as if he had been out of his profession for too long. It turned out that he was a gynaecologist, who had arrived in July from somewhere in Western Slavonia, and since none of the rear echelons would take him he had decided to join the bare-handed fighters instead.

After lunch Luka submitted to a haircut. He watched impassively as the hair he had been growing for two years and seven months fell away and dropped to the floor. Bosa clicked the scissors around his head and chatted away to Bižo about this and that, just like a real hairdresser. The cutting went on for so long that Luka started to fear for his ears.

'Keep your pants on, I have a diploma in hairdressing!' Bosa said, giving him a vicious look, and went on trying to persuade Bižo to install a boiler.

'What d'you need a boiler for? Cold water's good for your lungs,' he said, thinking of her breasts.

'I don't know what kind of a pigsty you grew up in, but we had hot water in our house. It'll be autumn in a few days, then you'll see. Look, Luka, all done, open your eyes!'

Looking at himself in the mirror Luka saw no major damage had been done. A pile of his hair lay on the floor like the fur of a skinned animal. 'Hey, I'll fetch you a boiler from the first house we take,' he told Bosa.

'Thanks,' she snorted.

Bižo led him out to where the weapons and ammunition were stored, and picked himself an M-70 automatic in fairly good condition, then they went to register him at the village hall. The building was decorated with the Federal flag with a red star, the Serbian tricolour with a cross, and the Chetnik Jolly Roger with the Cyrillic inscription 'Freedom Or Death!' Inside they woke up some half-deaf old man, and Luka spelt out his name and military service number. The old man stamped his army booklet with the insignia of the Territorial Defence Force, and hugged and kissed him. Then they returned for a well-earned afternoon rest.

Back home Dule told them that they would be on sentry duty for the next seven days because there was a ceasefire, and according to HQ's unwritten rules the checkpoints were always reinforced at such times.

In the yard they found five of the six television sets switched on, and Doctor drinking with Old Krsto, a neighbour from over the road. Krsto was a massive chap weighing around a hundred kilograms, an old veteran and local prophet. During the great peace-making of 1945 he had soberly predicted another war fifty years later, and had prudently kept renewing his ammunition supply for his 1943 trophy machine-gun. He was a legend in the village, because he had quarrelled with his old friends on political grounds the year before Yugoslavia split with the Soviet Union in 1948, and he still wore the proletarian five-pointed red star on his collar. He was always keen to chat with Doctor about Tito, socialism and the good old days, and clear up unresolved historical contradictions: 'They're all dumping on Tito now and saying he fucked their mothers – who knows, maybe you're one of his sons?' He turned to Doctor, downing his fifth or tenth glass. 'Krsto says fuck the lot of them. I had just one wife, one party and one machine-gun. See, it works perfectly. I shot five thousand bullets in the last war, and I've saved five thousand more for this one. That should be enough.'

'You're sure your ammunition won't let you down?' asked Doctor.

'Let me down? It's a bad fighter who blames his ammunition! I've looked after this lot like my life all these years, it'll see me through.'

On Croatian TV there was a spot of Franciscan Band Aid as a group of monks sang for the motherland. Doctor looked dolefully at the box, then turned to the old man. 'Five thousand won't be enough my friend, it won't get you anywhere.'

'What do you mean?'

'I killed over three thousand with my bare hands.'

'Three thousand! Hear that, kids?'

'I swear on my mother's life, over three thousand abortions in twenty-five years of devoted work. Some did more, and now they're the first to go running to church. If there's a God, he'll be pissing on them from on high.'

'You're right, the priest was complaining to me just the other day. "Sod it, Krsto," he says, "all your reds are coming to church now, I can't deal with them all." They're probably shitting themselves in case they get killed without being baptized. Do you know when I quarrelled with them?'

He turned to face Dule, who was cleaning his weapons on the sofa under the porch; Bižo and Luka were half-listening to him and half-watching the Eurosport channel on satellite TV.

'It was in the autumn of 1947, on account of your great-uncle Đuro Tomaić. I was secretary of the local Communist Youth Association of Yugoslavia. Two comrades from the Committee come round – I won't say their names, they're still hanging about – and they say, "Krsto, tonight you must confiscate five pigs and a ton of wheat from Đuro, and if he says anything fuck his wife." So I say, "You want me to fuck my neighour Đuro's wife? He looked after me like a father, you want me to steal his pigs and fuck his wife?" "It's your party duty," they say. So I tell them, "It's only you and the party who give me duties like that. I'll fuck who I like." So they throw me out. Not for long though. The comrades were sent to the Island, where they had a chance to die like saints. But oh no; after only a year of brainwashing they realized their mistakes and came back singing hymns to Tito.

'So a few years ago when this business started up, they came round to my place with some friends, and I invited them not to bear a grudge. And just imagine, after a couple of drinks the idiots started dumping on Tito again. Well, they went too far, so I told them to shut it. "First you're for Stalin, then you're for Tito, then it's Šuvar, now it's Slobo – the next monkey that comes in from the jungle, you'll be supporting him. Some Serbs you are!" Then they say to me, "So weren't you the first to take Stalin's picture off the wall in 1948?" I go, "Who says, motherfucker?" They say, "You did. It was hanging right there, where those ducks and the hunter are now!" "You mean this picture? Go on, take it down," I say. So they take it down, and discover on the back a page of a party newspaper hammering Stalin in 1948. "Tear the page," I say – and they find Stalin beneath it. "What do you mean, take it down, motherfucker?'" I say. "I kept him there not for his sake or mine, but because of you and your kind."

'So the first time I chased them out of the house because of Đuro Tomaić, and the second time because of Stalin. I've had one wife, one party and one machine-gun, and if I get fucked I'll know why, but no Serb cause will make me friends with shit that always was shit and always will be, however heroic they end up.'

21

LAST DAY OF SUMMER

It was late when Luka was shown to his room. His bed had one of those peasant mattresses, all puffed up like a doughnut, and he slept worse on it than he had on the steps in Belgrade. They had to get up before dawn to start their sentry duty at four, although it wasn't so much sentry duty as lying in the cornfield beside the road. The day started by freezing their bones in the morning cold and ended by drowning them in sweat. The hours between were filled with big buzzing flies, clouds of stinging mosquitoes and razor-sharp stalks of corn. It seemed to Luka an unbelievably pointless exercise. Every so often a distant shot would ring out, and the even more distant roar of a canon, but it wasn't enough to rouse the little detachment from their lethargy. Luka noticed a gingery glint of rust on the gun that he had cleaned only three hours earlier, but it didn't excite him, and a few times through the day it would fall out of his hands as he dozed off to sleep. Soon the barrel was full of earth, so he ended up making a protective cling-film top for it, like people put on jars of home-made jam. For the next three days he carried his gun with its virginal hymen to the sentry point and back, shaken in his faith that he would ever get a chance to use it.

At dawn on the fourth day they had crept through the

dewy corn to their positions as usual. Luka was lying soaked
through in a trench dug for someone much bigger than him.
Shivering with nerves and dampness, he watched the first
streaks of light pushing above the stalks, which told him that
in fifteen minutes the sun would appear. He was trying to
warm his hands when a clod of frozen earth fell on him from
the next trench. It was Dule, warning him that someone was
coming. Dule had played this trick on him several times over
the last four days, but to be on the safe side he sent the signal
to Bižo, who was waiting in another trench seven or eight
metres up the field. Bižo's face was black with grime and mud
and almost impossible to see through the corn, but Luka
could make out the grenade in his right hand, its ring having
been thrown over to the trench where Doctor was sheltering.
For a moment he saw something move out of the corner of
his eye. Then he heard the muffled jingle of metal, and
silhouettes floated by, the colours of their uniforms merging
in the blurred boundary between light and darkness. Luka's
gun was fixed on the edge of the dugout, the bullet was in the
barrel. Now they had to wait for Old Krsto to fire the first
shots from his machine-gun as they had arranged.

Luka managed to count eleven figures when the machine-
gun started rattling. Bižo threw his grenade, and the little
column ducked and weaved out of the way of the bullets that
harvested stalks and people alike in a whirlwind of slashed
grain, smoke and blood. Dule was inserting his second clip
now, but Luka's first bullet still rested quietly in the barrel. A
moment later three desperate-looking men jumped into the
field from the other side of the road and ran into one of the

cunningly laid mines. Through savage screams and an avalanche of bloody flesh Luka caught the bewildered look of the
fourth man, who was stumbling along the side of the field
towards his trench, breaking the corn and digging up the earth
as he came.

Luka noticed with complete detachment that his finger on
the trigger was numb, as if glued there. He glimpsed the
blinding white teeth of the man advancing towards him, but
he distinguished nothing more of that grease-painted face
before the blast from his gun drew a final line between its
horror-crazed mouth and the merciless mouth of the gun
barrel.

The gun exploded in an eddy of blood and mud and
splintered corn. The storm trooper's war cry fell silent with
Luka's shot, and death was discreet, like a well-preserved
secret between friends, because he was dead before he hit the
ground; Luka had pulled the trigger from less than ten metres,
the guard had seen him too late, and the bullet had gone
under his chin and out through the back of his head,
transforming his scream of wonder and rage into a barely
audible mutter.

The storm abated, and the silence roared like a wolf. Dule
jumped from his trench and ran over the harvested corn to
the road. Bižo called to Luka from above and stood up lazily,
his gun dangling from his right hand and touching the earth,
as if rooted there. Luka came up and lay down on the ground,
staring at the boots of the sprawling guard. As he stood up he
became aware that after seven days of trying he had finally
had a shit; it was hanging there in his pants, warm and firm,

as Dule shouted from the road in a voice hoarse with celebration and excitement, 'We got twelve! Twelve mother-fuckers!'

Unbuttoning his flies, Luka cut his underpants from his trousers with his bayonet and threw them aside, together with the unwanted shit. Bižo called him again, more tentatively. He pulled up his trousers and whistled back, and Bižo once more appeared above him. Jumping over the body, he glanced at it, grabbed the gun and handed it to Luka. 'There, now you've got your own gun.'

The dead man's eyes were wide open and still wet.

'Thirteen!' Bižo shouted back to Dule, walking round him.

Dule crouched, telling them to keep down, and the bloody line, broken in several places, made its way through the broken stalks.

Little Dule was shaking all over, his nostrils flared like a hound pointing at its prey. 'There were fourteen of them! Another one walked into the mine, he crawled over there!' He pointed at a puddle of blood in the middle of the field. 'He can't be far, I'll get him!'

He crept off towards the sounds of moaning and breaking stalks. The moaning stopped and turned into a wheezing, gurgling sound, and Dule jumped up smiling darkly and waving a bloody Rambo knife over his head. 'The man brings this baby to slit my throat and then cries for help! No problem, I helped him!' He moved the edge of his hand quickly over his throat, and wiped the blade with a leaf of corn.

'Fourteen!' Bižo said.

Doctor was walking in the middle of the road, avoiding the

pools of blood and speaking into his walkie-talkie. Then he ceremoniously fired a green rocket flare towards the newborn sun.

'Nice work, boys, we're being replaced two days early, we just have to wait for the trailer.'

The replacement shift took their time, and it was an hour before the tractor arrived dragging the trailer behind it. They were in a foul mood, and cursed obscenely as they wrapped the bullet-riddled bodies in tarpaulin. Most of the uniforms were so torn and bloodied that no part of them could be used, even the boots.

'Undress this one of yours, everything on him's in one piece,' said Old Krsto, but Luka couldn't do it; it was a thin summer uniform, he noticed.

'Last day of summer, eh, Doctor?' A balding, tubby man with a moustache smiled at the group leader.

Doctor shrugged. 'Depends. No more summers for these gentlemen anyway.' He pointed to the dead meat being loaded on to the trailer. 'I hope I live to see the next one.'

A man called Lopez dragged Dule's quarry with the slit throat out of the corn and laid it by the wheels of the trailer.

'Fucking hell, who decorated this one?'

Dule laconically raised three fingers.

'Nice work, son,' Lopez said in a teacherly tone. 'Now listen to what your Uncle Lopez is telling you. Take a good look at that hole, that's what the cunt looks like. Warm, wet and sometimes bloody.'

'Don't poison the child's mind,' an older man admonished. 'If it wasn't for cunts none of us would be here.'

The tubby guy, nicknamed the Beast, who addressed Doctor,

was the chief of local Territorial Defence. He had come to see for himself the results of the ambush. 'How was your new cadet?' he asked, looking at Luka through narrow brown eyes.

'Fierce as a viper,' replied Doctor, clambering aboard the trailer.

The tractor started up, leaving dark stains of blood behind in the dust and a torn-off camouflage cap with the chessboard symbol.

'What a beautiful start to the day,' Bižo said, pushing the corpses into a heap in the middle of the floor and sitting down.

Luka smiled broadly, holding his new gun between his knees.

The space set aside for the burial was on the waste-disposal site outside the village. A small bulldozer was already there digging trenches, and after the bundles of tarpaulin were thrown inside it scattered a thick layer of mother earth on top.

'These are now *glebae adscripti*,' Bižo commented, wiping the blood from one of the wrapped corpses off his hands; dropping a bit of professional terminology into his everyday conversation helped him feel secure in himself and what he was doing, and what he would probably be doing one day in the future too.

Bosa was waiting happily for them at home and tried to warm them up for some housework, but Bižo spent the rest of the day sleeping. Luka sat on the porch examining his new gun, which had gone a bit rusty in Croatian hands. In the far corner of the courtyard Dule had set up a small gym where he was trying to build up some muscles, and he asked Luka to show him his best exercises. Leaving the gun dismantled on the table, he accompanied the kid there. He picked up a weight, and as the morning was very hot he took off his shirt to show how each muscle worked.

'Take off your shirt too,' he ordered.

Dule did so to reveal the most impressive collection of scars imaginable on a living man; there were scars from knives, scars from a knotted rope and from blunt objects, and scars evidently from a red-hot iron and the gas ring on a cooker.

'They're all from Osijek jail,' he apologized.

'Put your shirt back on,' Luka ordered, feeling inadequate because his only scars were from vaccination jabs. Around his neck he was wearing a bunch of keys as an amulet.

'What are those for?' Dule demanded.

'For my old flat.'

'You can flush them down with the shit. The only thing that can get you back home is this.' Dule pointed at the gun on the table.

'Okay, forget it, let's see how you do with weights,' Luka said.

He was showing Dule how to work his muscles for days, and by night there was the cannon's roar from Vukovar to listen to. The windows trembled, and the Beast put the village on strict alert, expecting a more massive attack in retaliation for the successful ambush. But nothing happened. Over the Danube, trucks routinely set off loaded with electrical goods and furniture, and Luka watched satellite television all night, prevented from sleeping by the annoying vibrations coming through the air and the earth. Bosa and Bižo were having fun in their room. Doctor and Old Krsto were making grappa at a neighbour's place. Dule and little Gugi slept through it, Gugi because he was young and carefree and deaf as a post, and Dule because he had learnt to sleep in jail even while being beaten to a pulp.

Mornings started with Bižo yawning and saying he was dead on his feet. This irritated Luka, because he used to say the same thing every Monday after a weekend spent with Maria, or rather on top of her, when he and Bižo met at the Economics Faculty canteen for their early morning beer and gossip about the professors, in the days when they had something to study together.

Bosa would sing folk hits all morning and cook up her desperate lunches, which were always three hours late, and Krsto and Doctor would return bleary-eyed from their still, sober up under the tap, sit down in the yard on two red chairs they had taken from one action, and start drinking all over again. Doctor regaled them with stories about the time he spent drinking at the house of the farmer whose grandchild he had brought into the world, and Krsto recounted various alcohol-related partisan tales, lingering particularly over the one in which he was allowed to avail himself of a litre of home-made plum brandy as an anaesthetic before having shrapnel extracted from his stomach.

On one such day Luka was sitting on the porch exposing his left, less representative profile to the sun, when little Gugi came up with a piece of thin electrical wire, the kind kids used for making catapults when Luka was small. Gugi babbled and waved the wire in his face as though convinced he could do something with it. Tapping him on the forehead, Luka went to the kitchen and came back with a mug of diluted detergent. Then he knotted the wire to make a noose, dipped it in the mug and blew. Gugi looked in amazement at the bubbles trembling on the wire and floating off into the sky, round and shining like rainbows. Then Luka gave him the mug and the wire, and he ran around the yard in his rubber boots ten sizes too big for him, chasing the bubbles in the breeze. Luka stayed where he was, sunbathing with his own bubbles in his head. One burst, releasing his first memory of Maria.

They had met outside the physics room at secondary school. She was a sweet little first-year, and he passed her as she was arriving with the others for their class. He managed to exchange a few words with her in the break before his IT lesson, and suggested she skip her boring class and take a walk with him until it was over. But Maria was wary, and followed the others in.

Luka generally spent IT sitting on the window ledge like an eagle in his eyrie, looking down at the park beyond the school building while the other eagles in the classroom pecked at the liver of the unfortunate teacher nailed to his over-head projector. Everyone was soon playing cards and getting drunk, and as the chaos spread, Luka jumped out through the window on to the scaffolding that surrounded the façade of the building (it was forever being repaired and reno-vated), and ran along it to the physics room to grab Maria's attention.

The others noticed him at the window, and when the teacher went to the lab to collect things for an experiment,

Maria climbed out of the window to join him on the scaffolding and they ran off to the fields together. That was how things started between them five years ago on a September day just like this one. He took her picture from out of his pocket, the one he always carried around with him. It was crumpled. He smoothed it, and at that moment the bombardment started.

Three columns of dust shot up from the field behind the house, and lumps of earth rained down on the straw roof. Everyone jumped to their weapons except Bosa, who stood on the doorstep calling the little boy, forgetting that he couldn't hear. A moment later Luka, Dule, Bižo, Doctor and Krsto were out on the road hurling themselves into the ditch that ran alongside it, and trying to work out what to do next. Doctor was receiving a lot of confusing messages on his walkie-talkie, and the ones he was sending back weren't much clearer. There was no telephone in the village apart from the field telephone down at HQ, which was connected to an anonymous military command post manned by some officer who was invariably uninformed, pissed off or just drunk.

Krsto and Doctor were also drunk, and a good five minutes passed before it occurred to them that they should spread out a bit in the ditch. Luka lay on the bottom and killed time counting the explosions. He stopped somewhere around three hundred, and lay flat on his back staring up at the sky, waiting for them to pass.

A minute after the last explosion, they dragged themselves out of the ditch and saw the Beast hurtling towards them from the village in his war trophy, a camouflage-painted

Omega. He screamed something at Doctor, and raced back. Then Doctor sent Bižo and Luka to check on their replacements on sentry duty, who weren't picking up his calls, while he and Dule went to the village to see if there were any casualties. Luka was not overjoyed with his task, because the risk of being ambushed seemed great, but he followed Bižo to the field. They found the trenches empty, with no bodies or signs of a fight.

'What happened?' he asked Bižo. 'Do you think they cleared off?'

'Fucked if I know,' Bižo said.

At that moment they heard a rustling behind them. They turned around with their weapons raised, and saw two unshaven villagers, Lopez and Banija, looking contemptuously at them.

'What's up, shat your pants?' Lopez asked Bižo.

'I don't know who shat more,' Bižo replied. 'Why did you go? Why didn't you answer our calls?'

'You think I'd answer *you*?' said Lopez. 'Who the fuck do you think you are?'

'I've come to save your arse, bumpkin,' Bižo announced, deliberately exaggerating his honourable liberating role.

'You can fuck off back where you came from. I didn't invite you, as if you didn't know. Just don't hang around my cunt any more, okay?'

'I didn't know you had a cunt.'

'You know now, so piss off.'

'Okay, big dick, do your shift and don't fuck around next time you're called.'

'We'll be seeing each other,' Lopez promised.

The rest of the shift were slowly making their way back from the reserve position to the trenches.

'Just say when you want a fist down your throat.' Bižo shrugged.

Stepping backwards they slipped away, taking the longer road home.

'Did she really go with that idiot?' Luka asked when they were almost at the village.

'She was married to his cousin, fuck it. He was killed in action a month before I came. Lopez thought he could pull her, but she didn't want to know. I've already cracked his skull once, he knows there's more where that came from.'

When they reached Dule's yard they found a huge crowd of peasants standing there. Luka hadn't realized so many people lived in the village, and they all seemed to be in the yard, listening in respectful silence to the Beast as he addressed them angrily about the nearby Croat village.

'A fortnight ago we could have taken that pigsty in ten minutes and straightened up the line! I've had it up to here with their strategic plans. Whose side are they on? I don't give a flying fuck what they're doing in Knin, we all know what happened in Western Slavonia – do we want it to happen to us? The Ustashe are bringing in over a hundred reinforcements and mortars – now *you* show up and ask for our numbers. As far as *you're* concerned our numbers are zero, I'm giving you no one!'

The Beast swung round and pointed as he said this, and for the first time Luka noticed the presence of a number of officers, sitting together at a table slightly apart from the rest. The meeting was progressing in an atmosphere laden with accusation and incomprehension, when a tanned, grey-haired Montenegrin captain stood up and gave his side of the story:

'Listen, folks, I haven't come here to give you orders or listen to your complaints, I've come here to carry out orders. I have more criticisms of the High Command than all of you put together, and if I were in charge things would be very different, but this is how it has to be for now. You, Comrade' – he pointed to the Beast – 'I'm seeing you for the first time in my life, like you're seeing me. Neither of us knows what the other was doing before, but we should know from the start who's breaking the . . .'

At this the Beast went berserk. Banging his fist on the table, he screamed at the tanned captain:

'No, you listen to me, "Comrade"!' He spat out the word with evident disgust. 'I don't know where you've come from or where you were born, but everyone in this village knows me, and I'd sooner lose a hundred of yours than one of mine! I don't give a shit about your friends in Belgrade, any more than they do about me. We've managed without you so far, and we'll manage without you now. If you want to go with us, you'll do as we say. If your brain comes from Belgrade, you can forget it. Piss off, have your war there, you've plenty of Ustashe waiting for you. I'm not moving from this place till I see your orders and plans in black and white with every detail worked out and explained to us.'

The Beast's words were greeted with loud applause and cheers of approval. The captain threw up his hands, sat down at the table, threw a long calm look over the gathering and poured himself more grappa. The Beast collected himself and sat waiting for the others to speak. The officers sat in silence. They were wearing red five-pointed stars on their caps while most of the peasants wore various Chetnik insignia and Serb tricolour badges. The silence continued. They were all waiting for someone to break it with a conciliatory word.

At last Old Krsto, the most venerable fighter present, walked up to the officers' table and poured himself a glass of grappa. Turning to the crowd, he pointed at the star on his collar, then looked back at the captain. 'Four years I fought in the last war, while your generals were still pissing in their pants,' he said. 'After that I worked like a horse for forty years and paid my taxes and supported the army. Now I'm carrying a machine-gun again. Fuck it, son, both of us are grey, I just went through a bit more, that's all.'

The villagers cheered, and the officers nodded wisely as Krsto went on: 'We defended ourselves the best we could. Now the bandits are stronger, and without weapons and artillery we won't be able to see them off. You can't do it on your own either. I've already watched this village burn once. Twice would be too much for me. We have to sort it out, we're in this together.'

The captain stood up and shook Old Krsto's hand, and the tension slowly diminished. Bottles appeared, and people once more talked about how and where the army had screwed up, and about the volunteers, the police and the Territorial Defence Forces, but in a much friendlier tone. By noon everybody was pretty drunk, and ready to forgive and forget. Then the singing started. Pigs were roasted on a spit, and the atmosphere became more like the celebration of some great battle than the preparation for an even greater one. Everyone was soon roaring drunk. Dule was bored and sat whittling the tops of his bullets and bracing himself for the forthcoming fight.

Embarrassed by being so sober, Bižo and Luka left the happy crowd and walked to the village hall. Against the wall, big red Cardinal wine grapes were ripening in the September sun. The grapes hung practically to the earth, as big as plums, with pear-shaped seeds and thick, bitter skin. The friends sat in the shade of the wall putting the fruit in their mouths. It was crying out to be harvested, but the villagers were more interested in their stills now.

Far off, from the direction of Srem, Bižo and Luka could hear the noise of approaching trucks. The noise became louder. The trucks passed the building, stopped, turned back and stopped again; the engine of an ancient Deutz was clearly dying. Then they heard a door open, brisk footsteps approached, and a tall, slim man in ugly sunglasses walked through the gates of the yard and asked if this was the Territorial Defence Force headquarters. On the wall by the entrance to the hall a large table was clearly visible, with a large sign in Cyrillic saying 'Territorial Defence Force Head-quarters'; the man's eyes weren't on the sign but on Bižo and Luka looking at it.

He asked them again, with his back to the table; it evidently mattered to him a lot. Bižo finally put him out of his misery by pointing to the table. Then they heard more footsteps and three dusty, bare-chested individuals came in. They were all overweight, and wore their shirts open to the waist with their bellies pulled in by innumerable belts, making them look more like sausages than fighting men. One of them went to the tap on the wall and started splashing himself. The pipes made a lot of noise and woke Doctor from his early afternoon nap. He came to the door, and needed only a scythe in his hands instead of his old sub-machine gun to look like Death had risen from HQ. The new arrivals saw him and stepped back.

'What do you want?' Doctor asked in a cracked voice.

The man at the tap spluttered and explained politely that they were volunteers who wanted to fight. Doctor congratulated them, then went out to see what else they had brought.

Waiting in the trucks were twenty-three fierce fighters of all shapes and ages, from gentle youths to respectable old men, dressed in an assortment of shoes and uniforms. They lined up in the yard, and it must be said they brought a fair bit of colour to the early autumn afternoon. Then Doctor took their names and sent them off to the village, from which happy marching songs could soon be heard.

This didn't last long, because at three the mortars started falling, and exploding too, and the chaos really began.

The first big mortar bomb flew over the headquarters and crashed on to the hen house behind it, raising a mass of flying feathers and squawking. After that five more big ones fell in quick succession on to the yard. The shell must have been dug in too deep, and the back-up boys ran frantically around the village looking for somewhere to hide. Luka crawled into a deep ditch by the side of the road, resigning himself to finding nothing better, and listened to the pandemonium that continued on all sides for the next fifteen minutes.

The yard was filling with a thick, acrid smoke from the piles of carpets and linoleum that Old Milosav kept in his house next door. Milosav was a wealthy farmer, a suspicious, unsociable man who suffered from bad circulation in his legs. After every action he would bring back more carpets and stack them up in his house and yard, despite everyone telling him not to. His house was burning down now, and everything in it. Milosav was on afternoon sentry duty. Luka knew that no one would go out of their way to put the fire out unless it spread too far, and he himself couldn't care less. But the smoke was making his eyes water, so he crawled twenty metres down the trench and waited helplessly, as in the dentist's chair, for the bombing to stop.

The last shell fell at a quarter to four. By this time the smoke from Milosav's house had already thinned, and Bižo and Doctor appeared in the yard, at least half an hour too late, with fire extinguishers.

In the lean-to by the house there were welding tools, and the oxyacetylene meant the house quickly burnt to the ground. The walls were still too hot for anyone to approach, so Bižo emptied the extinguishers on the rolled-up carpets, which smoked like big cigars as Doctor went round the burning building bashing things with a pickaxe handle. Then the three of them leaned against the fence.

'Eh, what's a life? One cracker fucks up your property in half an hour,' Doctor said bitterly, kicking the tail of a mortar and exposing his teeth, which were like old piano keys.

'Never mind, Doctor, he has two more houses in the village, he can build another in a month,' Bižo said.

'Of course he can, fucking *kulak*,' Doctor agreed, throwing another mortar-stabilizer on to the pile. 'And, I'm telling you, he'll burn down at least ten of theirs tomorrow.'

A half-dead chicken, her feathers stained with blood, staggered past the wall and stopped by Bižo's feet. He pushed her aside with the toe of his boot, and went with the others to the hen house to see what was left of it. It was a direct hit. Burnt feathers and grains of buckwheat were spread all around, with ten dead white hens in the middle and a big rooster, unharmed but distressed by the loss of his harem.

'The fun's over, old man,' Bižo told him. The rooster went off picking with his yellow feet over the still-warm site of the fire, but almost nothing was left now of his ménage. Luka picked up a fat, dazed-looking chicken for Bosa to stew for *paprikos*, but it started wriggling so he let it go. Behind him in the kitchen garden he heard the squealing of pigs. They had broken the fence of their sty in a panic and were rooting for potatoes, leaving a trail of chaos in their wake. Luka couldn't imagine why pigs were called cultivated animals; they were at least as wild as people.

It was as they were walking out of the yard that they noticed one of the new recruits lying in the ditch. They turned him over, but Doctor could find no visible wounds. He put a mirror under his nose. Nothing. He touched his pulse. It was as if his heart had never worked. Soon a crowd of people had assembled, and Doctor could do nothing but pronounce the man dead: '*Mors subita,* as we say. Sudden death.'

'We didn't need a doctor to tell us that,' said an old peasant woman with a gun on her shoulder and a cigarette in her toothless mouth. 'What are we going to do with him?'

'How should I know, woman? We must inform the Command, they can bury him. He'll have to wait till tomorrow though. Let's go, folks, what are you standing here for? Find his papers and wrap him up in a blanket. He isn't the first and he won't be the last.'

This was all Doctor had to say on the subject, so they walked slowly back to Dule's house, observing the signs of bomb damage along the way; it appeared Milosav had come off worst, but he didn't know that yet.

As they were nearing the house, the Beast roared up in his Omega again with two army officers.

'Get in, Doctor, I've been looking all over the place for you!' he said, opening the door. 'You two, hurry up!' he shouted to Luka and Bižo as Doctor eased himself into the front seat.

Kicking pieces of roof and glass up the middle of the road, they walked on to the house.

Apart from a small hole in the thatch where a mortar had gone through the roof and fallen into the yard, it had been undamaged. Bosa was sitting in an armchair in a tracksuit and trainers watching several televisions all tuned to different channels, with six or seven remote controls on the table in front of her. Dule was still sitting at his table butchering bullets, and didn't look up when they appeared. Bosa didn't seem that pleased to see them either, and Bižo kept his distance from her; for people who slept together every night, they seemed unusually restrained.

'Anything to eat?' Bižo fired out his usual question.

Without batting an eyelid she turned up the volume on Croatian TV, at which Bižo stormed into the kitchen where he could be heard rummaging. Bosa jumped up from her armchair and went after him with a step that promised heavy shit. Dule went on doing his homework. He had already cut over two hundred bullets, but he still didn't stop.

Croatian TV was showing one of its demented propaganda shots, with some loser firing from a howitzer as happy as a child, and Special Forces guys jumping up and down in four lines and singing sacred Herzegovinan songs. Luka used Bosa's absence to find the right button among all the remote controls and silence the thing. He turned down the volume on MTV and threw an anxious look at Dule's homework, but the kid didn't look up. He was arranging the bullets upright so they looked like the metal eye-teeth of some beast of prey, working in a spiteful, sombre silence that was driving Luka wild. He had the feeling that all this would never stop – the ominous hush, the killing and the settling of bad debts – that chickens, people and pigs would go on being slaughtered for ever, and that this slaughter would become routine if everyone abandoned themselves to television and hatred. But he couldn't say any of this to Dule; Dule had got his education in Osijek jail, where after forty days he knew things he shouldn't have known in a lifetime.

Bižo and Bosa were shouting at each other in the kitchen now, and Luka turned the other televisions down so he could hear what it was about. But Bižo was speaking with his mouth full and Bosa was screaming at the top of her voice, so he turned the TVs up again. He had eaten nothing all day but grapes, but he wasn't hungry. He followed the pictures on the sets lining the yard, while next to him a kid tortured in prison made soft-nosed bullets, and in the kitchen his friends calmed down and prepared for their afternoon exchange of tenderness.

Dule finished cutting the bullets and packed them away gently, like the seeds of some rare plant that would one day bear a precious fruit. Luka wanted to say something to him but he didn't know what, so he joined him at the table and started packing bullets into clips and joining them with insulating tape.

Dule handed him one. 'You know what I'd like to do tomorrow? I'd like to get a pump-action shotgun and fuck everyone alive.'

'Yeah, right,' said Luka, staring at one of the screens.

Bižo and Bosa had finished their quarrel now and she was cooking something, so he went off to take a shower.

22

SUDDEN DEATH PLAY-OFF

Around six that evening, Krsto, Doctor and the Beast arrived with a number of army officers. They looked like a group of old business partners, all on the same wavelength and about to strike a deal together. They sat with their plum brandy and compulsory meze snacks, watching television and chatting about neutral subjects such as how the harvest was getting on, how much remained to be done, why life was so much better abroad and so on – like people at a village feast. More men and officers arrived, the chatting stopped, and maps of the various sectors were handed around the tables. Officers took compasses and questioned the Beast about the disposition of the minefields. Then a young, sympathetic-looking lieutenant stood up to deliver a brief analysis of the situation. Skipping the comrades bit, he said that he regretted the attack earlier on, and the loss of life and material damage, but he wanted to assure those present that things would soon settle down and that the army would provide all the necessary material and human resources for the forthcoming action, which was of vital importance to the future course of operations. This action would start early the next morning, when the army would fire on enemy positions in the neighbouring village. Protected by rockets and artillery-fire, mechanized infantry and tank units would advance simultaneously on the village. Preparations would continue as they moved to their starting positions outside the town. Then volunteers and Territorial Defence Forces would go into action with the tank units to neutralize the enemy's anti-tank groups and remaining points of resistance. While the enemy positions were being captured and cleansed, a new line of defence would be established, which would shorten the gap in the line by a full eleven kilometres. Within this line it would be possible to push units deeper into enemy territory, which would facilitate and speed up the transfer of operations to the enemy rear in a wider sector of the battlefield.

The young lieutenant sat down and the older captain from Montenegro took the floor. He explained that the original battle plan had involved cutting the enemy off from their provisions, then encircling and capturing the town, but the plan had to be dropped because of their excellent fortifications and food supplies. This meant they were now having to muster all their forces to smash the enemy's bastion in one push, and drive them out. Should they bring in reinforcements, he added, the army would provide additional airpower to neutralize them as they arrived.

He then wished everybody luck, and the officers turned their attention to the tactical details of the operation, so as to ensure that everything went according to plan, and risks were reduced to a minimum. They also issued stern warnings that the enemy were mostly drug-crazed fanatics who would stop at nothing. This raised a certain amount of laughter on the lines of 'give me a break'. Then the Beast stood up importantly and announced that there would be two fighting groups, and the plan would be explained more fully by the leaders of these groups. After this he called the names of those in his group, including some of the latest volunteers, and left the rest for Doctor and Krsto.

'Jesus, Doctor, what was all that about? We didn't hear bullshit like that even after the battle of Neretva, pardon my language,' said muddled Old Krsto when there were just twenty of them in the yard.

Doctor pulled a handkerchief from his shirt pocket and wiped the sweat from his bald head. 'We'll go on doing what we've always done.' He shrugged. 'Go where they tell us, take what they give us, make sure we have a way out in case they screw up, as is quite likely from past experience. Although if they hit them hard like they say, and they have the tanks, there'll be no need. Just to let you know I'm going first, but I'll go back first too. And I don't want anyone running ahead of me, understood?'

Everyone said they understood; they didn't mean to shout, it just came out that way. Few of those present had any proper military training, and it took Luka and Bižo an age to show them how to dismantle a gun. They spent the rest of the evening teaching them how to aim and fire.

After dinner Doctor appeared, looking worried. 'Do you think they should go with us? Maybe we should wait till they've had a bit more practice?'

'Screw them, Doctor, they're not for slaughtering but they're not for keeping. If we go, they go,' said Dule, observing the faces of the new volunteers in the flickering light of the televisions. These faces were very serious. For many of these

Serbians it was the first time in their lives they were watching Croatian TV directly, without adverse comment; some had never seen a living Croat. But whatever their motivation for fighting, they had no moral reservations. The night was warm and dark, the sky was full of clouds. From the ditches the frogs started up their noise, and shadows tilted on the walls of the yard, breaking on the surfaces of the few unbroken windows.

There weren't enough beds for everyone, so the men stretched out on armchairs, sofas and settees; some shared double beds, some lay on the grass with their weapons beside them. There was no word about waking-up time, but they knew it would be before dawn.

It was still dark when Luka was woken at five to four by the alarm on his new watch. Freezing cold and sleepy, he dragged himself to the tap to wash his face and drink some water. The water was lukewarm and tasteless and glinted slightly in the darkness as he splashed a few drops on his face. Doctor and Old Krsto were sitting at a table in the yard drinking their first plum brandy of the morning, washing it down with the remains of some coffee from a thermos flask. There was a satellite programme on one of the TV sets, and rustling on the table was a good old RUP-33 short-wave radio, a goodwill gift from the army. Krsto was showing Doctor something in the plans.

'I don't doubt the Beast knows what he's doing, but once they capture the tower, everything else is simple. Behind the village is the irrigation channel, after that it's the forest. They can hide there, but they can't come back. The Danube's up, the stream's high, you couldn't cross it with weapons. Hi, Luka, sleep all right?' Krsto interrupted his lecture as Luka emerged from the darkness.

'I heard your watch,' said Doctor, looking at it glowing on Luka's wrist. Everyone at the base had seen his watch; Luka knew he wouldn't keep it for long if anything should happen to him.

'Shall I wake them?' he asked, stretching.

Doctor waved his hand. 'No, we're waiting for the signal. Have some coffee.'

'I don't drink coffee,' Luka replied.

Krsto shook his head. 'My son, let me give you my recipe for a long and healthy life. First thing in the morning I eat one lump of sugar as a bait for all the bacteria in my stomach. Then I gulp some coffee to make it dark down there for them. And then I kill them all off with plum brandy. That's what I call medicine, not the stuff the doctors give you.'

Doctor didn't manage to give his opinion on this because there was a sudden crackle on the radio. 'Isnogood, where are you? Isnogood, answer me!' a voice shouted through a fog of interruptions.

'This'll be for me,' Doctor said, grabbing the receiver. 'Where are you, Shoemaker? Same place as yesterday? Twenty to nine?'

'C'mon, I can take you with my rook!'

'I'll give you thirty rook, but that won't help. Are you up for a championship match?'

'Sure am. Get ready, I'm coming.'

'Good lad,' Doctor said, breaking the connection. 'Get the boys up, we're starting the engines.'

He grabbed his ammunition belt and downed the rest of his brandy, while Old Krsto looked down at the bottom of his coffee cup. He moved it to the light to see it more clearly, then said, 'Today I see a big victory. Too bad my wife's not around, she'd be able to explain it better.'

A moment later the yard was in confusion as the clumsy sleepers awoke. All twenty-five of them were on their feet, some washing their faces with grappa, some washing their throats.

Doctor walked around, making sure no one was still asleep. 'Right, all present. Take your weapons and line up two by two. No need to hold hands, but we're going, fast!' he gabbled.

They went out on to the street. Some dogs barked, then fell silent. Bižo was ahead of Luka, behind Dule and next to three new army recruits, one of whom was waving his gun around under Dule's nose. Dule kicked his arse. 'Turn that weapon away from me, pal, we haven't started yet.'

Soon they left the road and cut across a cornfield. The stalks were heavy with dew, and the dampness came in through their noses and up to their foreheads, making their eyes twitch and stiffen. Luka heard the buzz of mosquitoes and the sound of boots cutting across the thin layer of dried earth. The darkness was imperceptibly melting away and on the horizon a thin line of light appeared, cut by a few lonely trees.

The group dispersed over a good hundred metres, and after four hours' walking they stopped in the middle of a field for a break. Paka, a Montenegrin from somewhere beyond Petrovac, was breathing heavily; only his wide-open eyes and teeth were visible in the half-light. Dule was wiping the dew from his gun with a piece of newspaper. Luka was trying to find a drop of water to drink from a leaf that had fallen on his shoulder. The surface of the leaf was unpleasantly rough, with not enough dew to wet his lips, which were dry from waiting. He also felt fear; it was there, like the filling in a tooth, no bigger and with much the same taste. Time stopped moving, the minutes seemed to be going backwards. The big hand seemed nailed to his watch.

At half past five, a second before the operation was due to start, Luka was convinced he would spend the rest of the morning waiting in the cornfield. A second later the deafening roar of the big artillery started, and flaming rockets snaked across the sky. The evil sound intensified in volume to the point of being unbearable, and Luka felt almost relieved when the explosions started with a volley of mortar-fire from the big cannons. Everyone put their hands over their ears and dug their heads against the shaking ground. The explosions came continuously through Luka's head, as though it were in a drum being hit with full force. A message was passed from mouth to mouth through the file, but he didn't understand anything until he felt Bižo pulling at him to move on. He was shouting: his face was distorted with the effort, and the veins were bulging on his neck and forehead, but Luka couldn't hear a word. Everything was swallowed up in the hellish thunder.

Suddenly the field was lit like daylight by the explosions, illuminating the headlines of the newspaper that Dule had been using a moment ago to clean his gun. When Luka's ears started functioning again, he heard a voice shouting: 'Go, go!'

It was his own voice, and he followed it. Crouching down, crawling on all fours and rolling on the ground, which trembled like a scared animal, he came to the edge of the field, where Doctor and the rest of the group were sitting in a ditch.

Before them, some half-kilometre up the road, the village was a boiling soup of sulphur and gunpowder. The stench from the volcano's crater was spreading upwind, and pieces of hot shiny metal were falling all the way to the group at the edge of the field.

'Jesus, see those fireworks?' Doctor shouted in an unearthly voice. The rest of them watched spellbound and shitless as tides of hot thick smoke belched from the village and the shadows of the houses vanished in the force of the bombardment, which melted everything into one shattering sound. Millions of sparks spread the smell of horror and the screams of smoking concrete and metal, as though mother earth were throwing up her hot womb.

'Fougasses! Fire!' howled a voice, carried along by fear, and the syllables vanished into the chaos of the storm.

As Luka stepped off the road he felt a rhythmic shuddering, as though someone was whipping the ground with chains. The tanks were approaching.

They were moving along slowly, looking for them. Doctor pointed his torch at the bonnet of the leading tank, a trusty 55, but in the noise and flashing it didn't see him, and he had to jump out into the road to stop the troop carrier rolling up behind. The column stopped. The young lieutenant looked out and gesticulated to them to get in.

'What's happening?' Doctor yelled at the top of his lungs.

The lieutenant explained something to the group leader with his hands, then Doctor moved back to let them climb on board.

Dule and Luka found themselves in the first personnel carrier with two volunteers, Paka and Bolan. Just four men made up the carrier's firing crew; at least six were missing.

'Where are the others?' shouted Luka.

One of the men rolled his eyes and leaned across the plastic sheeting between the two periscopes.

The vehicle moved very slowly, changing direction at every moment. Luka picked a helmet off the floor and put it on. The tank jolted and he banged his head against the metal wall. The firing crew pushed the barrels of their guns beside their periscopes and screwed them in position, while the BVP rocked and stumbled on like a boat on the open sea.

Flashes of explosions came through the windows, tapestrying the walls with intricate patterns, and Luka experienced in a slightly different way what he had felt when he was sheltering in the basement at Osijek from the bombing. It was a foretaste of death, not his own death but someone else's, whose witness he would be, and it wouldn't be something sudden and unpredictable, like an ambush, it would be certain and unmistakable, like a fire from the sky.

As the column approached the village his tension vanished, and he felt light as a flame. He had no eyes or ears or name any more, just the desire to crush and destroy everything in front of him.

No more than twenty minutes had passed from the start of the operation, and the bombardment was moving to the other end of the village and to the irrigation channel behind it. The tanks advanced into the village in tight formation, like bulls in a cabbage patch, meeting no resistance. Then the order came to halt.

On the floor of the carrier lay some unopened cases of ammunition, still with the mobilization letters on them, a bunch of ten bazookas and grapes of grenades.

Dule looked at them and shouted at one of the army recruits: 'Hey, Bolan, what happens if they throw this shit in here?'

'Then you'll be the youngest Serb launched into orbit, brother!' Bolan pinched his cheek; he was the joker of the crew, from somewhere in Bosanski Šamac.

Dule started to feel claustrophobic, though he didn't know what the word meant. 'What's this shit? What are we waiting for? Let's get out!' he yelled, pushing the lock until he opened the door.

The rest jumped out after him. Behind the BVP stood another personnel carrier with a three-barrelled PAM anti-aircraft machine-gun on the bonnet, firing ammunition sporadically at the house opposite, which was already burning anyway. The crews emerged from the other vehicles, red-faced and sweating from the heat. The shelling overture was a few octaves higher than necessary, and they walked around looking dazed by the mayhem raging around them without so much as a shot being fired from the other side. The PAM went on making patterns on the house's walls and windows and the gates of the yard. All around, holes bloomed like big flowers. Old Milosav, his eyes red with sweat and the desire to avenge his burnt house, was rallying his group: 'Let's go, why are you standing there? Follow me!'

'Where are the fuckers, where the fuck are they?' his son Nenad kept saying, turning on the burning ruins as if expecting them to jump out from the flames.

The PAM machine-gun swept the landscape, harvesting mindlessly, until Bižo took a pickaxe from the tool set in the carrier and hit it a few times.

There were a couple of short rattles and the firing stopped.

'Spread out, boys, spread out!' Doctor's voice could be heard shouting hoarsely as he arranged his newest volunteers, clustering around him like chickens around a mother hen.

Dule and Luka stepped back to the wall of the destroyed house and stood there with their crew, not knowing where to go next. From the middle of the advancing column of tanks they heard a drunken tenor voice shriek: 'Move your arse down there! I fuck your Indian country!'

The young lieutenant, red in the face, gave quick orders: 'Three tanks and thirty men to the church now, move, at the double!'

Three tanks left the column, moving their turrets left and right, dispersing clouds of black smoke, and making the stroll to the church more pleasant. The thirty chosen men gathered instantly and walked down the road, while the young lieutenant kept bucking them up: 'Heads down! Keep close to the tanks! Walk on the concrete or the tracks! Check every yard and house!'

They advanced slowly, metre by metre, but there were few houses left to check. Before them, the tanks crushed mounds of plaster and wattle, fragments of furniture and walls, but they didn't find animals or men.

Luka followed an M-84 tank. Under its tracks, water-pipes and straw from the walls were breaking up. The tank passed through the remaining wall of a house, and arrived in the neighbouring courtyard. In front of them an unfinished new three-storey house was burning. The roof had fallen in, but the ground and first floors were still intact.

Dule hit the turret with a brick from a collapsed wall, and the commander's snout appeared at the opening.

'Cover the windows, we're going in!' Dule said, and the commander waved his hand.

The entire corner of the building had been smashed, and Luka and Dule entered through the opening. A shell had gone off in the room, making a hole in the floor through which they could see the cellar. There were three overturned camp beds in the room, soaked in fresh blood. Under one of them they found a guy without a face, just a bloody porridge with a few ginger tufts poking out.

'Fuck, he's so yellow, he looks like he was made with four eggs not two!' said Dule in disgust, going through the dead man's pockets. Then he made another discovery. 'This one's a Kraut!'

He showed Luka some documents with German stamps. Luka shrugged. There was nothing of interest in the room, apart from a few pieces of soldiers' uniforms and a small broken television set.

Paka and Bolan squeezed into the house after them and went round the other rooms, and Luka and Dule jumped down to the cellar. A mortar had exploded next to a hydrant and made a big puddle of water on the floor, swimming with sawdust and chips of wood. The rest of the floor was covered with bits of plaster and sand. Going through the torn-off door, they explored the other rooms. In Luka's, amongst bits of uniform and dirty washing, he found a police pump-action shotgun and ammunition-belt. On the floor were some straps. They seemed good enough for Luka, so he picked them up and put them in his knapsack.

'What did you find, Dule?' he shouted.

'Nothing, just cans!' Dule shouted from the next room.

Luka went in, giving the kid the shotgun and ammunition, then focused his attention on the boxes of cans laid out before him on pallets.

'Fuck, this looks good.' Dule slobbered over the metal and plastic of the shotgun. Then he put his old M-70 on his shoulder.

The cans he had been so disparaging about were not the usual shit given to the army, but posh food from foreign donations: salmon, tuna, crab, beef, pineapple and similar goodies, all stacked neatly.

Paka and Bolan were upstairs, seeing if there was anything there for them. 'Get the tank up close!' Luka called up. 'We need something to carry this load of stuff!'

The tank moved to the edge of the house and, with the help of a winch, the pallets of cans were hauled from the cellar. Then they were pulled up to the yard with a wire cable, and covered with a sheet of tarpaulin.

The commander of the tank kept hurrying them up and telling them to climb aboard, until Dule started showing off his new pump-action shotgun. 'What's the matter, Lizard? Think the action will fall through without you? Why are you running off in that tank?'

The commander gave him a strange look; he didn't appreciate the kid's comment. He closed the lid, and pushed on quickly, and the column crawled on through the village towards the church, from which the sounds of explosions and machine-gun fire could be heard. A personnel carrier was standing by the ditch and its crew was trying half-heartedly to fix one of its tracks, which lay a couple of metres behind them on the road; they looked as if they couldn't care less, as though they were on army drill.

It was almost completely light now. On the road outside the church, Doctor and the Beast were discussing with the young Lieutenant the destruction of the tower.

'Where have you been, boys?' Doctor asked, when the BVP had come to a stop.

The tank commander lifted the lid and addressed his boss. 'Comrade Lieutenant, permission to fire some mortars too!'

'Right you are, Commander. Next target, the enemy retreating over the irrigation channel, two fougasses, fire!' said the lieutenant, swigging from his canteen. 'The bandits are hiding in the cemetery. We'll have to wait until there's a bit more light, then we'll chase them out, eh?' He looked at the Beast, who nodded. 'They'll have at least fifty dead and wounded and nowhere to run.'

The conversation was accompanied by renewed thunder from two three-barrelled PAMs, and from a few machine-guns scattered around the cemetery. The bullets had made a visible dust on the gravestones, and bits of stone had broken off, making it look more like they were there to build a tunnel through the rock than to fight. After a couple of minutes the firing stopped, and the young lieutenant climbed into the tank to address the men inside the cemetery through a loudspeaker. His voice sounded excited; this was the high point of his life.

'Ustashe, you are surrounded and you have no chance to get out! An officer of the YPA is talking to you. Surrender and we'll treat you in accordance with accepted international law. If you refuse to lay down your weapons, nobody's life is guaranteed!'

No noise came from the cemetery, then there was a movement among the tombstones and a white cloth appeared, and ten men in multicoloured uniforms shyly approached the tank, where the brains of the operation, Doctor, the young lieutenant and the Beast, stood waiting. In front walked the man with the white flag, tied to a branch. He stopped when the lieutenant shouted at him, 'That's all right, don't come any closer, is this all of you?'

'No, Comrade Lieutenant, the wounded stayed, they couldn't walk,' answered the man with the flag, not daring to put it down. He was balding, with a moustache, a bit taller than average, bony and muscular, but scared.

The Beast was looking at him as if he would eat him alive.

'What is it, Feldvari, aren't you going to say hello to me? Don't we know each other?' he said, his face distorted.

'Come on, you know what we agreed, don't screw up,' the young lieutenant urged him.

'I wouldn't do him any harm, I wouldn't touch him with a bargepole, motherfucker! Did you just shit yourself?' the Beast roared at his old acquaintance. 'Go on, pick up the wounded, you put them in that shit, fuck your Croatian Democratic Union, get lost! Dule, Bogdan and you two go with them so we don't have any more shit!' The Beast was mad with rage. He turned to the lieutenant. 'Screw it, Lieutenant, you and your international rules. For eight years I was at school with that guy, until yesterday he was plotting against my head, and now I should let him go? You think he'd let me go? Like fuck he would. He'd kill me like a dog, they'd kill us all...' The Beast was crashing on, nobody was trying to stop him.

'I shouldn't go in there, Doctor, someone might recognize me and I don't know if my people are still in town,' Luka said, trying to get out of it.

'Listen, the way you look now I promise even your mother wouldn't recognize you,' Doctor said, leaving Luka no choice but to follow.

The cemetery was deserted and thickly overgrown with grass. From the old tombstones most of the letters had been erased, and there was thick moss and lichen everywhere. They were abandoned after the Volksdeutscher minority had left in lovely 1945. The prisoners went around the graves picking up the dead and wounded. The dead looked better than most of the wounded.

'You donkey over there, hold that gun by its barrel or I'll blow your arse away!' Dule shouted at a small fat man who was gathering abandoned weapons and armaments and throwing them on a black marble tombstone. Soon there was a heap of Kalashnikovs – Romanian and Hungarian – old semi-automatics, pistols, batons and grenades. Luka walked round the tomb, slipping on streaks of blood and spent bullet cartridges jingling under his feet. Sitting on the stone he opened a can of pineapple slices, and looked at the wide-open eyes of a bullet-riddled corpse in the grass. After they had played a staring game for a while, he took off his helmet and laid it over the dead man's eyes. Then he drank the juice from the can and went through the bits of pineapple. He was on his third when Dule came up. 'Give me some,' he said, so Luka gave him the rest and sat back against the tombstone.

Further up the cemetery, people had found some foreigners. They had crawled into a family vault, two Krauts and two Poles. Old Milosav had found them there. 'What the fuck are you doing here, motherfuckers? Who sent you? Fuck you, Kohl, fuck you, Genscher, fuck you, Pope!' Milosav stood there foaming at the mouth. He was mad as the devil, his brain was blocked.

'What's the matter, Milosav, got some tourists?' some people shouted at him from the other side.

There was a fair bit of noise, and the Beast arrived in person to see what was happening.

'*Was ist los, Ausländer?*' He addressed a man with a gingery moustache who was peering from the family vault, not wanting to come out.

'*Nichts verstehen, entschuldige,*' the Beast replied to the man's protestations. He gabbled more broken German and some Polish, then shouted at those with him to pull back the stone of the vault. When it was almost back he threw two grenades inside. They exploded like thunder, and the stone jumped and broke in two.

'That's the way to do it, guys. Let's go on,' he said, grabbing two guns from the pile of captured weapons. 'Carry all that stuff, let's go.'

'There must be a hundred guns there,' Bižo said to Luka, taking an old M-53 machine-gun.

'We moved a ton of cans to the side up there, we should

load them,' Luka said, bringing a happy smile back to Bižo's face.

They walked away from the cemetery, picking up Dule on the way, who was hanging around the carrier showing off his pump-action shotgun.

'Dule, have you seen a truck that could carry a ton of stuff?' Bižo asked him.

'Yeah, there's a van down there, we can see if it has any petrol. Come on!'

The small bottle-green van was sprayed with holes and the bonnet was destroyed, but the rest of it was all right, and they managed to start it after fiddling with the wires. In front of the church some guys were playing football with a captured ball, twenty-a-side, still in their boots. The purpose of the game was to kick the ball as hard as possible, until it broke or someone broke their legs. They were letting go their unpurged tension and fear, and the game wasn't pleasant to watch, let alone play.

Bižo drove with Luka and Dule to the destroyed house, where they found the cans waiting for them. There was no need to hurry, they loaded them at a leisurely pace. Trucks were passing back through the destroyed village, it was the right time to pick up some souvenirs, and the afternoon was passing in a fiery haze of expropriating the expropriators.

'What the fuck's this one?' Dule said, picking up a crate of cans with a dappled cow on the front.

It was French corned beef, and if Luka had learned anything in the army, it was how to open a can in five seconds.

Outside the yard the trucks and carriers rolled on. The taste of the meat in Luka's mouth was strange and heavy, the taste of an animal killed far away, and many years ago if the numbers engraved on the metal were to be believed. The French cow was dying for the last time, beside the warm ruins of a burnt-out house. The killing of chickens, pigs, cows, people – for the first time Luka asked himself if there was any difference. He envied Dule his good mood. The kid was eating away and had switched on the radio in the carrier. God was on his side in this raid; God was a charming old man with a long beard and a tall Chetnik hat, and he was working for him, at least that was how it seemed to Dule.

Luka felt as though the day was filled with heavy metals, as if a church bell had been pushed into his mouth and was vibrating dully in his head. Throwing away the can, he wished he was sitting on the red chair opposite the wall of TV sets, which was the nearest he could imagine to home.

The breeze was slowly diluting the smoke and the smell of burning, when in the distance he heard something hiss. A second later he saw over his head the belly of a plane, shining like a fish and instantly disappearing. Another plane swept overhead, the roar of its engines mixed with a weird exploding noise, like marbles being thrown down stone steps. Another explosion – and a curtain of dust and smoke came down over the remains of the church. The plane disappeared, as if they hadn't been invented yet, and Dule bounced out of the truck as if catapulted from it.

'Fuck, did you hear that?'

'Cluster bombs.'

'Are you crazy, what fuckin' bombs?'

'Air bombs,' Luka said, too tired to explain.

'What fuckin' planes?' Dule squeaked, looking at the curtain of smoke from the middle of the village. Then he ran over to the ruins of the house, breaking the fence on his way.

'What happened?' said Bižo, getting out of the truck where he had been rearranging the cans.

Luka pointed to the smoke cloud rising over the village, and they started the van and caught up with Dule in front of two long crevasses right on the spot where the forty men had recently been playing football. They were all gone, even their shoes. There were just the two cracks in the earth, as though made by a big whip. On the cratered asphalt and the torn-up earth by the road, strips of grey and khaki mingled with patches of burnt blood and slime.

'They were our planes!' roared a desperate voice.

'What the fuck do you mean, *our* planes. To hell with your Red Indian country! Whoever said they were ours, I'll rip his throat with my teeth! If they're yours, go fuck yourself!' screamed the tenor from the rear, hoarse with rage and alcohol.

Dule came out of the truck vomiting pieces of corned beef on the ground, where it mixed with the bloody strips of fabric and the remains of forty people who had disappeared into the darkness, leaving nothing but dandruff and ashes behind.

The young lieutenant, the Beast and Doctor appeared. Luka and Bižo sat in the van, glued to their seats, unable to get out. Outside, there was a storm. They heard the voice of Old Milosav, a voice unlike any heard anywhere, before or afterwards. He was calling for his son Nenad, the best football player in the village, who had found the ball and organized the game. The old man was cursing the ball, football, himself, his son, God, the planes, the army. He was crawling over the grass looking for one thing of Nenad's among the bits of cloth. He knew it made no sense, he knew his life made no sense, and he was screaming this until Old Krsto and two middle-aged men came over and lifted him up.

Dule vomited again. Someone gave him a bottle of plum brandy, and he drank and vomited some more. The young lieutenant gathered around him the rest of the soldiers and reserve troops and spoke quietly and gently to them, as if scared of his own voice. He kept looking round, trying to read from their faces what he should say, but all the faces looked as shocked and blank as his own. 'Men, I have no words for this, believe me someone will pay, it will be dealt with in a proper military court, all we can do now is to make a list of the dead, until further ... If someone remembers who went to play football...'

The soldiers started remembering. The one with the best memory was a young corporal. The kid had tears streaming down his dirty face, and he took a grimy, brown-checked handkerchief and blew his nose. Someone smiled bitterly and cursed, and they tried to remember the names of a few reserve soldiers who had arrived at the unit just two days earlier.

At the church, Milosav and some of the distressed witnesses took five prisoners to the wall and shot them. No one tried to stop them. The young lieutenant turned up when they were preparing to kill the second round. He was incandescent with rage. 'What the hell are you doing? To hell with you, didn't I tell these people nothing would happen to them! Let them go immediately, or I'll arrest the lot of you!'

'You motherfucking greenhorn, don't tell *me* what to do! Didn't you promise nothing would happen to us too, and you fucked up! Back off! If there was any justice you'd be one of them!' screamed Milosav.

The lieutenant went mad. Blazing with command fever, he unlocked his M-70 and aimed it at Milosav and his firing squad. There was dead silence.

'Come over to me, bloody peasant, I'll kill you all if you don't put down your weapons!' The lieutenant waved at the BOV with the three-barrelled PAM, and the vehicle slowly rolled towards the cemetery fence and aimed it at the church wall. Had he given the order he would have killed all participants in the argument, plus the prisoners involved. Milosav and his followers unlocked their barrels without putting their weapons down, and the old man raised his bloody eyes to the young lieutenant and said quietly and memorably: 'Kid, may you never say that to me again. My people and I are going, this is the last you'll see of us, we did our bit, we gave more than was needed. And if you ever come to my village again I swear you won't get out alive. Got that? Now we're going home.'

The young lieutenant lowered his gun, and the soldiers put the prisoners into the carriers to take them to HQ.

Milosav stumbled over to the Beast, who was following the scene with a weary calm. The old man hugged him and clapped him on the shoulder. Then with eyes full of tears he shouted at Dule: 'Come on, son, don't stay with these fucking commies while you're still in one piece. Your parents won't have anything to bury!'

He hugged them all, smelly with sweat, smoke and brandy, then he and his followers walked to the head of the column.

Luka drove the van at the back of the column, very slowly, at a snail's pace. The army wasn't watching them, they were busy wrapping the shot prisoners in tarpaulin, and the unit passed through the village in silence, accompanied by the lonely creak of someone's boots and the occasional jingle of equipment.

23

THE BORED SURVIVORS

The trenches by the cornfield where they had crouched that morning watching the fireworks still bore the traces of their rolling, with flattened grass and uprooted bushes all around. They weren't walking back through the field, they were driving up the road, but not as winners. In front of the village a posse of old women armed with semi-automatics was waiting. They already knew that people had been killed, and that there would be no burials, and they stood there in their black shawls as the guard of honour.

In the village the column spread out and the green van almost sped to the cottage, where Bosa threw herself on her brother.

It was too early for lunch, so they sat out in the yard and drank. They got drunk, so they poured more and watched lies on the televisions. Then Paka turned up with his knapsack and a video recorder.

'Hey, look at this, you'll die laughing! Lopez, Banija, Bolan and I raided a good house, a *Gastarbeiter* one, and we found these!'

He brought some tapes out of his knapsack and connected the recorder to the television. On the screen was a wedding, a Croatian wedding with a forest of chessboard signs. The church they had destroyed today appeared in close up, with more chessboard flags and tambourine players and Mercedes with German plates. Paka fast-forwarded the film to the wedding service, and they saw the priest in his white surplice moving about like a penguin. Then the bridal couple waddled on. Paka slowed the picture down. 'See the bride, look at her!' The camera was moving around the couple. The bride looked nice from every angle.

'Yuk, the groom!' Paka said.

The groom had a thin moustache, and the standard trendy peasant hairstyle, with a fringe and layers at the back. The quality of the picture was not very good.

'Now get this!' Paka put in a new tape. 'This one is Love.'

On the screen, the bride and groom appeared in a more intimate pose.

'Sh-it!' Dule was amazed, rubbing his eyes. The view was amazing. The bride was like thunder.

Bižo was grinning. Paka was commenting on each change of position in an official voice. 'This one fucks like a fish, boys. It's not the Croatian army you're up against, it's Croatian cunts. Look at the kid, she's not eighteen and the moustache guy isn't twenty, and they're making babies already. Hey, Slavonians, when are you getting married?'

'I'm going to as soon as the war ends,' said Dule, engrossed in the pictures.

'And you, Bižić? Little guy? You doing it soon too?' Paka asked.

'Yes, I will, as soon as we take Osijek,' he replied distractedly, not moving his eyes from the screen.

The guy on the tape was extremely loyal; he was screwing

his wife under a poster of Hajduk, a Croatian football team, and beneath a calendar with a chessboard and some holy pictures, the house was furnished with a million cheap knick-knacks.

'This one's a big Ustashe,' observed Paka. 'There's no room without a chessboard. I asked the Beast who he was and if we'd captured him. I'd let him go just for his wife. Look at her...'

'Fuck, what did he miss in Yugoslavia? He had everything. What did he need independence for?' Bižo said fervently. There was no place in the house or yard where these two didn't have sex.

'Look at them going at it so shamelessly,' burst out Old Krsto, who had arrived unobserved. 'I know both their parents,' he said, following the action with a fever unusual for one of his age.

Paka put on some fresh tapes. The guy was really cruel; he screwed his wife fully armed and dressed in a Guards uniform. The thing was becoming tedious.

'I'm taking these tapes home to show who I was fighting,' said Paka. 'And to show my little girl some things.' And that was the end of the presentation.

The company fell into depression again. Paka packed his tapes, picked up his video recorder and went off to his friends. Bižo threw aside another empty bottle. Dule, who had drunk enough to last him a lifetime, retreated to his corner to exercise his muscles.

Afternoon set in, lukewarm and boring, *piano pianissimo* with horseflies and crickets. Distant rattling was heard first. Then a longish column of tanks and soldiers crawled through the village to their new positions, raising clouds of dust to the sky. They thundered through the place for at least ten minutes, but no one came out to throw flowers; people had had enough of the army for a while.

At that moment the gates of the yard burst open and in walked the tanned Montenegrin captain, the one who had wanted to make everything clear at the first meeting. With him came three bumble-bees from the army police, dressed in new green uniforms and olive berets.

The captain looked around the yard as if he had never been there before. 'Looting, looting,' he said, as if to himself. 'Not directly, God forbid. My army got wiped out and the brothers are loading stuff. Where's that Command of yours?' he asked, looking round the yard again.

Luka pretended to be asleep behind his dark glasses. Bižo put his feet on the table and looked at the sky. The captain and his fighting trio looked indecisively at each other then left, and soon their old jeep was heard starting up and driving down the road after the column.

The dust from the column settled on all the objects in the yard. Bižo took out his house-pistol and shot at the empty bottles by the wall. He used up three clips, filled them with more bullets and shot again. It was getting on Luka's nerves. He turned up the volume on Croatian TV, where the current Minister of Defence was speaking. Bižo filled the screen with five bullets. The thing was dying and smoking, but Luka decided not to complain about it.

At this moment the Beast and Doctor arrived, fairly deranged, having evidently had an argument.

'Fuck it, Doctor, you don't give a toss about what I'm

telling you. Who's in charge, me or them? They already screwed us. It couldn't get any worse.'

'Unfortunately it could get a lot worse, my friend, don't worry, that's the army for you. Who would you get your ammunition, uniforms and food from without them? If you're with them, at least they won't shoot you. They're a bit touchy now, stay away from them for a while, let things settle down.'

'Doctor, we're not moving from the village until this shit is investigated!'

'It won't be investigated for another five years, my friend, they need people now.'

'I can't lead people to an army that bombed us this morning. To me they're worse than the Ustashe. Old Milosav has lost his mind. He can't bear to look at the red star now, he'd rather have the chessboard.'

'I'm not talking about Milosav. He has to stay at home and pull himself together. He's no good for this any more. To kill those prisoners like that – his nerves are shot, do you hear me?' Doctor said in a professional tone.

'I hear you, but which house should he stay in? His was burnt down yesterday, his son was killed today. I pray to God he dies soon. He doesn't care who he kills. Fuck it, this isn't war, it's the deluge. To lose fifteen of my people without any bullets being fired, eh, Doctor!' The Beast clutched his head.

'Listen, you're in no way to blame, you couldn't have done anything. It was an industrial accident. Screw it, if they come after us now, you'll be guilty. Yes, it's the deluge, my friend, the tide is rolling forward, we may all drown and never come up again. Think about it a little. We've got some good guys, they'll come out alive if we go with the army. We're not going to the ends of the earth, it's only three kilometres.' Doctor's voice was calming down.

The Beast sat down. 'Motherfuckers, I'd go three hundred kilometres if I knew they wouldn't screw us. Why should we get killed for the fuckers? I've been watching them, they're all rotten, where can they lead us if they don't know where they've come from?' The Beast was talking more to himself now, just to hear his own voice in the sombre silence of the sunny afternoon.

'I don't know, my friend,' replied Doctor. Then he leaned towards Luka and Bižo and looked at them. 'What do you say, guys? Are we going with them?'

'We are going to three hells,' Bižo replied instantly, putting up three fingers.

'Eh, are we going, or do we stay here until we rot? Do you prefer to burn or to rot?' shouted Doctor, kicking away the lizards of doubt. He picked up a bottle and took a swig.

Bižo was sitting in the armchair with his head in his hands. Turning his back to everyone, Doctor rummaged for the remote controls and switched off all the televisions. 'Right, it's closing time, guys. Pack your bags, we're off tomorrow!'

Then he went into the house, from which his husky snores could soon be heard.

Luka's chair tipped over and he was sprawling on the ground, paralysed by sun and alcohol. He lay there like that until Bosa came to call them into the kitchen for lunch. 'Hey, get up, the food's ready,' she said looking at him, suspecting he might be wounded or something. 'Are you okay?'

'I feel like hell,' he said, trying his best to stand up. Yeah, he was making it, only he kept tipping to the right, as if he had had a stroke.

Bižo was in a deep drunken sleep in the afternoon sun. There was no chance that he would wake up in a good mood. Lunch passed in a tense atmosphere. Luka didn't find it easy eating Bosa's soup, which seemed to be full of unrecognizable ingredients.

'Fuck, what's this?' Bižo asked, pulling out a long wavy hair, clearly Bosa's.

'Hair, Bogdan,' said the cook.

'Fuck our mother, Bosa, you could have put another plate out for your hairs, you'll be bald in a month!' Dule fussed, pulling another hair from his dish.

'I don't care about the hair, I'm not eating that. What the fuck *am* I eating?' Bižo teased her.

'It's good, considering it was for us,' Luka said, trying to calm things down.

'Maybe I have cancer,' said Bosa enigmatically.

'Yes, on your brain by all appearances,' Bižo said.

'What a shit you are. The world has never seen such a shit!' she said, storming out into the yard.

Bižo looked at Luka, and at Dule a bit longer, then he stood up, letting his spoon drop into his soup. 'Good, I'll see what's wrong with her. She didn't used to be like this, did she, Dule?'

'I think it's your doing too, brother-in-law,' replied Dule significantly.

At this Bižo went wild. 'Hey, you did your bit, if you think

I'm guilty I also have at least a thousand reasons to go mad, motherfucker, but I'm still standing!' he screamed, and went outside.

Dule and Luka sat quietly downing Bosa's slops, while the two in the yard argued. It was very loud.

'This isn't going to be fun, there's nothing for you there.'

'Really? What shall I do with the kid? Have you thought about that?'

'What do you want me to do? Are you mad? We have to go on, you know that.' Bižo was losing his temper.

'It's not that — we know each other. I'm in my fourth month and you want me to disappear!'

'I told you, fine, have it, but don't expect me to stick around till then. Go to Dejan's parents and have it there. Fuck it, make peace with them, then you won't lose your crown!'

'Who's Dejan?' Luka asked Dule.

'Her husband, he got killed at the beginning of the war and her in-laws threw her out, the cunts!'

'Why doesn't she have an abortion?'

'She won't. She promised him she'd have it even if he got killed,' replied Dule.

Outside, Bosa was roaring: 'I've told you a thousand times, I'll have it and give it to its grandparents, then we can ...' Her voice trailed off, but Luka knew what she was going to say.

'WHAT?' he heard Bižo scream. 'ARE YOU MAD?'

'What now? How come? You're drunk! I've lived with you for two months, what did you expect?'

'And what will you do if I get killed? Give birth to something for my parents?'

'Don't worry. Your kind don't get killed.'

'So what is my kind?'

'You know yourself. You'd better say if you're going to marry me.'

There was no word from Bižo, and Luka concluded that he was defending himself with silence.

'Fuck your mother!' Bosa was already at the door. Then she rushed through three rooms, slamming the doors behind her and making enough noise to wake the dead.

Doctor snored on quietly. The two at the table finished their soup and wiped their bowls with pieces of bread. Bižo came in like a moonwalker and sat down at his bowl. He didn't notice that his spoon was lying in his soup, and he took Dule's before he realized he had two. Suffering seemed to have impaired his senses, and he laughed a little. Dule and Luka didn't laugh. They chewed their crusts and took no notice of him.

Bižo took another sip of cold soup. 'Why don't you two fuck off?' he said.

So they dragged themselves out to the yard, where Bosa was already throwing most of Bižo's stuff from their room. She threw it out of the window crying, then she closed the window and drew the curtain.

Luka switched on the television and remembered similar moments from his life. All those arguments, so unhappily, genetically programmed, without anyone being at fault. On television they were saying the Belgrade Red Star Football Club had a good chance of becoming world champions, and what a big encouragement this would be for people. He switched to Croatian TV. Someone was really doing a good job of it there — bullshitting round the clock. The remote control fell from his hand.

Everything had gone, even the rage, as if someone had broken into his soul and ransacked it. Once there had been a boring little town and many people like that in it, and he had to go and squeeze himself into this brick yard with the grass and weeds. He was in the herd again, with all the rejected, desperate people, full of hidden hopes and open wounds, bored to death until this new game of shooting and killing started. He saw fanatics with revenge as their only ideal, materialists whose only goal was to loot, and above it all life, senseless and unpredictable, like a drunken bully turning on people randomly and without explanation.

Bižo emerged, wiped out by his argument with Bosa, and sat down next to Luka in the armchair. Further off on the sofa, Dule was playing with his pump-action shotgun. 'Hey, Bižo, what would our mothers say if they could see us now?' he asked his old friend, who groaned in response.

The days were terribly long for the survivors.

24

AS BLUE AS A HINDU DEITY

The promised positions were three kilometres west. Squeezed into the ruins of a progressive rural household, Luka had the chance every day to see how things were getting better. Half a kilometre behind them yawned the big tubes of the rocket-artillery, from which mortar bombs were fired a few times a day. There was new ammunition coming, and new lists of targets, and after every night more soldiers would disappear from the artillery crew, either Croats or Albanians, who could tell? It had already become something of a routine; next morning the Beast would just call someone else from the artillery crew to pick up the uniforms, which were usually found by the sentry in the unpicked corn.

Old Krsto would see off the disappointed artillery man on duty saying, 'What a shame, the irony of it, you're missing half your artillery but the main thing is all your uniforms are numbers complete.'

But the man on duty didn't give a damn for numbers or rank.

The regular soldiers with whom Luka's group shared their position never stopped complaining; they should have left the army in September and all their leave had been cancelled, even for a weekend. But at least the post was coming from home, and they knew their families were safe.

The soldiers didn't get on very well with the volunteers, and the volunteers didn't get on with each other. The atmosphere was absolutely rotten. The bad news kept coming, and even worse rumours. They were forever waiting for some big order from Belgrade, some big cleansing, but it seemed there was no washing powder left there.

One night at three a.m., shooting was heard from the fields. Everyone jumped to their weapons. If there hadn't been categorical orders not to shoot, everything would have been different. As it was, they took cover outside and shot into the darkness without restraint. This went on until the ammunition from their fighting-kits was spent.

It turned out that the shooting earlier had been Dule, who appeared in the light of their torches leading a man he had caught on sentry duty. He was a little puckered man, and on his back he was carrying a big-catch guard, who must have weighed a hundred kilograms and was stitched around his waist with gunshots. 'They were hanging around the cornfield,' explained Dule, looking at his half-asleep team.

'You shot this one straightaway, right?' Doctor pointed at the fatty on the skinny one's back.

'Not me, one of you when you were shooting. The good thing is that fatty was first, so his lard sucked all the bullets in.'

There was a short silence. They heard the blood dripping down the fat man's boots.

'Put him down, what are you waiting for, monkey?' said Dule kindly to the little man, who threw his load on the ground with relief. The thunder produced by the fall seemed to wake the team from their sleep. The fat guy was dead, or something like it. There was still something dripping from him. His uniform was pierced with bullets, and therefore unusable. Some of the men kicked him to make sure he was dead, and in the process they didn't notice how they moved to the living one. But they threw him in the mouse-wheel and beat him wide and long, until Dule came to his senses and stopped things with a short burst from his automatic. His man was already half-blue.

'Fuck off, he's mine, there's nothing for you, I'll kill him if I feel like it. No "cons" I hope?'

It turned out they were all for it, but they were still watching the prisoner with evil looks as he pissed and shat himself, green with anguish and disfigured by fear. The frustrated crowd then gave him rough descriptions of what would come next, and he rolled his eyes, melting away like a snowman in spring. The threats hung in the air as Dule, with the help of Bižo and Luka, took his catch to the orchard, handcuffed him to a pear tree, and went back to finish his sentry shift.

Bižo and Luka sat on a bench, keeping the prisoner company.

'Mind you, this one's as ugly as a dog. Dule'll kill him as soon as he gets a better look at him,' Bižo said. 'Why did you shit yourself, scum? So many younger and more handsome guys than yourself were killed.'

All the talk was in vain. The man lay sunk in lethargy against the tree, like a martyr on the chessboard calendar. He seemed to have fallen asleep with his eyes wide open. His upper body was covered in the blood of the man he had carried, and below he was wet where he had pissed himself.

His hair was thinning and dishevelled, matted in some places with blood, and his face was badly swollen. He was wearing camouflage uniform trousers and an old zipped-up tracksuit top. On his feet he wore green rubber boots. If he had any insignia he was wise enough to have got rid of them on the way. From his clothes he looked like a peasant who had come out of the fields to do his autumn work. But there was something bitter and cheated on his face, such as Luka remembered on the faces of redundant workers, and he had seen plenty of those in his neighbourhood. All in all, the man didn't look his best, and Bižo began to feel sorry for him. 'Eh, Ustashe, have a smoke,' he said, lighting one of his ultra-stinky cigarettes and putting it in the man's mouth.

The man roused himself and nodded.

'Fuck my mother, when I look at you like this...' Bižo stopped and went off into his thoughts. 'What the fuck are you to me?'

The Ustashe man was squatting against the tree as if having a shit. He exhaled anxiously, as Bižo loudly pursued his thoughts: 'Look at him, what a cockroach, what a turd, he'd slaughter us for a case of beer!'

'Not bloody likely any more,' Luka said. He stood up to pick a pear from the branch, but the fruit had already died.

'It's not that, the Beast is right, I've nothing personal against this poor devil. Hear that, scumbag?' Bižo addressed the man. 'What was I guilty of? Fuck it, they blew up my house on the Feast of Our Lady – did I tell you, Luka? Beni and I were on our way back from the Tufna at five in the morning with some girls we'd picked up. We were taking them to my place for a bang. But when we get to my place to screw them, it's not there. Blown up. Beni was pissed as a newt and kept singing, "Left and right, my place is gone!" and asking me, "Where's your place, man?" It was smashed to the basement. Luckily my folks weren't in, they were staying at our weekend cottage. Eh, what can I say? My place was gone, and our neighbour's was untouched. He had our key, he let them in. Boras, what a shit that man is. In the morning, Beni and I are loading what was left of my stuff on a trailer and Boras and his wife are at the window. He says, "Oh dear, Bogdan, were you hit by those Chetniks from Tenja?" And he laughs. "The fools," he says. "They must have got it wrong."'

Bižo turned to Dule's catch. 'You're like that. You say, "I don't give a shit. Kaput tomorrow."' He shrugged. 'See, Uncle Ustashe, we don't hate you the way you hate us. We're the guys you chased out of the better-off houses, that's all. I'm not saying we're better, we're just different. I can't hate you just because you hate me, what do you say? Bad business partner, ha? No, I was lucky. What's a house? It comes and goes, comes again. But if I'd had done to me what they did to Dule you wouldn't be smoking here, hell no. He'll tell you about it tomorrow in more detail.'

Bižo finished his favourite chapter of the sad story of his fucked-up life, and looked up at the sky. It was clear and empty. The wind had cleansed all the clouds. 'Go, Luka, you have a sleep, I'll smoke another one with my uncle. I never had an uncle. We just found each other.'

Luka didn't feel like going into the damp and farted house with his twenty unwashed drunken colleagues, and he couldn't leave Bižo alone with the prisoner. Since he had broken up with Bosa, his moods had been swinging with the wind; he could have chopped the guy into pieces or let him go, either of which would cause additional problems with Dule.

Next morning found Luka wrapped in a sleeping bag on the narrow bench. Bižo was sleeping on the chair next to the prisoner, who was still handcuffed to the tree, both of them covered with a film of morning frost.

When day broke, Dule returned from his shift carrying the officer's bag he had found in the field, containing maps of all the sectors. He handed Luka a topographic map with fairly precise markings of their positions, trenches and fortifications, plus the positions of their rocket-artillery, some command posts they themselves didn't know about, and a couple more details that were of interest only to spies.

Seen in this light, Dule's man seemed more enigmatic, and they looked at him with new respect; he had borne up relatively heroically under his beatings, and he had survived Bižo's sob stories all night. Luka could have sworn he was a retard, but it turned out he was a spy.

Dule wasn't put out by the discovery. He gave the guy such a spinning kick that he went round the circle of the tree and woke up. Then Dule untied him and drove him to the yard.

'C'mon, pull yourself together or I'll pull you apart,' he said drily, while Bižo was still rubbing his bloodshot eyes.

Outside the house they were handing out tea and opening tins. Doctor came and called Dule and Luka to go in, while Bižo stood outside, zealously guarding the prisoner; he kept angling for Bosa, but she paid him little attention these days.

'Listen,' Doctor cleared his throat. 'I don't know what it is you've found, but I wouldn't send him to the Command yet.

Have a poke at him first, just try to avoid the rough stuff.'
He blinked at Dule.

'Yeah,' Dule said, going out. 'They won't notice anything.'

Doctor held Luka back. 'Try to make sure the kid doesn't
go too far.'

Luka shrugged.

Dule and Bižo were already driving the prisoner out of the
courtyard. The air shook around the little canister Bižo was
carrying with him, and the wind carried back the smell of
petrol. The wind was carrying everything – dust, stray leaves
and the clouds over the October sky. The rain had soaked
and softened the entire countryside, making everything slimy,
oozing and cold. Luka knew only two seasons, hot and cold,
and would have exchanged a hundred winters for one summer.
He could stand the cold except in the form of ice cream.

They left the village. Dule pushed the slave all the way to a
sign in the road that read: 'Borovo Welcomes You and Wishes
You a Safe Journey'. On the back, someone had cynically
added, 'Now you've had it!' The sign was pierced with bullets,
like all the other street signs and billboards for fifty kilometres
around. With a couple of bursts from his shotgun, Dule
ripped it from its frame. Then he took out a couple of pairs
of handcuffs, crucified the guy to the frame and wordlessly
took off all his clothes. Leaving him there, he joined his
friends in the leeward side of a tall poplar. They stood there
for about a quarter of an hour, while the north wind howled.

'Okay, let's move or we'll freeze,' Dule said, walking back
to the candidate, who was already very cold. Luka followed to
prevent Dule overdoing it. Bižo stopped by the side of the
road to finish his cigarette.

'It ain't half hot!' Dule gawped comically at the guy, who was shivering savagely and looking at them with icy horror in his eyes.

When Dule rubbed his back with a cloth soaked in petrol, he jolted as if hit by electricity. Dule worked slowly and systematically. He anointed him all over with petrol, then stood back to let it evaporate. The man was violently throwing himself around, the air around him seemed to shiver, his chattering teeth stopped him from cursing. After the second anointing, he claimed he didn't know anything, swearing this way and that, and after the third, he begged Dule to stop and said he would tell him everything. But Dule wasn't so curious about what he had to say, as about the blue colour that was appearing around the man's mouth and spreading over his skin. His screams had a worrying tone now. After the fifth unction he was already as blue as a Hindu deity, and Dule went up to him with a tape recorder and said, 'Sing.'

The song of songs followed: names, surnames, dates, amounts, passwords and so on, and after it was over Dule put the tape back in his pocket and anointed the singer once more for luck.

When they took him off his frame the man threw himself in the mud to regulate his body temperature; he was shuddering like a truck in neutral. In the yard, they hosed him down with water and the incident became a sensation. They spent the time until lunch inventing far-fetched rumours about the prisoner's role, and predicted for Dule at the very least a war hero's medal.

During lunch Bosa started playing one of her little games with Bižo, punishing him for the day he had rejected her in such an unmanly way. Bižo felt guilty and tried to make peace, but she was untouchable, and this didn't pass unnoticed by the rest of the group. As an urbane and honourable guy, Bižo suffered from the taunts Bosa was getting from some of their colleagues. It happened most often when Dule was there, and at mealtimes, and so regularly that it spoilt the appetite. The one who usually started it was Lopez, who according to the story had been beaten up by Bižo – but just once.

25

THREE BASIC KILLING TIPS

After the fall of Milosav, Lopez had taken over his clan and turned himself into the hero of the uprising. He had a good vocabulary and an excellent memory for some action that no one else could remember, and his name reached some of the newspapers. He had become involved in the export of electronic goods and had made useful contacts, and there were rumours that he would soon go into politics.

For lunch they had beans brought in from the rocket-artillery, and they ate them lukewarm, like salad, along with the looted tins. The tins had some rust on them, but there were no complaints about the contents. Dule, Bižo and Luka were sitting at the table in the yard. Next to them sat Lopez, Paka and Banija.

Bosa kept coming up, ostensibly to offer her brother more beans, and asking him if they were any good, as if they weren't the same beans every time, as if she didn't eat them herself.

Bižo, carried away, replied, 'They're the best, sweetheart!'

The romantic, unfucked longing in his voice made Luka want to throw up.

Then drunken Lopez got involved. 'They're not bad, Bosa, I just need something warm and wet on mine, have you something by any chance?'

'I didn't ask you,' Bosa said curtly.

'Hey, is your migraine still bothering you, would you like Señor Lopez to sort it out for you?' He grabbed her.

Bosa hissed, 'Fuck off, dog, you're getting on my nerves!'

She walked off in a rage, while Bižo and Luka exchanged looks.

'Warn your sister not to keep hold of that little cunt of hers, or it might grow together, and then...'

Lopez stopped suddenly, because Bižo hit him on the head with a recoilless rifle he found under the table.

Luka grabbed an M-70 leaning against the wall. Dule was already holding a knife at Banija's throat.

The beans spilled over the table and on to the floor. Paka managed to save his, and appealed to the conscience of both sides in the argument: 'Leave it out, guys, at least while we're eating, aren't we Christians?'

As he spoke, Bižo kept knocking the seven-kilogram steel barrel against Lopez's head.

As the game went on, people started gathering from all over the yard. Luka put a bullet in his barrel and told the crowd to fuck off. Bižo threw aside the recoilless rifle, leaving in the mud a corpse with a mass of disfigured flesh for a head.

'That one's fucking dead,' concluded Dule, removing the knife from Banija's throat, whereupon its owner walked away quickly to find Daddy Beast.

'Tell me about it,' gasped Bižo, barely able to speak.

Bosa pushed through the crowd to him, and hung on his neck.

'What did you do, you fool? You must run away from here, they'll kill you, run!'

Bižo took her hands, still breathless. 'It'll be all right, pick up your stuff as quick as you can. Dule, bring the car . . . !'

As inspired instructions poured out, Luka bent over the seemingly dead Lopez and checked his pulse. He still showed a few signs of life, but they weren't exaggerated.

'Leave that shit to stink, we're out of here!' Dule shouted, driving up quickly in his Citroën, and pushing his sister and brother-in-law inside.

'Where are we going?' Luka asked.

The three looked confused. That was the question.

'Get in, we'll decide later!' Bosa shouted.

Luka calmed her down: 'Don't panic, Bosa, he didn't take out the President of the Republic, only Lopez.'

Dule turned to Bižo on the back seat. 'So where to?'

The question was a big one, and Bižo made a big decision: 'Okay, to hell with it, get out.' He climbed from the car, leaving the door wide open.

Doctor appeared over the yard with a sub-machine gun on his shoulder. He looked down at the corpse, and addressed Dule. 'Shit again, eh, Dule?'

'It wasn't me this time either, my brother-in-law beat me to it!'

'Doesn't matter.' Doctor waved to Bižo. 'There won't be many tears for him.' Doctor didn't like the deceased, who had given him a new war nickname: the Cuntologist. 'Just take him away from there.' He pointed at the corpse, which was taking up a great deal of space in the yard. 'Throw him in the old well in the garden, and let that be an end of it.'

Dule brought a sheet of tarpaulin from the shed and they wrapped Lopez's body and his head, so they wouldn't spill his brains around as they carried him to the well. The well was in fact a dried-up hole covered in planks, so they buried him in accordance with navy ritual, and put the planks back.

When they came back to the yard, there was nobody there. The unit on duty had gone to their positions, and the morning shift had come back to rest. The only noise came from HQ, where the Beast had just come in and was arguing with Doctor and Bižo about the latest incident. His howls could be heard echoing through the closed door: 'Don't, Doctor, we're not little kids, killing each other over pussies! If we were shooting for that we'd all have been killed long ago!'

'I know, my friend, but it wasn't like that, it happened in a moment...' Doctor spread his hands. 'You know yourself what he was like.'

'I know.' The Beast calmed down, and looked with clenched teeth at the table in front of him. 'I've known him longer than anyone else. He was a thief and a fool, he'd kill you just like that – as you killed him – but he was a good fighter and he had friends, and if you don't get out of here you're in trouble. If you go, his people will go, that'll leave me with twenty people. Fuck it, I needed this. We had something here, it was a good unit, and you've fucked it up for me. I don't know where you'll go, but there's nothing for you here.'

'We're not orphans,' Bižo said when Luka and Dule came in.

The Beast looked at them pityingly. 'Woe is your mother, that's all I can say. Woe is your mother, and safe journey.'

'Where are we going?' piped up Dule, looking at the mud on his boots and the mud on the boots of all present, then straight into the Beast's pupils. 'Where to, Daddy?'

'It's best not to tell anyone, don't let it out. I'll stamp your army-books. You, kid, will get a certificate so you can report wherever you like.'

'Is that all?' Bižo said a little impatiently.

'No, it is not all. I can give you some advice for the future. Next time you're going to kill one of ours, fucking kid, fuck you, remember three things well. In the night, from the back, and without witnesses — if you'd done that my unit wouldn't have fallen apart because of three motherfuckers. You're going with them, aren't you?' He addressed Doctor.

Doctor stroked some invisible hair on his head. 'You know me, an eternal adolescent, always on the move.'

'Fuck me, you're crazy. If you weren't, you wouldn't be here,' said the Beast, wistfully pouring himself a full glass.

'C'mon, Chief, don't drink now, put those stamps in, we should go. Krsto's coming with us, he's bored of rockets,' Doctor said, tugging at an imaginary beard.

The Beast shrugged, drank up his glass and pulled out a wrecked typewriter.

Outside, Bosa was throwing clothes in a trunk, and Old Krsto was suspiciously measuring the space in the Citroën.

'You'll go with me, Krsto!' shouted Doctor when the others came out.

The old man put his machine-gun and ammunition in the boot, and Bižo and Dule brought over their weapons. The Beast appeared at the door of HQ, waving the army-books and Dule's certificate. 'Here they are, take care of yourselves!'

'No worries,' replied Doctor. 'Take care of yourselves and your bare-handed people.'

In the car, Dule switched on Croatian radio, gritted his

teeth, raced up through the gears of his Citroën and drove faster and faster into the cold grey afternoon. Doctor and Krsto followed fifty metres behind in a grey Peugeot that had once been white, and behind them howled the rocket-artillery, which had just started up. Sitting behind Dule on the back seat, Bižo and Bosa had made friends again, which made Luka think of Maria, but that didn't make it any better for him. There was no help, no hope, and the future was just a bullet in his barrel.

26

CAVIAR TO THE GENERAL

The same feeling came back to Luka later when he stood listening to the live speech of some high-ranking major general about what was happening and what was going to happen.

Herded together on the field was a mass of different muddy uniforms: regular soldiers, reserve soldiers, Territorial Defence and volunteers. The Territorial Defence and the volunteers were in rebellion against incapable commanders and suspected traitors. The reservists were going mad because they had been called up for military exercises and then pushed into the war; instead of fifteen days they had done forty-five, and they had had enough. The regular soldiers were angry because their leave had been cancelled and, in short, all of them wanted to go home.

This was fine by Luka, but his home was in the opposite direction. He was standing with Bižo, Dule and Doctor in the crowd. Krsto and Bosa were looking after the cars, and the quiet autumn drizzle was turning the sacred soil into this cursed mud. The more decisive members of the crowd were already moving off when three officer-escort vehicles appeared, two Campanolas and five Pinzgauer jeeps.

From the Pinzgauers a team of anti-terrorist parachute-commandos jumped out in YNA camouflage uniforms, with olive-green berets on their closely trimmed heads. They carried K & H guns in their hands, and love for the motherland in their hearts, just like in the song. These were experts, real professionals who knew what they were fighting for, took a shower at least every other day and wore clean clothes. Facing them was a mass of men. None of them, apart from a few young soldiers without beards, had been shaven according to regulations; nothing was being done by the regulations within a circle of fifty kilometres, because no regulations could last four months of these bloody fuck ups.

The commandos lined up by their vehicles, and asked the crowd to pull back another three metres so the general could make his official speech. Playing the same psychological trick as the cops in the football stadium during the wilder matches, and with a minimum of discipline, step by step, the commandos got their three metres. Everything was ready for the legendary speech.

The general appeared from his Campanola jeep looking like a large intestine that had not been emptied for a month. Olive-green in the face, he scrabbled for a piece of paper in the pocket of his combat uniform, looked for his glasses, then turned the paper over to find the beginning. The rain was falling harder now. A fat reserve captain took out a nylon sheet from his ABC decontamination kit, and some people stretched it over their heads like spectators at a village match, caught suddenly in a summer storm.

'Fucking idyllic.' Beside Dule stood a bearded Chetnik volunteer wearing a Serbian tricolour on his black beret. 'Take a good swig of that, brother!' he said, handing Dule a flat bottle with a pale drink inside.

Dule took a good swig, contrary to habit.

The general coughed behind his firm hand, and started his speech:

'Comrades, officers, soldiers, volunteers and territorials – good to see you!!!'

'I hope your eyes fall out!' shouted a half-drunk voice from the back of the crowd, starting up laughter in all the lines and melting the last grain of piety.

The speaker was an old fighter, and paying little attention to this remark he continued with his forceful oration. The less they listened, the more he was convinced he was right. The voice from the speakers positioned on the roof of the Campanola threw up sausage-like phrases gathered from many annual ceremonies, rites, openings and parades. It was an unbelievably boring speech, and those listening were as interested in it as in last year's fart. The story started a long time ago in the days of the glorious outlaw ancestors, and continued with the achievements of the National Liberation Fight in the last World War. The debt to the motherland was mentioned, which had to be repaid, and if it was not, the motherland would take it for herself. The speech was also about naive, seduced brothers, and even worse things.

Luka took the plum brandy from Dule's hands. The volunteer said, 'Listen to that guy shitting up there. Yesterday we got three of ours slaughtered. They had their ears cut off.'

'Did you pay them back?' Dule asked, and the volunteer, a man in his late thirties, put his finger in his mouth and looked enigmatically up at the sky. The bottle passed on, but others kept coming from all sides.

Probably under the influence of the volunteer's story, Dule

turned Luka's attention to the general's ears, which were enormous, like bat's wings. 'Look at his ears, he'll live to be a hundred!' he said, not without envy. His and Luka's ears were small, normal; what if the seduced brothers cut them off and hung them on their car mirrors for souvenirs?

The general strayed from his text for a second, because some drunken boys had come out of their lines and were trying to piss over the three-metre boundary of dreams that separated them from the commandos' stony faces.

A buffalo-like colonel from the convoy bawled at the pissers and took out his gun. In reply, the sound of gunlocks clicking spread through the crowd like a disease.

Suddenly everyone was whistling, and for a moment it was like the awakening of spring, or a revolution. Then the football supporters' voices rang out, cursing the Yugoslav Army, the faggots, and the colonel for having no balls. A hundred unshaven mouths were hurling curses. The crowd smoked with anger, like an enraged animal. The colonel shouted at the commandos to keep the crowd back; they asked for another three metres, and the moment was full of tension.

But they got their three metres, then thirty, and soon three hundred, as crowds of men moved off slowly to the muddy crossroads. For them the war was over, they were going home.

The colonel cursed into his beard and joined the general in the Campanola. The commandos crammed into their Pinzgauers and drove off, either to fight the war or photograph some new propaganda shots, which would probably never be seen.

Behind them in the mud the crowd had left empty bottles

and cans, boxes of cigarettes, epaulettes and pieces of equipment.

'What a shame it is, what an irony,' Old Krsto said, looking back at the field, where the rain had made an ocean, and archipelagos of molehills. The rain had wet Krsto's grey hair, drops fell from his nose and moustache, and he would have stood there for a hundred years if Doctor hadn't pulled him into the car.

Further down the road, they found a few nice houses. They picked one with intact windows, missing only its front door. The reservists tramped mud through the rooms, dumping straw and clothes all around. Standing in the middle of the largest room like a good fairy was a rusted stove, its pipe pushing up through the ceiling into the dark sky.

They unloaded their baggage and weapons from the car and hung their wet clothes on a couple of rickety chairs, and Luka tried to light a fire with rotten straw and pieces of beech parquet that someone had piled up neatly round the stove. He was busy with this when Dule came up holding some books, and handed him one with a warped green cover: Ernest Hemingway, *Across the River and into the Trees*. 'What's this book?' Dule asked.

'American retired colonel screws young Italian countess in Venice,' Luka said.

'Does anyone die in the end?' Dule was interested.

'He does, yes.' Luka frowned. 'Did you think you might read it?'

'No, I was thinking about Bosa, she reads those love stories.' Dule was embarrassed.

'Leave Bosa out of it, give me that for the fire.'

Luka wasn't usually so hot on Hemingway, but now he had no option. He tore a couple of pages from the middle and put them in the stove, and when the fire was burning he threw the whole book inside. The old man and a sea of quixotic crap. The man loved Corrida and Venice, what could you do with him in this Balkan pig slaughterhouse, fuck it.

The stove grew warm and cast classical shadows on the heads, which were eating pineapple and crab from tins. The atmosphere was slowly melting. Old Krsto was talking with Doctor about the past, and his eternal predicament about whether socialism had screwed up people, or people had screwed up socialism. Krsto had spent all his working life in his profession, and he was terrifically proud of that. As administrator of the selection of pigs on the VUPIK pig-plant, he had been one of the best workers, until he got into a dispute with the boss of bosses. He started up his own farm then, and became one of the biggest animal-breeders in the municipality.

Krsto held with none of the complexes of the modern age, and talked with nostalgia about the old days. As he spoke he farted and handed round photographs from his partisan days. The old man was full of wind and statistics, and gave both out copiously. His municipality had the highest per capita income in Yugoslavia, out of sixty thousand people over forty thousand were employed, and at least half of them had land, the most fertile land in the country. While they cared for brotherhood and unity, they boasted of having twenty-four different nationalities living in the town.

Old Krsto spoke in a voice full of sincere sadness, and as his emotions overcame him he farted even louder, and his speech returned to the routine reality of blood, mud and tins.

'Fuck these tins,' he said, throwing away some meat slices and salmon. 'When I remember a pig-slaughter at my place before the war — I could feed a hundred people just by telling them about it.'

Bižo, Dule, his sister and Luka smiled bitterly at him. The old man looked at them sadly. 'Damn, whatever you kids are guilty of, you'll never have what we had before. I see these new ones, and it's like socialism's screwed us up and didn't let us breathe; then I look at this, and I don't know who screwed who.'

He stopped and thought for a while. A terrible wind blew outside, tugging the sheets of tarpaulin they had knocked up for a door. In the distance, silenced rifle shots could be heard, and the roar of cannons. In the room the atmosphere was warm and festive, as though they were expecting guests.

'How many children can a woman give birth to in seven years, Doctor?' Krsto asked.

Doctor was surprised by the question and counted for a while, then said uncertainly, 'In theory she could have eight to nine, if there were twins, but I haven't seen it. Perhaps down in Kosovo, dammit. Why do you need to know?'

'Let me tell you. On my farm, after I left the plant, I had one record-winning sow, who in seven years produced exactly two hundred piglets. That was a God-given animal; not a piglet stillborn, not one deformed. The newspapers wrote about her. She fed every one of those piglets herself and looked after them like no other sow, she never even squeezed

one by accident, let alone suffocated them like some do. So
see now, she had piglets this year in April. There were sixteen
of them. She had a good birth, she was suckling them as
always. The piglets were like an attraction. I invited my people
over from the plant for a christening, and they couldn't believe
they were all hers.

'Then in May this crap started, the cops were whacked in
the village of Borovo, and my pig got nervous and started
biting her young. She bit their ears and tails, and one morning
I found them in pieces, she'd torn them apart. Just one piglet
made it, she survived by hiding under the pieces. She was
quiet, as good as bread. The same thing happened to me in
1941. A sow slaughtered her piglets, and later people slaughtered each other. I didn't tell anyone, so as not to have any
trouble, I just gave her away when they were collecting
donations for the army. Not to be ashamed, you know.'

Krsto was justifying himself. 'The same devil enters people
too, who knows where from? But I know it's not from a bad
life. We've lived the last years as we never lived before; it's
more the other way round. I've watched all those congresses
in the last three years, and I felt sorry there was no one over
those fools, no God to put a fucking end to all the palaver.'

Krsto took his flat bottle of plum brandy from Doctor and
drank. 'Every time I mention God I think of my mother. She
kept telling me after the war, "All right, my son, even if
there's no God, at least there's something." And I can't get it
out of my head that there was something in hers, something
like nothing, fuck it. See, she died the day before Tito, and
the whole village cried for Tito and I was crying for my
mother.'

'What happened happened,' Doctor said to the old partisan, trying to save his bottle from Krsto's safe embrace. But it was too late.

'Ha, ha, ha, it's empty.' The old man grimaced.

Doctor pulled another from his shoulder pocket. 'Can't go without disinfectant, eh?'

After the meal, Luka unrolled his sleeping bag and took off his mud-encrusted boots. Dule, Bižo and Bosa were preparing for sleep too. Old Krsto watched them quietly with sadness and a little envy. Insomnia was his second mother.

'Where does it come from, Doctor? I can't sleep, I just look up at the ceiling and think,' complained the old man.

'You've got nothing to think about, this is your life now. To live, you have to sleep.'

'All right, this is my life, I've had a hundred times worse in my life, it's not hard for me. See those kids, fuck it. How much money was spent on their vaccinations, their swimming pools and sports halls, and see what they're doing to them. Before this war started I sold all my pigs to Serbia, I gave my son money to take his wife and children there and buy a house ... "Rade, son, I fought for four years and that was my war, I don't want you to finish it. You don't need a father now, but your children need one, don't get involved in my things." What have we done to our children, Doctor? I can't sleep because of them, it seems if I fall asleep there'll be no one to think about them any more. When I was young I thought the world could be good, and people were shit because they were just missing some little thing, like a fuse, so when I see a bastard I think, look at him, how little he needs to be a man. But medicine has no cure for that, eh, Doctor?'

'Yes, we should air this room a bit so we don't die of carbon monoxide poisoning,' Doctor said, moving to the window.

27

WELCOME TO PIG CITY

In the morning they all had heavy heads and almost didn't hear the clank of the armoured column, lighting the foggy autumn sunrise with its headlamps. Big-arsed self-propelled artillery and tanks passed the houses and stopped half a kilometre down the road. It seemed they wouldn't wait much longer, so Doctor and Krsto hurried out to catch up with them while the others packed their things into the cars.

The first face they saw belonged to their old friend Captain Radulović, the Montenegrin with three stars on his shoulders and rocks in his head. When he saw the old man he blossomed.

'Is that you, Krsto, my old friend?' he said, and the two red stars went into an embrace.

'Rumour has it that you're in shit, so we've come to help you,' Krsto responded cordially.

Radulović accepted them with open arms, and took them down to his battalion commander, who was something of a living legend.

From the beginning of the war, the battalion commander, Four Stars Captain Thunder-Uncle, had cruised in his tank around the whole of Yugoslavia, visiting the battlefields in Slovenia, Banija, Kordun and Western Slavonia, and ending up at his wish in Vukovar, to see what the hold-up was there. Uncle was straight, firm and dumb as a dick, exactly as a good soldier should be. Here, where the brain of any normal civilian arsehole would stop functioning, he was inspired to create bullshit that would become of lasting historical significance. Uncle didn't give loud speeches, but they were full of wise advice. He looked through the periscope for a while, bracing himself before his crew.

'Radulović, don't get on my dick with these prisoners, give them to the Chetniks and get them fucking out of here.'

'No, no, Uncle, these are volunteers, they're ours.'

'Look at them. Ours? All dressed up like Ustashe, as beautiful as Christ's five wounds. Welcome on board Uncle's train. What can I say, you don't look like cunts, but these ones here don't choose who they fuck. You've nothing to be afraid of, just don't fall into their hands alive. Don't surrender either. When you're outside the town take care not to separate too much and don't keep too close together. Everything may be laid with mines, you must watch out for that, especially when you're looting. And if anyone gets hurt stealing I fuck their mothers straightaway.'

'Uncle, this man is a doctor, he's been fighting from the first day, what are you saying?'

'A doctor and fighting? You're crazy then, brother,' Uncle said to Doctor with a smile.

'He's not crazy, he lost everything in Požega,' Radulović explained, and Doctor and Krsto exchanged looks.

'Just so we understand each other,' Uncle said. 'I don't give a fuck if you're thieves or junkies, drunk or crazy, because they're drunk and crazy out there, and who gives a fuck about them? They can't win but they won't surrender, that's their problem; our problem is to kill them as fast as possible. I don't like it when my soldiers get killed, and if we need to we'll destroy all of this, crush it like a drunk on shit. Not a brick will be left standing, we won't spare a mortar, but I don't want to lose one man. If my command was the highest this war would have been over long ago, but the Command's jerking on dry, they want to fuck and stay virgins. That's why they'll get this town – without streets, the streets without houses, the houses without walls, and the walls without bricks, but they'll get this town. Give people their body-armour to make sure it fits.'

They brought out long bulletproof vests weighing ten kilos, which covered them to their hips.

'What's up, kid?' Uncle addressed Dule. 'Bulletproof, but too heavy for a poof. Are you a poof, my son?'

'No, I'm not,' said Dule.

'If you're not, put that armour over your balls, you'll need them when this shit is over. You won't need balls if you're a poof, you can just get fucked in the arse and be a man of the world.' Uncle finished his speech and turned to Radulović. 'See people eat and shit. In half an hour we're going inside, and inside there's no jerking.'

Inside there was a fucked-up street. On the place where it intersected with another there was nothing, the crossroads had been wiped out. A popular café had once stood on the corner, the headquarters of the Ustashe, full of explosives. That's what the paratroopers said as they swept the area like a new broom, with Uncle's boys bringing up the rear like little shovels.

A few houses were standing, and people were sitting in the cellars. They didn't believe freedom had come, they were expecting another kind of freedom.

'Chetniks, Chetniks,' a woman wrapped in a knitted shawl repeated mechanically. Ten seconds' pause, then 'Chetniks, Chetniks,' again, and silence.

'Got it wrong, Madam,' Bižo told her. 'We are the Serbo Communist Yugo Army. If we were Chetniks, you wouldn't have time to fart.'

'Chetniks, Chetniks,' she repeated, staring into empty space.

In a corner by the door sat a wounded sniper from the 63rd Parachute Brigade. He was holding an SAR-15 gun in his arms, the kind Luka used to see on Karo's Special Forces in Osijek; he said he had captured it at Pleso airport.

The sniper had the smallest feet Luka had ever seen on a soldier, a small nose shaped like a comma, and childish blond hair. They wheeled up the food, but he couldn't eat; his broken hand was shaking too much. Two days before, his group had raided a house in which there was an Ustashe sniper. Two officers went in last and got killed first, because the firing was from behind. The Ustashe was firing randomly from a closed wardrobe with an MGV-176, and tore the three apart in their body-armour, and when the others jumped on him he activated a mine and sent another two down with them. The little sniper was the only one to survive. After that he killed for two days and nights without a break. Meanwhile they advanced five hundred metres up from the place where he left his friends in pieces. Three times they were ordered back, then sent on again. The last time he had slept was sixty hours before, and his hand was shaking so much he couldn't hit his own mouth with the spoon.

Bosa tried to feed him like a little child, but he didn't feel like swallowing. He was waiting for the 63rd Brigade to finish cleansing so he could return to base with them. He sat talking about this like a robot with a factory-fault. Luka tried to catch the eyes of this man who had been killing for forty-eight hours non-stop, at a speed of two hundred and fifty metres a day, but they were just a bit tired. He didn't know himself what he'd been expecting; clock hands instead of pupils, maybe.

The guy was blinking his swollen, red eyes. Doctor gave him an injection for the pain and bandaged his broken hand. He had been hurt when the wall he was hiding behind fell down, and he had raised his hand to protect his sniper.

Outside, a bearded procession of angels with tails was passing along the street, carrying the Chetnik pirate flag with the Jolly Roger, and firing machine-gun shots instead of singing.

'Doctor, fuck, give us a doctor!' a bewildered voice was shouting.

'I am a doctor, what is happening?' Doctor pushed his head through the hole where there used to be a window.

'Doctor!' screamed the voice from the darkly approaching column.

'Here I am, people, what do you need?' Doctor leaned out of the window.

A stocky gypsy with white teeth jumped out from the formation. 'Tell me, Doctor, how do you like this war?'

The Chetnik crew congratulated their joker with spontaneous applause, and Doctor calmed down and came back to the shelter.

The woman wrapped in the shawl went on repeating, 'Chetniks, Chetniks.' Next to her a young, frowning mother was holding her frightened daughter. There were no men in the house apart from two old guys on a dilapidated sofa. In a separate room, an old woman was falling apart from cancer.

Bosa opened a tin of pineapple slices and offered them to the girl with the frowning mother, but got no response. 'Take it when I offer it, I know you haven't seen fruit since September.'

The girl shook her head and her mother frowned even more, maybe because Croats do not have the same names for their calendar, or because of Bosa's uniform and the gun at her belt.

'Why are you handing them out? Keep them for yourself,' said Dule, leaning towards one of the old men. 'Tell me, Grandpa, were there any Serbs hiding with you?'

The old man shrugged and didn't speak.

'You know nothing, like you were born yesterday,' Dule said.

The only person in the mood to talk was the old woman in the next room, but what she said made no sense. Doctor hastily gave her an injection to reduce the pain, and fled from the unbearable stink.

From the least damaged house in the street the paratroopers

appeared, their boots bloodied to the ankles. One of the clumsiest slipped and fell in the thick mass of blood curdled like pudding on the ground. Quietly they brought out the bodies. The hands were tied in front of them, with holes from meat-hooks on their heels. One body, one and a half, two bodies, two and a half, twelve corpses and a half, and then they ran out of body bags. The disposal unit went to look for more and didn't return.

Luka and Dule were given orders to keep watch over the corpses, and see that the pigs and dogs who were gathering at the smell of rotten blood didn't tear them apart. The pigs came wriggling over the yard and lazily started sniffing around the bags. They were huge, at least two hundred kilos each. Paying no attention at all to the guards' 'Eh, go away!', they went on stretching the bags in search of meat.

Disgusted by the sight of their bloodied jowls and expressionless heads, Luka strode off to one of the tanks and returned with a pickaxe. He went for the first pig, which didn't move until he had hit it several times on its hairy back. The animal looked at him with wondering eyes, squealed indignantly and went on doing its thing. Luka went mad. He waved his pickaxe like a lunatic and managed to drive away the pigs with a series of bloody blows. The armour was heavy. He was tired of hitting, the sweat was dripping down his face. When he sat down, the pigs came back again.

Still out of breath, his face and gloves covered in blood, he unlocked the gun. But Dule took his hand. He had brought a canister of oil from the tank-driver, and now he carefully poured the contents over two of the most stubborn sows. A small slimy trace of oil travelled to Luka, and he lit the match.

A flame flew to two muddy heaps of lard that didn't move until they smelt the stink of their own burnt hair. They started rolling in the mud of the yard, then rushed out to the street with unearthly screams, spreading panic among the bearded volunteers who threw themselves into the shelters and started shooting in fear of some new enemy trick.

Old Krsto stared spellbound at the flaming pigs. He had stopped his conversation with Doctor, and hurried into the yard to see who was blaspheming his sacred animals. The old man's eye fell on the chewed pieces of people in the plastic bags, and on the two guards, pushing the rest of the pigs and the dogs into the corner of the yard as they prepared them for their baptism of fire, and he walked away without saying a word.

In the course of the afternoon the paratroopers captured the last street in the vicinity, which closed the circle around the factory building where the guards had set up their headquarters. Shooting was heard continuously on all four streets leading to the factory, and Uncle spread his crews along them, counting on a short blast from all sides to deliver him another solid surrender.

Night started at around six in the evening, when the red points of the snipers' laser optics danced their deadly round on the bullet-pocked walls of the factory building. Uncle gave orders to answer every bullet from the snipers with a hundred from the tank machine-gun, and all night jets of artillery and machine-gun fire sprayed the circular walls of the building and ran off, making little fires in the dying weeds of the yard below.

That night, radio-connection was made with the guards and police surrounded in the factory. They wouldn't hear of surrender, referring to news on Croatian radio about some so-called humanitarian EU convoy that would get them out of the shit. The convoy had in fact set out from Osijek, but there was no chance that the military authorities would let them through, so they returned a day or so early in their little white vans and boiler suits.

And so because the news on the radio was too good for the surrounded to surrender, straight after dawn the tanks started firing on the factory from four sides. Fifteen minutes later the building was wrapped in dust and smoke. Over the short-wave radio came a lot of satirical chat about the wider and closer family, nation and religion, the usual formalities, and not a word about surrender.

The effect of the bombing was zero. It was noticed by all inside, but Uncle thought it wouldn't hurt to give them a few more. So he ordered the same target, same distance, and went on bombing unnecessarily until the hour was over.

After that a new voice came on the radio and asked very politely to speak to no less than the High Command.

Captain Thunder laughed from his heart for a long time, perhaps too long, then he picked up the handset of the RUP. 'You can't talk to the Command, they're on their annual holiday, I'm the chief of the parade here, and to me you can only surrender, which means get your hands up and come out by the east gate.'

'Yes, but there's a fire here.' The voice hesitated. 'We're not in touch with all our people, it'll take time.'

'You want me to speed it up, sonny? You want me to hit

you for another half hour, then set the Chetniks on you so no one will ask later what happened, and you won't give me a headache?'

For some time nothing was heard on the radio except crackles and interruptions. They moved it to a safer spot, and the voice answered again, much weaker now.

'You went underground, or what?' Uncle said.

'We're in the shelter with the wounded, they're putting out the fire upstairs. We can surrender in two hours, if your High Command guarantees our personal safety.'

'Are you crazy or on drugs, man? What Command? They don't give a fuck for you or me. This is all under my direction, understand?'

'Yes, I understand you completely. But can we take it that your word guarantees our safety?'

'What am I to you, a credit reference? I can't guarantee you anything but I can grenade you, so think about it!'

28

THE SMOKE THINS

Negotiations continued for a long time, and the process of surrender lasted until noon. On the north side of the factory a group of Croatian black-shirts tried to slip through the encirclement. There was a short burst of gunfire, followed by silence. Then there was another, longer roar of machine-gun fire, and the news on the radio that everything was falling into place. It was two in the afternoon when the commander of the guards announced that a certain number of civilians, together with a hundred and thirty armed and uniformed men, were ready to surrender and lay down their arms.

Uncle concealed his joy, and asked them to wait another hour until lunch was served because the men had breakfasted in a hurry, which made many of them nervous, and there were problems with the delivery of the food, and the beans had gone cold so they had to cook more.

The thing with the beans was a lie; they were regularly delivered cold, and the army would devour them in five minutes. But Uncle needed to preen a bit, and no one minded too much.

At three o'clock, when the smoke had dispersed from the factory, a group of twenty guards appeared at the gates bearing the wounded and dead on stretchers and in their arms. They walked slowly to the tanks, which were formed in two cordons.

'Pass down the tanks and lay down your weapons!' Uncle bellowed through the ceremonial silence. There were some distant bursts of machine-gun fire. The Guardsmen approached fearfully.

'What is it, Ustashe? Did you shit yourself?' shouted some drunk territorial, which didn't help them feel at ease. But no one else said anything.

Those on stretchers were carried first to the end of the cordon, where they were searched thoroughly and Doctor checked their bandages and wounds. After the stretchers it was the turn of the less badly wounded. Limping and twitching, with bandaged limbs, they laid their weapons on the road. One kid, wounded in the leg, dropped his gun and it clanged a bit louder than the rest; it was just an accident and no one paid any attention. The next man threw his gun on the heap. The man after him hit the asphalt with his sniper so temperamentally that its optics broke into a million pieces. He was dressed in the black Croatian Special Forces uniform without a cap, with a bandage on his right hand, and one on his left eye. Dule hit his other eye with his rifle butt, and when the man stumbled and fell he fired a load of shot into his stomach.

He practically split him apart.

'Come on, let someone else throw their gun!' Dule shouted, reloading his, and the laying down of weapons went on with extra care.

'Calm down there, kid,' someone warned Dule. 'Don't make us call your sister to a parents' meeting!'

Dule picked up the broken sniper from the road like a wounded bird. 'Who knows how many of ours he killed, motherfucker,' he hissed, rolling the black-shirted one over into the ditch.

Just in time, the little convoy of one Campanola and two Pinzgauers drove up from the command position. Six army policemen jumped out, looking like dog-catchers, and stood in a circle around the major and the captain, dressed in camouflage fighting uniforms.

'You are not an easy man to find, Comrade Captain!' the major said to Uncle.

'To find me, Savo, you must sometimes come to the front of the front line.'

'What private war are you running here?' shouted the major. 'Stand to attention!'

'First it isn't a private war but a collective war, and I can't stand to attention until everything's finished.' Uncle shrugged, which he found difficult in his body-armour. 'The Ustashe are surrendering.'

'Ustashe, eh? And didn't you hear our orders? Didn't you catch our frequency on the radio? You exposed these people to the danger of our own bombardment! For three days you have been deaf to the orders of the High Command! If you don't pull back within ten minutes to the lines drawn in the orders, I'll have no option but to arrest you and take you to the Command.'

'And what about the surrender?' asked Uncle.

'What surrender? That's not your problem now. You'd better prepare yourself for the brigade report.'

'Comrade Major,' Old Krsto spoke from his corner, 'I want to tell you you're wrong about him.'

'What?' screamed the major.

'The captain's a good officer, he didn't expose anyone to danger more than himself, and he led this action professionally and soberly,' Krsto said.

'And who are you to judge?' the major fumed. 'The captain is an officer and has to execute orders. If he doesn't he has to account for it to his superior command. Is that clear to you, old man?'

'It's clear to me, but let me make one thing clear to you. If the captain doesn't show up tomorrow morning at eight o'clock, at this same place, then this unit is coming for him, if need be to Belgrade.'

The major opened his mouth to say something, but Uncle was already climbing into his Campanola. 'Let's go, Savo, I'm in a hurry to get back here.' Then he clapped Old Krsto on the shoulder. 'Everything's all right, they're jerking me off a bit, but they can't fuck me. Radulović, you finish this off and don't pull back whatever you do.'

The Pinzgauers dashed off, followed by the Campanola, and the prisoners looked at them for a while, not understanding anything.

Dule was the first to snap out of it. 'Let's go, donkeys, finish putting your weapons down!'

Captain Radulović remembered to issue commands: 'In the column, two by two, straight to the red house! Forward, march!'

The herd crowded into two columns. The wounded went

in front. They were handed over to the military police at the end of the street and piled into trucks, and the war for them was happily over; waiting for them across the Danube was accommodation at the Ministry of Justice's pleasure.

29

THE CHASE
Time to Duck Down

On the smashed street corner outside their headquarters, Bižo, Dule and Luka were on sentry duty on the eight p.m. to eight a.m. shift. The night was clear and cold, illuminated by the half moon and the oil lamps made from tin cans that some believers had lit after their evening sardines in memory of those killed.

They were sitting in a deeper shelter than usual, in the crater of a demolished building. Bižo and Dule were sitting on the edge, having fun practising their aim with a captured sniper.

'Fuck, you can see everything like daylight.' Dule was delighted. 'You wanna see, Luka?'

'No thanks, maybe someone's watching you with one now.'

'Fuck you,' said Bižo, taking the optics from Dule.

The area around them was quiet. Here and there in the distance they could hear shooting, and the mute trembling came through the ground to where they sat. Nearby, they could hear soldiers singing in an improvised wine cellar. Along with the guards a substantial amount of bottled wine had been surrendered, which they were using for their personal hygiene since the town was without water. The red wine they used for washing their hair, and the white for all the rest. It was like the decadent days at the end of the Roman Empire.

Before dawn it suddenly grew much colder, and vapour started to rise through the manholes along the street. Big clouds gathered and the fog came down, opaque and grey like the screen of a switched-off television.

The darkness was paling, but the fog was still as dark as night. Luka was stretching in the shelter, numb from lying in an unnatural position, when Dule gave a signal. A group of hooded apparitions was quietly passing by. With his thumb and index finger Dule made the letter 'U', for Ustashe. Their guns were locked, and in the moment it took Luka and Bižo to unlock them, the newcomers spotted them.

At that moment, which stretched like a performance in five acts, Dule fired his shotgun, and from the other side of the street came a noise as if someone was throwing a handful of gravel in water, a long, enquiring burst from a silenced automatic.

Bižo, who had been standing at the top of the shelter, fell on his back, firing from his automatic, then slipped down to the bottom of the crater. Luka held his finger on the trigger until he reached the last bullet and felt the heat of the cartridges falling in his hands. But he wasn't paying attention, or aiming at anyone, he was looking down at Bižo, stretched out not making a sound.

Dule lay outside the shelter firing short bursts from Bižo's automatic. From the other side nothing more came, apart from the sharp smell of the first morning gunpowder.

Luka slid on his backside down to Bižo, shining his torch on him in the darkness as he tried to find the traces of

wounds. His head and neck were all right. Luka pushed his
hand under the armour. The material of his bulletproof vest
was pierced in a few places, but there was no blood. Everything seemed okay, but the right arm of his blue windcheater
was torn to shreds, and beneath it was his wounded elbow,
from which the blood dripped steadily. Bižo was slowly
coming to. Luka was finishing the first bandage when Dule
called him: 'Let's go, Luka, fuck it, they'll get away!'

Not half a minute passed before the first soldiers came
running from the side, and Dule and Luka ran before them
up the street.

On the field of battle lay the corpse of a Croatian policeman
in camouflage uniform with his head blown apart. The trail
of blood led to Dule. There were also bloody trails leading to
Bižo and Luka. Staggering and stumbling through the darkness, Dule followed his quarry more with his nose than his
eyes. Luka's hair was standing on end. He shook himself like
a young retriever, completely awake and in a sweat. A flaming
thread burned inside him as he ran on after Dule, following
the distant and unclear signal.

The whole street seemed to pulsate in time to their steps.
They were on the trail. Dule pointed at a group of broken
shadows dragging a bulky object some twenty steps or so
ahead of them; four figures were carrying one wounded.

Dule lifted his gun to his shoulder and rested it against his
cheek. The smoke signals of breath from his mouth stopped
for a moment, while he aimed and opened fire on the shapeless
object that was disappearing into the gate of a half-destroyed
bungalow.

In response they heard a sound resembling a loud sigh, then that other sound, of someone throwing pebbles in the water. Then two bursts of machine-gun fire came from the yard, covering them with plaster from the gate where they were sheltering. After that the four masked figures disappeared down the street, while the wounded one stayed inside the gates, hit in the legs and back.

'Never mind that now,' said Luka, pulling Dule along the trail of the masked four.

Now they were running along the tracks that the tanks had left the day before. The tracks finished in front of the last house in the street, opposite the factory.

'Maybe it's mined,' said Luka.

Dule listened to the rumble of the tanks that were still too far away. 'They're searching house by house. Fuck, they'll be here by New Year at this rate,' he said, dashing into the yard firing short bursts from Bižo's automatic.

It was a stupid cowboy trick, and after it finished he ran to a dead corner of the house by the little window on the ground floor, and waved to Luka to join him.

Luka was preparing to go, cursing Dule for everything, when he saw the gun barrel poking out of the first-floor window. He just had time to duck down on the concrete slab outside the front door, when bullets started pouring from above. He crawled up the street to the next yard and inched his way to a place in the fence where he could clearly see Dule under the window, fidgeting and peering around for him. He came to something resembling a shed, which covered the fence from view of the first floor. He rolled over it with difficulty, like a tired turtle in his body-armour. Moving silently forward, with his back to the wall of the shed, he reached the corner, where a few steps separated him from Dule.

He was about to join him, when the door of the shed opened up with a bang. In fact it flew up from its hinges, and a guy in black jumped out from inside the shed and shot at Dule with a burst from his silenced machine-gun. He fired at his legs, and Dule responded by blowing him back to the shed with his pump-action shotgun. Luka was clumsily scratching his back against the wooden wall of the shed, when another figure fired from inside the house, piercing the wooden door panel with bullets. Luka moved to the entrance of the shed and threw in two grenades, and after the bangs he dropped inside.

He found a half-burnt corpse in black in there, curled up against the wall, and Dule lying on a concrete paving stone with his right shoulder against the wall of the house, trying to stop the bleeding from his legs. His handkerchief was hanging from the pocket of his bulletproof vest, but he didn't manage to get it out because new bursts of gunfire came from the window, tearing off the tufts of dead grass by the paving stone he was lying on.

Crouching behind a pile of sacks smelling of damp mortar, Luka started firing towards the first-floor window of the house, until the barrel disappeared from view.

'That's it, fuck their mothers,' Dule shouted as he dragged himself towards the corner of the building, leaving behind two bloodied lines as he went.

'Eh, Chetniks!' a voice called from above.

'We are not Chetniks, motherfuckers!' Dule shouted, emptying the last bullets from Bižo's automatic in the direction of the window. 'We're YPA!'

'So it is, Lizard. Have you got many days left?'

'More than you, shitface!' screamed Dule, his guttural accent more pronounced than ever.

From the window fell a white box of Cedevita vitamin powder, from which poked a slow-burning fuse. 'Swallow this, kid, maybe you'll speak better!'

The box stood two metres from Dule, and the same distance from Luka. They knew everything about it, except how much time they had left before the thing blew up. Luka was looking at Dule's face over the white box with the green top and the fuse dangling from it. The box wasn't guilty of anything; Dule had got them into this mess.

'This was your clever idea!' Luka shouted at him.

'Hey, stay there and stop shitting!' shouted Dule.

Luka thought how much he hated that little idiot.

Dule shouted at him again to take shelter, but Luka pushed on towards him. He was borne along only by the desire to tread on him and hit him till he was crushed, that stupid kid without a brain, but instead he grabbed the box and threw it towards the window. The burst from the window covered him on the back and nailed him to the ground. After that he felt only the hit of the explosion, and a squid poured black ink into his consciousness.

30

THE MUFFLED STEPS

The first thing Luka did on regaining consciousness was to curse the day Dule was born. The kid was shaking him and trying to drag him along the ground, and he was hurting all over. 'I fuck your holy picture, don't touch me, you retarded monkey!'

'You threw it in and no one came out!'

They were lying at the corner of the house, near the front door, and Dule was pulling him on. His legs were wrapped in bandages, through which the blood was slowly seeping.

Luka moaned as he tried painfully to stand up. He crawled to the wall and leaned his back against it, sweating with the effort. The power in his muscles was coming back, but the fire of the chase had gone, God knows where.

'I could cut your throat, you big donkey!' he told Dule, tearing his trousers at the seam. 'Press there and there and don't let go.'

He soaked the bloody fabric with plum brandy from the little bottle in his pocket, cut a bandage and wrapped a new one over the trousers. Dule clenched his teeth. Sweat poured from his face.

Luka took Dule's shotgun and cocked it. Then he pulled his pistol from his boot, unlocked it, and pressed it to the kid's temple.

'Take this, if someone comes down from there besides me.'
'Don't go, Luka, wait for our people.'

Tell me about it, Luka thought.

He put Dule's knitted cap on one foot and his own cap on the other to muffle his tread, and with the gait of a knocked-out boxer he walked to the front door. It was open. He cast an eye over the ground floor. There was nobody there. Muddy footprints led up the wooden stairs.

He climbed them slowly, feeling more and more sharply the pain in his back where the bullets had hit his bulletproof vest. At the top of the stairs lay the splintered bedroom door, and someone's ripped-off arm clutching the handle of a Heckler & Koch sub-machine gun.

In the bedroom, next to the double bed, lay the armless guy who had been shooting from it. His spine was broken; it seemed as though half his body was lying down, and the other half standing up. On the carpet, where the bomb had exploded, a big hole of dishevelled burnt ends bloomed, and beneath it fragments of broken floor.

The body of a guard sprawled next to the hole, covered in pieces of shattered glass from a television set. He had been nearest to the bomb when it exploded; maybe he had been holding something in his hands when it went off, but he didn't have any hands now. The room had been a neat suburban bedroom, a museum of kitsch furniture. There wasn't a chessboard or a picture of the President of the Republic to be seen; the owners clearly weren't Croats.

From the bathroom leading off the bedroom trailed a thin line of blood. Luka followed it and carefully pushed open the door with the tip of his barrel.

The fifth body was on the floor, twisted as though something had eaten it from inside, lying in a pool of blood coming from he couldn't see where.

He stepped over the stretched-out arm to turn the body on its back. His boot wrapped in Dule's cap slipped in the blood, and he accidentally moved the cuff of the windbreaker. Between the jumper and the glove was a cheap Swatch, like thousands of others, and among these thousands he recognized the watch he had given to Maria when they were separating. Next to it was the woven chessboard bracelet that little Ivana had made for him back in the basement to protect him from the mortars, and he felt the same sense of astonishment he used to feel when Maria appeared where he wasn't expecting her.

He felt as if someone had pulled a cord over his neck and was strangling him slowly. But no one was behind him, the suffocation was coming from inside, a swarm of bloody fears.

He slowly moved his foot from the arm. It seemed smaller and more slender than before. With his feet he turned the body on to its back, and the sight pushed him to the floor. There was just one ghastly wound. The stomach had been slashed at the navel by three angular pieces of thick glass, whose points vanished somewhere deep inside. He trembled as he looked at the wound, and thought of the pain that had come from it. Kneeling in the blood, he looked at the pale marble face, the dry, greyish lips, and the hardest thing, the stiff guard-of-honour look, the dry eyes that didn't know anything more about him, or about anything else.

Long ago, when he was a child, he had broken his mother's old porcelain doll. It was the only toy from her childhood, and Luka remembered the fear he had suffered waiting for her to find out, although the punishment was just symbolic – to stand in the corner.

Once more he was being pushed into that corner, and once more by a broken body, Maria, and a fear like then. No one would hit him for it now, but the fear came black and enormous, in the flood of horror from Maria's frozen eyes. He embraced the porcelain doll and took off her knitted cap, and her hair spilled out, glowing reddish brown and smelling of Erdut red wine.

He imagined her washing her hair for the last time with wine because there was no water. She must have been thinking of him then, because they were always drinking red wine, as if they had always known, the two of them. His eyes were wet, his throat tightened.

Instead of the coasts of Spain, sunset and a beach, and her voice dark as wine, he was stumbling over her blood and carrying her down the stairs through the door.

Dule was sitting outside, his legs propped up by the wall. Wrapped up happily in his bandages, he was squeezing his gun in his hands when Luka appeared. 'What happened, Luka?' he asked. 'Where are you going?' he shouted after him.

Luka said nothing, he wasn't sure what he could say: Maria this is Dule, Dule this is Maria.

The roar of tanks and shouting of soldiers became louder. You came, he thought as he left the yard. But you didn't find me. And the town, what does it look like? What a pigsty, the biggest pigsty on the planet.

On the wall he was passing were some pre-war graffiti. Sid and Nancy. Not bloody likely, he thought. There were ruins and shooting all around, and worn-out graffiti and fucking propaganda posters on the wall, like Berlin in 1945. Adolf and Eva? His smile was made more bitter by the tears that were pouring down his throat. Walking over the street he reached the patch of ground outside the factory yard, tall with dried weeds. A field of weeds, and something else. Death was spread beneath it like a net swinging in front of his eyes, heavy with golden bait. He was ready to take a bite and, holding Maria's body tightly, he staggered on towards the Gates of Forgiveness.

NOTES

The author scribbled these notes in pencil on the manuscript of the English translation of *Made In Yugoslavia*. When they were read by the publishers it was felt that they had to appear in the book – not to explain the novel (that is why there is no reference to them in the text) but as a unique and captivating insight into this rich and complex region.

p. 3 'It was time for Bili to come home'. It was the last Tuesday in June 1991 – the day after Slovenia declared independence and the day before the war in Slovenia began. This was *the* day for Bili to get out of the army before being mobilized to the Slovenian border crossings.

p. 3 'Bili': in different parts of Yugoslavia people's names are used differently and there is a marked difference between what you would be called in town and the name you are called in the country. For example, Bili's name is Domagoj Bilek (see p. 45) and Gogo is a standard nickname for any child named Domagoj. For his friends he is Bili, except when they are angry at him and then they call him Domagoj. For his father and uncle he will be Gogo, especially when they are addressing him as if he were a child. The same is true of Bižo

— the name Bogdan is rare in the urban population but quite common amongst the rural community. This cultural polarization is almost as important for the genesis of the conflict as the ethnic confrontation.

p. 6 'The "vap"': this is a strictly local custom in Osijek. The custom is so local that Yugoslav readers outside Osijek would have no idea what it meant.

p. 7 'USTASHE ONLY!' The Ustashe were the Croatian militia. Serbian nationalism was driving people throughout Yugoslavia to revive the Serb Chetnik movement. It was the end of June 1991. Osijek, in Eastern Croatia.

p. 8 'The massacre in the village of Borovo': just as there were, and still are, towns in Croatia with a large Croatian majority with strongly chauvinist views towards other nationalities, so Knin and Borovo Selo were places with concentrated Serb majorities and a similarly chauvinist commitment from its people. During the fifty years of their rule the communists were fairly successful at maintaining a kind of balancing act and suppressing the ancient antagonisms that existed between these sides, but with the victory of the Croatian nationalists in the election in 1990, the communist balancing act proved to have been a total failure. In 1991 the attempts by the new Croatian rulers to impose their politics by armed force in areas with Serb majorities resulted in a massive resurgence of old intolerance. Borovo was just such a place.

p. 13 'Special Police Force': as republics in the Yugoslav

Federation were not allowed to have their own armies each republic began to form its own version of a Special Police Force, which was more a military unit than a police force.

p. 40   'A little red Fiat': the Fiat 700, or Fiat 850, is manufactured in Yugoslavia. Nicknamed 'the Fićo', it was Yugoslavia's national car. It was so small that one American journalist once wrote: 'If the Volkswagen looks like a beetle, the Fiat 850 looks like a flea.'

p. 44   'Rise Up, My Lord!': Croatian patriotic song.

p. 45   'I gave blood three times': blood donors in the Yugoslavia National Army would be rewarded with two days' leave every time they gave blood.

p. 87   'Don't take your shoes off': this is a very serious matter. Probably the next thing we'll start fighting about. According to the polls 50 per cent of people in Yugoslavia think that shoes should be removed when visiting someone's home. The other 50 per cent think it is a disgusting ritual. It is an Eastern custom brought in by the Turks and as well as being cherished by Muslims it is widespread in many of the nations in this area. What many see as a token of respect, others see as quite the opposite.

p. 96   'The downtown Pentecostalists': the Pentecostalists were famous in Osijek for the wildness of their services. People would attend services at the Pentecostalist church just to see how outrageous they were — the congregation falling into trances, speaking in tongues, weeping, laughing hysterically.

p. 145 'Only a dead Serb makes a good Croat': Luka is quoting a Croat extremist slogan.

p. 154 'Lech Wałesa moustaches': a Polish trade union leader chiefly remembered for his grand moustaches.

p. 175 'Bežanija': this is an area of Belgrade. It also means a panic withdrawal, the act of running away.

p. 201 'The comrades were sent to the Island': many books have been written about Goli Otok (The Barren Island), where a concentration camp was established for Tito's opponents who supported Stalin in 1948. The purges were conducted so thoroughly that it was not uncommon to receive the death sentence for one remark in favour of Stalin. Many of the prisoners who survived the camp never spoke about what happened there and those who spent less than four years in the camp were often considered to be police in-formers. When Krsto says that his comrades came back after only one year, he is insulting their integrity. Having Stalin's portrait in your house was enough to send your entire family to prison. Krsto points out the portrait as proof of his moral superiority.

p. 287 'The same names for their calendar': Croats have

their own names for months whereas Serbs use a calendar very similar to that of Western Europe.

p. 307 'The Gates of Forgiveness': the word for 'forgiveness' is the same as that for 'farewell' in Serbo-Croat. There is no English equivalent.